**Presenting a sensual new miniseries
from Carole Mortimer**

A Season of Secrets

A lady never tells...

Elena Leighton and Ellie Rosewood might only be a
lowly governess and a lady's companion, but there
is more to these women than meets the eye!

For their meek and respectable demeanor
hides this season's most scandalous secrets...
and all is about to be deliciously revealed!

Lord Adam Hawthorne
makes a date with impropriety in
NOT JUST A GOVERNESS
August 2013

And how far will the Duke of Royston
go to lay bare the real Ellie Rosewood?
NOT JUST A WALLFLOWER
December 2013

and in ebooks from Harlequin Historical *Undone!*
Sylvie's Story
July 2013

D0288895

Dear Reader,

When you picked up your Harlequin Historical book this month, I'm sure you will have noticed that we've had a little makeover! But, rest assured, inside you'll still find the timeless stories you know and love and, yes, those deliciously sexy heroes—be they Regency rakes, Viking warriors or rugged, honest-to-goodness cowboys. Fall for every one of these men as they find love with spirited, unconventional heroines—and watch as they break all the rules!

We're proud of our beautiful covers here at Harlequin Historical and hope you like this fresh new take on them as much as we do. Drop by www.Harlequin.com to let us know what you think.

Don't miss this month's fantastic reads:

SMOKE RIVER BRIDE by Lynna Banning

NOT JUST A GOVERNESS by Carole Mortimer
(*A Season of Secrets*)

A LADY DARES by Bronwyn Scott
(*Ladies of Impropriety*)

TO SIN WITH A VIKING by Michelle Willingham
(*Forbidden Vikings*)

Happy Reading!

Linda Fildew
Senior Editor
Harlequin Historical

Carole Mortimer

Not Just a Governess

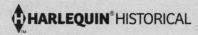

H HARLEQUIN® HISTORICAL

Recycling programs
for this product may
not exist in your area.

ISBN-13: 978-0-373-29748-1

NOT JUST A GOVERNESS

Printed in U.S.A.

To my very special Dad, Eric Haworth Faulkner,
6/2/1923–6/12/2012. A true and everlasting hero!

The dedication of this book says it all for me.
I lost my Dad in December, a man who was and
always will be a true hero to me, in every sense of
the word. He was always very proud of my writing,
but I am even prouder to have enjoyed
the absolute privilege of being his daughter.

I hope you will all continue to enjoy reading
my books as much as I enjoy writing them!

Chapter One

Late April, 1817—the London home of Lady Cicely Hawthorne

'I, for one, am disappointed that you do not seem to be any further along with finding a bride for Hawthorne, Cicely,' Edith St Just, Dowager Duchess of Royston, gave her friend a reproving frown.

'Perhaps we were all being a trifle ambitious, at the start of the Season, in deciding to acquire suitable wives for our three grandsons?' Lady Jocelyn Ambrose put in softly.

The three ladies talking now had been aged only eighteen when they had shared a coming-out Season fifty years ago and had become fast friends, a state of affairs that had seen them all through marriage and their children's marriages. They now had their sights firmly set on the nuptials of their errant grandchildren.

'Nonsense,' the dowager duchess dismissed that

claim firmly. 'You had no trouble whatsoever in seeing Chambourne settled—'

'But not to the bride I had chosen for him,' Lady Jocelyn pointed out fairly.

'Nevertheless, he is to marry,' the dowager duchess dismissed airily. 'And if we do not see to the marriage of our respective grandsons, then who will? My own daughter-in-law is of absolutely no help whatsoever in that enterprise, since she retired to the country following my son Robert's demise three years ago. And Royston certainly shows no inclination himself to give up his habit of acquiring a mistress for several weeks before swiftly growing bored with her and moving on to the next.' She gave loud sniff.

Miss Eleanor Rosewood—Ellie—step-niece and companion to the dowager duchess, glanced across from where she sat quietly by the window with the two companions of Lady Cicely and Lady Jocelyn, knowing that sniff only too well: it conveyed the dowager duchess's disapproval on every occasion.

But Ellie could not help but feel a certain amount of sympathy towards Lady Cicely's dilemma; Lord Adam Hawthorne was known by all, including the numerous servants employed on his many estates, for being both cold and haughty, as well as totally unapproachable.

So much so that it must be far from easy for Lady Cicely to even broach the subject of her grandson remarrying, despite his first marriage having only produced a daughter and no heir, let alone finding a woman who was agreeable to becoming the second wife of such an icily sarcastic gentleman.

Oh, it would have its compensations, no doubt; his lordship was a wealthy gentleman—very wealthy indeed—and more handsome than any single gentleman had a right to be, with glossy black hair and eyes of deep impenetrable grey set in a hard and arrogantly aristocratic face, his shoulders and chest muscled, waist tapered, legs long and strong.

Unfortunately, his character was also icy enough to chill the blood in any woman's veins, hence the reason he was known amongst the *ton* as simply Thorne!

Hawthorne's cold nature aside, Ellie was far more interested in the dowager duchess's efforts to find a bride for her own grandson, Justin St Just, Duke of Royston…

'Adam is proving most unhelpful, I am afraid.' Lady Cicely sighed. 'He has refused each and every one of my invitations for him to dine here with me one evening.'

The dowager duchess raised iron-grey brows. 'On what basis?'

Lady Cicely grimaced. 'He claims he is too busy…'

Edith St Just snorted. 'The man has to eat like other mortals, does he not?'

'One would presume so, yes…' Lady Cicely gave another sigh.

'Well, you must not give up trying, Cicely,' the dowager duchess advised most strongly. 'If Hawthorne will not come to you, then you must go to him.'

Lady Cicely looked alarmed. 'Go to him?'

'Call upon him at Hawthorne House.' The dowager

duchess urged. 'And insist that he join you here for dinner that same evening.'

'I will try, Edith.' Lady Cicely looked far from convinced of her likely success. 'But do tell us, how goes your own efforts in regard to Royston's future bride? Well, I hope?' She brightened. 'Let us not forget that a week ago you wrote that lady's name down on a piece of paper and gave it to Jocelyn's butler for safekeeping!'

The dowager duchess gave a haughty inclination of her head. 'And, as you will see, that is the young lady he will marry, when the time comes.'

'I do so envy you, when I have to deal with Adam's complete lack of co-operation in that regard...' Lady Cicely looked totally miserable.

'Hawthorne will come around, you will see.' Lady Jocelyn gave her friend's hand a reassuring squeeze.

Ellie, easily recalling the forbidding countenance of the man, remained as unconvinced of that as did the poor, obviously beleaguered Lady Cicely...

'Oh, do let's talk of other things!' Lady Jocelyn encouraged brightly. 'For instance, have either of you heard the latest rumour concerning the Duke of Sheffield's missing granddaughter?'

'Oh, do tell!' Lady Cicely encouraged avidly.

Ellie added her own, silent, urging to Lady Cicely's; the tale of the missing granddaughter of the recently deceased Duke of Sheffield had been the talk both below and above stairs for most of the Season, the duke having died very suddenly two months ago, to be succeeded by his nephew. The previous duke's granddaughter and ward had disappeared on the day following his funeral, at the same time as the Sheffield family jewels and several thousand pounds had also gone missing.

'I try never to listen to idle gossip.' The dowager duchess gave another of her famous sniffs.

'Oh, but this is not in the least idle, Edith,' Lady Jocelyn assured. 'Miss Matthews has been seen on the Continent, in the company of a gentleman, and living a life of luxury. Further igniting the rumour that she may have had something to do with the Duke's untimely death, as well as the theft of the Sheffield jewels and money.'

'I cannot believe that any granddaughter of Jane Matthews would ever behave so reprehensively,' Edith St Just stated firmly.

'But the gel's mother was Spanish, remember.' Lady Cicely gave her two friends a pointed glance.

'Hmm, there is that to consider, Edith.' Lady Jocelyn mused.

'Stuff and nonsense,' the dowager duchess dismissed briskly. 'Maria Matthews was the daughter of a grandee and I refuse to believe her daughter guilty of anything unless proven otherwise.'

Which, as Ellie knew only too well, was now the end of that particular subject.

Although she knew that many in society, and below stairs, speculated as to why, if she truly *were* innocent, Miss Magdelena Matthews had disappeared, along with the Sheffield jewels and money, the day of her grandfather's funeral…

Chapter Two

One day later—Hawthorne House, Mayfair, London

'Do not scowl so, Adam, else I will think you are not at all pleased to see me!'

That displeasure glinted in Lord Hawthorne's narrowed grey eyes and showed in his harshly patrician face, as he heard the rebuke in his grandmother's quiet tone. Nor was she wrong about his current displeasure being caused by her unexpected arrival; he had neither the time nor the patience for the twittering of Lady Cicely this afternoon. Or any afternoon, come to that! 'I am only surprised you are visiting me now, Grandmother, when I know you are fully aware this is the time of day that I retire to the nursery in order to spend half an hour with Amanda.'

His grandmother arched silver brows beneath her pale-green bonnet as the two faced each across the blue salon of Adam's Mayfair home. 'And may I not also wish to visit with my great-granddaughter?'

'Well, yes, of course you may.' Adam belatedly strode across the room to bestow a kiss upon one of his grandmother's powdered cheeks. 'It is only that I would have appreciated prior notice of your visit.'

'Why?'

He scowled darkly. 'My time is at a premium, Grandmother, nor do I care to have my routine interrupted.'

'And I have just stated that I have no wish to interrupt anything,' she reminded him quietly.

'Nevertheless, you are—' Adam broke off his impatient outburst, aware that his grandmother's unexpected arrival had already made him four minutes late arriving at the nursery. 'Well, you are here now, so by all means accompany me, if you wish to.' He nodded abruptly as he wrenched open the salon door—much to Barnes's surprise, as the butler stood attentively on the other side of that door—for his grandmother to precede him from the room.

'You really are the most impatient of men, Adam.' Lady Cicely swept past him into the grand hallway, indicating with a nod that her paid companion should wait there for her return. 'I do not believe even your grandfather and father were ever as irritable as you.'

Adam placed a gentlemanly hand beneath his grandmother's elbow as he escorted her up the wide staircase, in the full knowledge that Lady Cicely's overly fussy nature—to put it kindly!—had irked his grandfather and father as much, if not more, as it now did him. Nevertheless, his grandfather and father were no longer with them, leaving Lady Cicely alone in the world but for himself and Amanda, and so it fell to Adam, as the patriarch of the family, to at least attempt kindness towards his elderly relative. 'I apologise if my abruptness of manner has offended you,' he said.

His grandmother released her elbow from his grasp to instead tuck her hand more cosily into the crook of his arm. 'Perhaps as recompense you might consider dining with me this evening…?'

Adam stiffened as he easily recognised Lady Cicely's less-than-subtle attempt at coercion; he hesitated to call it actual blackmail, although he could not help but be aware of his grandmother's recent attempts to introduce him to suitably marriageable ladies—suitable according to Lady Cicely, that was. Adam was having none of it. The ladies. Or the marriage. 'I have to attend a vote in the House tonight, Grandmother.' After which he fully intended to retire to his club for the rest of the evening, where he hoped to enjoy a few quiet games of cards and several glasses of fine brandy.

'Then perhaps tomorrow evening?' Lady Cicely pressed. 'It is so long since the two of us spent any time together…'

Deliberately so, on Adam's part, since he had realised what his grandmother was about. He had absolutely no interest in marrying again and his life really was now such that he had little time for anything other than his responsibilities to the House of Lords and his many estates. The dinners and balls, and all the other nonsense of the Season, held no interest for him whatsoever.

'We are together now, Grandmother,' he pointed out practically.

'But not in any way that—never mind.' Lady Cicely sighed her impatience. 'It is obvious to me that you have become even more intransigent than you ever were!'

Adam's mouth tightened at the criticism. Well-deserved criticism. But his grandmother knew the reason for his intransigence as well as he did; having been married for over two years, and so been dragged along as his adulterous wife's escort to every ball, dinner, and other society function during the Season, and to summer house parties when it was not, Adam now chose, as a widower these past four years, not to attend any of them. There was no reason for him to do so. Most, if not all, of society bored him, so why would he ever choose to voluntarily put himself through those days and evenings of irritation and boredom?

Even so, he instantly felt a guilty need to make amends for the tears he now saw glistening in his grandmother's faded grey eyes. 'I may be able to spare an hour or two to join you for dinner tomorrow evening—'

'Oh, that is wonderful, Adam!' His grandmother's tears disappeared as if they had never been as she now beamed up at him. 'I shall make sure to serve all of your favourite dishes.'

'I said an hour or two, Grandmother,' Adam repeated sternly.

'Yes, yes,' she acknowledged distractedly, obviously already mentally planning her menu for tomorrow evening. And her guest list. Some of which would no doubt be several of those eligible females Adam wished to avoid! 'How is the new girl working out?'

'New girl?' Adam's mind had gone a complete blank at this sudden change of subject, not altogether sure he understood the meaning of his grandmother's question; surely Lady Cicely could not be referring to the woman he had briefly taken an interest in the previous month, before deciding that she bored him in bed as well as out of it?

'Amanda's nursemaid.' Lady Cicely clarified.

Adam's brow cleared at this explanation. 'Mrs Leighton is not a girl, Grandmother. Nor is she Amanda's nursemaid, but her governess.'

'Is Amanda not a little young as yet for a governess? Especially when you know as well as I that society does not appreciate a blue-stocking—'

'I will not have Amanda growing up to be an ignoramus, with nothing in her head other than balls and parties and the latest fashions.' Like her mother before her, Adam could have stated, but chose not to do so; the less thought he gave to Fanny, and her adulterous ways, the better as far as he was concerned!

'—and you never did explain fully why it was that you felt the need to dispense with Dorkins's services after all these years?'

Lady Cicely was slightly out of breath as they ascended the stairs to the third floor of the house where the nursery was situated.

Nor did Adam intend explaining himself now. Having the nursemaid of his six-year-old daughter make it obvious to him that she was available to share his bed, if he so wished, had not only been unpleasant but beyond acceptable. Especially as he had never, by word or deed, ever expressed a carnal interest in the pretty but overly plump Clara Dorkins.

Now, if it had been Elena Leighton, Amanda's new governess, then he might not have found the notion of sharing her bed for a night or two quite so unpalatable—

And where, pray, had that particular thought come from?

Since the death of his wife Adam had kept the satisfying of his carnal desires to a minimum, considering them a weakness he could ill afford. And, whenever those desires did become too demanding, even for his now legendary self-control, he only ever indulged with those ladies of the *demi-monde* whose company he considered he could stand for longer than an hour, possibly two. Less-than-respectable ladies, who expected nothing more than to be handsomely paid for the parting of their thighs.

Adam had certainly never so much as thought of forming an alliance with one of his own employees, hence his hasty dismissal of Clara Dorkins two weeks ago.

Admittedly Elena Leighton, Dorkins' replacement, was quite beautiful in an austere way; she always wore her silky black hair secured in a neat bun at the slenderness of her nape, the severity of her black widow's weeds emphasising the pale beauty of her face rather than detracting from it. Her eyes were a strange light colour, somewhere between blue and green in her heart-shaped face, and surrounded by thick dark lashes, her tiny nose perfectly straight above bow-shaped lips, her jaw delicately lovely, neck and throat slender. Nor did those severe black gowns in the least detract from the willowy attractiveness of her figure: firm breasts above a slender waist and gently swaying hips—

Dear God, he thought, appalled with himself. When had he noticed so much about the looks and attraction of the widow he had recently employed to tutor his *young daughter*?

'*Mrs* Leighton…?' his grandmother prompted curiously.

'I believe she was widowed at Waterloo,' Adam said distractedly, still slightly nonplussed by the realisation he had actually noted Elena Leighton's physical attributes. The woman was his employee, for heaven's sake, not some lightskirt he could take to his bed for a night and then dismiss. Moreover, she was a widow, her husband having died a hero's death during that last bloody battle with Napoleon.

'Old or young…?'

Adam raised dark brows. 'I have no information whatsoever on the deceased Mr Leighton—'

'I was referring to his widow,' Lady Cicely chided with a small sigh.

Until this moment Adam had given no particular thought to Mrs Leighton's age, but had assumed her to be in her late twenties or early thirties.

He scowled now as he realised, when he thought

about it carefully, that it was the lady's widow's weeds which gave her the impression of age and maturity, that, in fact, she was probably considerably much younger than that... 'As long as Mrs Leighton carries out her employment to my satisfaction then I consider her age to be completely immaterial,' he dismissed as he stepped forwards to push open the door to the nursery before indicating that his grandmother should precede him into the room.

Elena looked up from where she had been studying a book of simple poetry with her small charge, her expression one of cool politeness at the entrance of her employer and his paternal grandmother.

A cool politeness, which she hoped masked the fact that she had heard herself become the subject under discussion by grandson and grandmother before they entered the nursery. And that she had tensed warily at that knowledge...

She had hoped the fact that she was the widowed Mrs Elena Leighton, employed by the cold and unapproachable Lord Adam Hawthorne as governess to his young daughter, would be enough to ensure that she escaped such curiosities. But she could see by the assessing way in which Lady Cicely now viewed her that, in that lady's regard at least, this was not to be the case.

Elena resisted the instinct to straighten the severity of her bun, or check the fall of her black gown, instead straightening to her just over five feet in height as she stood up to make a curtsy. 'My lord.'

'Mrs Leighton.' Lady Cicely was the one to smoothly respond to her greeting, his lordship's expression remaining coldly unapproachable as he stood remotely at his grandmother's side.

Elena had already ascertained, before deciding to accept her current employment, that the chillingly austere aristocrat was a man who chose not to involve himself, or his young daughter, in London society, preferring instead to utilise his time in politics or in the running of his country estates. An arrangement that suited Elena's desire—need—for anonymity perfectly.

She had to admit to having been a little startled by this gentleman's dark, almost satanic handsomeness at their initial interview, having had no idea until that moment that Adam Hawthorne bore the dark good looks and muscled physique of a Greek god: fashionably styled dark hair, equally black brows over those dark-grey eyes, high cheekbones either side of a long patrician nose, sculptured and sensual lips, his jaw square and uncompromising, with not an ounce of excess flesh on his tall and muscular frame—as evidence, surely, that he did not spend all of his time seated in the House of Lords or behind the mahogany desk in his study…

But after only five minutes in his company that day Elena had also realised—thankfully!—that not only was he the most haughtily cold and unapproachable man she had ever met, but that he did not even see her as being female, let alone have any of the lewder thoughts and intentions towards her that another male employer might have shown to the woman he was to employ as his young daughter's governess.

Elena now clasped her trembling hands tightly together in front of her, as the warmth currently engulfing her body forced her to realise that was no longer the case, as Lord Hawthorne's narrowed grey gaze slowly perused her from head to toe in what was obviously a totally male assessment. 'Lady Cicely.' She nodded a polite greeting to the elderly lady. 'Stand up and greet your great-grandmother, Amanda,' she instructed as she realised her young charge was still seated at her desk.

Elena had found it strange at first to realise that there was none of the spontaneity of affection in this household that she had been used to during her own childhood, Lord Hawthorne spending only half an hour of each day with his daughter, and even that was usually spent in discussing and questioning what Amanda had learnt during her lessons.

Consequently, Amanda became a quietly reserved child whenever she was in her father's company, the perfect curtsy she now bestowed upon Lady Cicely also reflective of that reserve.

'Great-Grandmama.'

Which was not to say that Elena did not see a different side of Amanda when the two of them were alone together in the nursery, Amanda as full of fun then as any other six-year-old.

Tall for her age, Amanda's face already showed the signs of the great beauty she would become in later years, her eyes a deep blue, her cheeks creamy pink, her little mouth as perfect as a rose in bud, her hair the colour and softness of spun gold. Amanda looked especially enchanting today in a deep-pink gown that perfectly complemented the fairness of her colouring.

A look of enchantment totally wasted upon her father as he stood across the room, his attention focused on Elena rather than his daughter. The same gentleman whom Elena, after only a week spent in his employment, considered to be utterly without any of the softer emotions.

Which was why she now found the intensity of his regard more than slightly unnerving, as if those deep-grey eyes were seeing her as a woman for the first time…

And Elena had no wish for any man, least of all Adam Hawthorne, to see her as anything other than his mousy and widowed employee. Any more than she wished to acknowledge him as being anything more than her employer, even if he was devilishly handsome…

She straightened determinedly. 'I will leave the three of you alone to talk whilst I go and tidy Amanda's bedchamber. If you will all excuse me…' She did not wait for a response before hurrying from the schoolroom.

Only to find that she was shaking so much by the time she had reached the safety of Amanda's bedchamber that she had necessarily to sit down for a moment in order to attempt to regain her senses, pressing a trembling hand against her rapidly beating heart as she fought the rising panic at the thought of Hawthorne seeing her as a woman rather than an employee.

Circumstances had conspired to leave Elena completely alone in the world, and necessitating that she go out to work in order to support herself, and so surely making her life already desperate enough, precarious enough, without the added burden of the sudden interest of the forbidding and forbidden Lord Adam Hawthorne?

Elena was only too well aware that many gentlemen took advantage of the charms of the unprotected females in their household. Indeed, her own cousin—

She would not…could not think about it. Even to think of what that worm—for she could never think of *him* as a gentleman!—had done to her was enough to make her feel ill, the nausea rising even now inside her——

'Are you quite well, Mrs Leighton…?'

Elena stood up so swiftly at the unexpected sound of Hawthorne's voice that all of the blood seemed to rush from her head, rendering her slightly dizzy and causing her to sway precariously on her ankle-booted feet as she reached out blindly for the back of the chair in order to stop herself from falling.

But not quickly enough, it seemed, as he crossed the room in three long strides to take a firm grasp of her arm, allowing her to feel the warmth of his long and elegant hand through the thin silk of her black gown. 'My lord?' Elena looked up at him warily, her breath catching in the back of her throat as she realised how close he was standing to her. A closeness she had not thought she would be able to tolerate from any man. So close that Elena was aware of, and yet not overwhelmed by, how much larger and taller he was than she. So close she could see the circle of black rimming the deep grey of his eyes…

They were, Elena acknowledged as she found herself unable to do any other than continue to stare up at him, the most beautiful eyes she had ever beheld: a deep-smoky grey, with that black rim about the iris, his lashes dark, long and silky.

'Mrs Leighton?' Adam returned softly, frowning slightly as he realised he could smell the citrusy perfume of lemons in her silky dark hair.

Just as he had become aware, having studied her closely in the nursery a few minutes ago, that she was far from being in her late twenties or early thirties, as he had originally assumed her to be. Indeed, she looked possibly one and twenty at most now that he was standing so close to her and really looking at her intently; the alabaster skin of her face and throat was absolutely smooth and flawless, those wide blue-green eyes seeming to possess an innocence as she gazed up at him warily, her slender figure also seeming that of a young girl rather than a mature woman.

His mouth tightened along with the hold he had upon her arm.

'Exactly how old are you?'

She blinked long dark lashes. 'How old am I?'

Adam's jaw tensed as he nodded. 'A simple enough question, I would have thought.'

She moistened rose-coloured lips with the tip of her tongue before answering him. 'Simple enough, yes,' she confirmed huskily. 'But is it not impolite to ask a woman her age? I also fail to see the relevance…?'

Adam's mouth thinned at her continued delay. 'You will allow me to be the best judge of that and please answer the question!' He had little patience at the best of times—and this was far from the best of times; he disliked, above all things, being lied to, and he was very much afraid, that if Elena Leighton had not lied to him outright, that she had at least been economical with the truth.

'I— Why, I am—I am…' Elena paused to flex her nape where it ached from staring up at him for so long, as she weighed up the possibility of this man believing her if she were to lie and claim to be five and twenty, an age that surely even he would consider to be sensible. If untrue. 'I am one and twenty.' Almost. Well…in eight months' time, her birthday falling on Christmas Day, her family having always ensured in the past that they were treated as two separate occasions. Not that there would be any celebration of that event this year, for the simple reason Elena had no family left with whom she wished to celebrate…

'One and twenty,' he repeated evenly, his long and elegant fingers slipping down her arm until they firmly encircled her wrist. 'That would place you as being a mere nineteen when you were widowed and began your employment as tutor and companion to the Bambury chit, is that correct?'

Elena gave an inward wince at this reminder of the reference she had presented to the employment agency some weeks ago, when she had gone to them seeking a placement in a respectable household. A reference, having had no previous experience in employment of any kind, Elena had necessarily to write herself…

She met Adam Hawthorne's scathing gaze unflinchingly. 'That is correct, yes. If you are not satisfied with my work, then I am sure that—'

'Have I said that I am not?'

Her chin rose slightly. 'You implied it.'

Those chiselled lips curled slightly, into what could have been a smile, but was more likely, in this gentleman's case, to be a sneer. 'No, my dear Mrs Leighton, I implied nothing of the sort,' he drawled. 'Perhaps it is a guilty conscience which now makes you assume so?'

Elena's heart skipped several of those guilty beats as she looked searchingly up into Lord Hawthorne's hard and unyielding face; those grey eyes were narrowed to icy slits, the skin stretched tautly over high cheekbones, deep grooves having appeared beside his nose and chiselled lips. It was the face, Elena acknowledged warily, of a gentleman one did not cross. Not unless one wished to experience the full onslaught of what she believed would be his considerable wrath.

She had, she realised with a sinking heart, been lulled into a false sense of security these past twelve days of only seeing her employer for the half an hour or so he spent in the nursery with Amanda each day, occasions when Elena more often than not excused herself and left father and daughter to their privacy. Consequently, to date he had been a remote figure, a haughtily autocratic gentleman who appeared to have more than a little difficulty relating to his young daughter, and as such did not impinge greatly on her own routine and life in the schoolroom.

The gentleman who now regarded her so intently did not appear in the least remote, in regard to her at least. Indeed both he, and his questions, were far too close for comfort. To the point that she felt decidedly overwhelmed by the proximity of that deceptively hard and muscled body. Standing so close to her own as he was, she was able to feel his warmth and smell his deliciously spicy cologne…

She straightened to her own full height, ignoring the fact that she barely reached his broad shoulders as she met that piercing grey gaze unflinchingly. 'I am sure that if you care to check the reference I supplied from the Bamburys you will find it all completely in order.'

And it would be; Elena may be newly cast out upon on the world, but she knew for a fact that a young and widowed Mrs Leighton had acted as tutor and companion to Fiona Bambury before the family had departed for warmer climes at the start of the year, the doctor having recommended as much for the benefit of Lady Bambury's weak chest, from which she had suffered greatly during the harsh English winter. Mrs Leighton, having had no wish to move to the Continent with the Bambury family, had chosen to leave their employment and remain in England.

Except Elena was not, in fact, the aforementioned Mrs Leighton…

'Indeed?' Adam murmured softly.

'If you would care to release me…?'

'Certainly.' The grip he had maintained about her wrist had not been in the least incidental, or an act of intimacy. Rather, it had allowed him to feel the leap in her pulse when he had questioned her as to whether or not she suffered from a guilty conscience.

Adam was now even further convinced that this woman was indeed hiding something. Quite what that something was, he had no idea as yet. But he had every intention of finding out. At the earliest opportunity. After all, he had entrusted this woman with the day-to-day care of his young and impressionable daughter.

Adam looked at her down the length of his nose. 'I must return to the schoolroom now, but be aware I do not consider this conversation over.'

She gave a slight nod in acknowledgement. 'As your employee, I of course await your further instruction.'

Now there was something to contemplate. Having Elena Leighton—the young and extremely beautiful Elena Leighton, the *widowed* Elena Leighton—awaiting his further instruction…

Adam pondered the dilemma of what he might choose to instruct her to do first. That she take the pins from that unbecoming bun and release that abundance of silky black hair, perhaps? Or that she unfasten those widow's weeds and reveal the fullness of her breasts to him? Or perhaps he would enjoy something more personal to himself?

His gaze moved to the fullness of her lips. What, he

wondered, would it feel like to have Elena Leighton on her knees before him and those lips skilfully wrapped about his engorged length? Teasing him, testing him, satisfying him?

Damn it all! What was he thinking?

He was not a man to be led about by that part of his anatomy. If his ill-fated marriage to Fanny had succeeded in nothing else, then it had served to cure him of that particular folly!

Adam stepped away abruptly, a nerve pulsing in his tightly clenched jaw. 'We will talk of this further tomorrow.' He gaze swept over her coldly before he turned on his heel and strode from the room, closing the door forcefully behind him.

Elena staggered back to collapse down on to the chair once more, her breathing fast and shallow, her heart beating erratically in her chest as she endeavoured to calm herself and the panic which had engulfed her, and which she had tried her best to hide, when he had touched her.

She had no idea what had happened to bring about that sudden conversation with him, or the subject of it. Why he had chosen to follow her to Amanda's bedchamber at all even, let alone take hold of her wrist, albeit gently?

What she did know, from the tenor of his questions, and the merciless coldness in his eyes before he left so abruptly, was that he was not a gentleman who would easily forgive being deceived. As Elena had deceived him from the first...

For not only was her name not Elena Leighton, but she was not a widow either—indeed, she had never been married.

Nor had she ever been tutor and companion to Fiona Bambury, the real Mrs Leighton, after leaving the Bamburys' employment, having decided to move to Scotland to care for the elderly parents of her deceased husband.

All of which Elena knew because she had been acquainted with the Bamburys, their country estate some twenty miles distant from her own grandfather's home, the couple occasional guests at his dinner table, as Elena and her grandfather had been occasional dinner guests at theirs'.

Because her name—her true name—was not Elena Leighton, but Miss Magdelena Matthews.

And she was the granddaughter of George Matthews, the previous Duke of Sheffield, and the young woman whose disappearance, so quickly following her grandfather's funeral, still had all of society agog with speculation…

Chapter Three

'Thorne? Damn it, Hawthorne, wait up there, man!'

Adam came to a halt in the hollow-sounding hallways of the House of Lords before turning to see who hailed him. A frown appeared between his eyes as he recognised Justin St Just, Duke of Royston, striding purposefully towards him, several other members moving hastily aside to allow him to pass.

A tall, blond-haired Adonis, with eyes of periwinkle blue set in an arrogantly handsome face, and a powerful build that the ladies all swooned over, Royston was also one of the more charismatic members of the House. Although the two men were of a similar age and regularly attended sessions, and their respective grandmothers had been lifelong friends, the two men had never been particularly close. Their views and lifestyles were too different for that, especially so in recent years, when Adam had avoided most of society events, and Royston was known to have the devil's own luck with the ladies and at the card tables.

Also, Adam had never been sure whether or not Royston had been one of Fanny's legion of lovers…

'Royston,' he greeted the other man coolly.

The duke eyed him with shrewd speculation. 'You seem in somewhat of a hurry to get away tonight, Hawthorne. Off to see a lady friend?' He quirked a mocking brow.

Adam drew himself up stiffly, the two men of similar height. 'I trust that, as a gentleman, you do not expect me to confirm or deny that question?'

'Absolutely not,' Royston drawled unapologetically. 'You appear to have become something of a…recluse in recent years, Hawthorne.'

Adam's gaze became glacial. 'Did you have something specific you wished to discuss with me, or may I now be on my way?'

'Damn, but you have become a prickly bastard!' The duke's expression turned to one of deep irritation. 'Join me in a drink at one of the clubs so that we might talk in a less public arena?' he added impatiently as several people jostled them in their haste to leave and received a legendary St Just scowl for their trouble.

Adam's demeanour lightened slightly. 'As it happens I was on my way to White's.'

The other man grimaced. 'I had a less…respectable club in mind, but certainly, White's will do as a start to the evening. I have my carriage outside.'

'As I have mine.'

The duke regarded him enigmatically for several long seconds before acquiescing. 'Very well. We shall both travel in your coach and mine will follow. Unless you have it in mind to join me in visiting the other clubs later?'

'No.' Adam's tone was uncompromising.

'As you wish.' Royston shrugged.

They did not speak again until they were safely ensconced at a secluded table at White's and both nursing a large glass of brandy, the duke slumped comfortably in his chair, Adam sitting upright across from him.

The two men had met often in past years at one *ton* function or another. In truth, Adam had always liked the man's arrogant disregard for society's strictures. Indeed, his own reserve towards the man this past few years was caused by his doubts regarding any past involvement between Royston and Fanny; Fanny's affairs had been so numerous during their marriage that Adam was sure even she had forgotten half her lovers' names.

That Adam and Fanny had occupied separate bedchambers after the first month of their marriage had not been generally known and made Fanny's adulterous behaviour, after Amanda was born, all the more of a humiliation. It would have been easier by far if they had occupied separate households, but that Fanny had refused to allow, preferring the shield of the two of them living together to hide her numerous affairs. Unfortunately, she had held the trump card, and had used the excuse of their baby daughter to enforce that decision. For, despite the awkwardness he often felt in being able to relax his emotions and draw close to Amanda as she grew older, Adam loved his young daughter deeply.

'How does your grandmama seem to you nowadays?'

Adam's eyes widened at the subject of Royston's question; Lady Cicely had been the last thing he expected to be discussing this evening, with Royston or anyone else. 'What do you mean?'

Royston stared down morosely into his brandy glass. 'Mine's acting deuced odd and I thought, as the two of them have always been in such cahoots, that I would see if yours was behaving oddly, too?' He grimaced. 'I hope to God it has nothing to do with this Sheffield business, because I am heartily sick of the subject! I liked Sheffield well enough, but all these weeks of speculation as to whether his granddaughter bumped him off, then stole the family jewels, has become an utter bore.'

The tension left Adam's shoulders. 'No, I do not believe Lady Cicely and the dowager duchess's…current distraction have anything to do with the Sheffield affair.'

St Just perked up slightly. 'No?'

'No.' Adam found himself smiling tightly. 'I believe—and I only know this because Lady Cicely is obviously far less subtle in her intentions than the dowager duchess—that they have it in mind to somehow secure our future wives for us!'

The duke sat forwards abruptly. 'You cannot be serious?'

Adam gave a mocking inclination of his head, enjoying the other's man's consternation. 'They appear to be very serious, yes. Think about it, Royston—they are thick as thieves with the Dowager Countess of Chambourne, whose own grandson has just announced his wedding is to be next month.'

'And you are saying our grandmothers are now plotting our own downfall?'

Adam could not help but let out a brief bark of laughter at Royston's horrified expression. 'The three ladies have always done things together. Their coming-out Season. Marriage. Motherhood. Even widowhood.' He shrugged. 'My own grandmother's less-than-subtle attempts at matchmaking these past few months leads me to believe it is now their intention that their three grandsons shall be married in the same Season.'

'Is it, by God?' The duke slowly sank back in his chair. 'And have you made any decision as to how you intend fending off this attack upon our bachelor state?'

'I see no need to fend it off when my uninterest is so clear.' Adam frowned.

Royston eyed him pityingly. 'You are obviously not as well acquainted with my own grandmama as I!'

'No,' Adam stated, 'but I am well acquainted with my own!'

'And you agree that marriage for either of us is out of the question?'

His mouth tightened. 'I can only speak for myself— but, yes, totally out of the question.' His nostrils flared. 'I have no intention of ever remarrying.'

'And I have no intention of marrying at all—or, at least, not for years and years.' Royston looked at Adam searchingly. 'Even so, I cannot believe that even the dowager duchess would dare—yes, I can, damn it.' He scowled darkly. 'My grandmother would dare anything to ensure the succession of the line!'

Adam gave a slight inclination of his head. 'My own grandmother has also expressed her concerns as to the fact that I have only a daughter and no son.' Not that he had taken any heed of those concerns; Adam felt no qualms whatsoever about his third cousin Wilfred inheriting the title once he had shuffled off his own mortal coil.

'But I take it you do not intend to just sit about waiting for the parson's mousetrap to snap tight about your ankles?'

'Certainly not!' Adam gave a shiver of revulsion.

Royston tapped his chin distractedly. 'There's not much happening in the House for the next week, so now would seem to be as good a time as any for me to absent myself from town and go to the country for a while. I have it in mind to view a hunter Sedgewicke has put my way. With any luck the grandmothers will have lost the scent by the time I return.'

'Highly unlikely,' Adam drawled derisively.

'But, as I am genuinely fond of the dowager duchess, and as such have no wish to be at loggerheads with her over this, it is definitely worth pursuing.' Royston stood up decisively. 'I advise you to do something similar, for I assure you, once my grandmama gets the bit between her teeth there's no stopping her. Oh, and, Hawthorne…?' He paused beside Adam's chair.

'Yes?'

'I make it a point of principle never to dally with married ladies,' Royston declared.

His meaning was not lost on Adam as he answered cautiously. 'That is a very good principle to have.'

'I believe so, yes.' The other man met Adam's gaze briefly, meaningfully, before nodding to him in farewell, pausing only to briefly greet several acquaintances as he made his way out of the club.

Leaving Adam to mull over the predicament of how best to avoid his own grandmother's machinations and to consider his unexpected, and totally inappropriate fantasy earlier regarding Elena Leighton's sensuously plump lips and the uses they might be put to!

Elena assured herself of the neatness of her appearance one last time before knocking briskly on the door of her employer's private study, having received the summons in the nursery a short time ago, delivered by Barnes, requesting she join Lord Hawthorne downstairs immediately.

'Come.'

To say Elena was nervous about the reason for Lord Hawthorne's summons would be putting it mildly—the sudden tension that had sprung up between them yesterday, and their unfinished conversation, were both still very much in her mind. She had no idea what she would say to him if, as she had suggested, he had decided to check her fake references and somehow found them wanting.

She did not see how he could have done so, when she had been so careful in her choice of an alias, her acquaintance with the Bambury family allowing her to write as accurate a reference as possible, considering she was not really Mrs Leighton. But that did not stop Elena from now chewing worriedly on her bottom lip. If Hawthorne chose to dismiss her—

'I said come, damn it.' There was no mistaking the impatient irritation in his lordship's voice.

Elena's cheeks felt flushed as she opened the door and stepped gingerly into a room lined with bookcases halfway up the mahogany-panelled walls, with several original paintings above them, and a huge mahogany desk dominating the room.

At least…it would have been the dominating feature of the study if the gentleman seated behind that desk had not so easily taken that honour for himself!

Tall and broad-shouldered in a superfine of the same dark grey as his eyes over a paler-grey waistcoat, his linen snowy white, the neckcloth at his throat arranged meticulously, his stylish hair dark as a raven's wing above that austerely handsome face, Lord Adam Hawthorne effortlessly filled the room with his overwhelming presence.

But it was a presence that Elena did not find in the least frightening, as she did so many other men following her cousin Neville's cruelty to her. Indeed, Adam Hawthorne, despite—or because of?—his air of detachment, was a man who inspired trust rather than fear…

His mouth thinned disapprovingly as he leant back

his chair. 'Did you have some difficulty just now in understanding my invitation to enter?'

'No. I—' She breathed out softly through her teeth before straightening her shoulders determinedly. 'No, of course I did not,' she answered more strongly. 'I merely paused before entering in order to...to adjust my appearance.' It took all of her considerable self-will to withstand that critical gaze as it swept over her slowly, from the neat and smoothly styled bun at her nape, the pallor of her face, down over the black of her gown, to the toes of her black ankle boots peeking out from beneath the hem of that gown, before once again returning to her now-flushed and discomforted face.

He observed her coolly. 'Might I enquire why it is you still choose to wear your widow's weeds when your husband died almost two years ago?'

Elena was visibly taken aback by the directness of his question. Nor did she intend—or, in the circumstances, was able—to explain that she chose to wear black out of respect for the death two months ago of her beloved grandfather, George Matthews, the previous Duke of Sheffield!

He raised a dark brow. 'Perhaps it is that you loved your husband so much that you still mourn his loss?'

'Or perhaps it is that I am simply too poor to be able to replace my mourning gowns with something more frivolous?' Elena felt stung into replying as she easily heard the underlying scepticism in his derisive tone.

Adam eyed her thoughtfully. 'If that should indeed

be the situation, would it not have been prudent to ask me for an advance on your wages?'

Elena's eyes widened. 'I trust you are not about to insult me further by suggesting I might use your money with which to purchase new gowns, my lord?'

Adam frowned his irritation with this young woman's prickliness. He tried to not remember Royston had accused him of having the very same fault only yesterday evening…

Adam owed his own withdrawal from society to the adulterous behaviour of his deceased wife. His fierce pride would not allow him to relax his guard when in the company of the *ton*. Elena Leighton's surliness also appeared to be a matter of pride, but in her case, it was pride over her lack of finances. 'It would be money you have earned in taking care of Amanda,' he pointed out calmly.

'Except, as I suggested might be the case yesterday, I believe you may be dissatisfied with my services…?'

Damn it, Adam wished she would not use such words as that!

The word 'service' once again conjured up images of this woman performing all manner of intimacies he would rather not be allowed to distract him at this moment…

Adam found had already been distracted—and aroused—enough already by the pretty pout of her reddened lips when she entered his study a few minutes ago. So much so that the material of his pantaloons was now stretched uncomfortably tight across the throb of his swollen shaft beneath his desk.

He stood up to try to ease that discomfort before re-alising what he had done and turning away to hide the evidence of his arousal, gazing out of the window into the garden at the back of his London home. 'I do not recall making any such remark.'

'You implied it when you questioned my lack of years—'

'Mrs Leighton!' Adam turned back sharply, linking his hands in front of him to hide that telltale bulge as he observed her through narrowed lids. 'I believe we have already discussed my views regarding you making as-sumptions about any of my comments or actions. If I have something to say, then be assured I will not hesi-tate to say it. How long will it take you to make ready to leave Hawthorne House?'

Elena stepped back with a gasp, her face paling as she raised her hand in an effort to calm her rapidly beat-ing heart at the mere thought of being cast out alone into the world once again. 'You are dismissing me…?'

'For heaven's sake, woman, will you stop reading meanings into my every word, meanings that are sim-ply not there!' Adam exploded as he scowled down the length of his aristocratic nose at her. 'I have several things in need of my attention on my estate in Cam-bridgeshire, and it is my wish for you and Amanda to accompany me there.'

'To Cambridgeshire?'

He nodded tersely. 'That is what I have just said, yes.'

'Oh…'

He flicked a black brow. 'There is some problem with that course of action?

It was a county in England that Elena had never visited before, but of course she had no objection to accompanying Lord Hawthorne and his daughter there.

Not as such…

The truth of the matter was that Elena had made a conscious decision to move to London after her grandfather had died so suddenly, and following the terrible scene with her cousin, which had occurred after the funeral.

Her grandfather, once a soldier, had told her that the best way to hide from the enemy was in plain sight, which was the reason Elena had chosen to change her appearance as far as she was able and adopt an assumed name, before accepting the post as governess to Amanda Hawthorne, a post that largely involved staying inside the house with her charge. Even if Neville Matthews, her cousin and abuser, and the new Duke of Sheffield, did decide to come to town, then he was unlikely to accept any but private invitations following the recent death of their grandfather.

She did not believe that she had any acquaintances living in Cambridgeshire, but she nevertheless felt safer in the anonymity of London…

'Perhaps,' Adam continued relentlessly as he saw the uncertainty in her expression, 'it is that you have…acquaintances, here in London, you would be reluctant to be parted from, even for a week or so…?' Just because the woman had been widowed for almost two years, and she still wore her black clothes as a sign of her continued mourning, did not mean that she had not taken a lover during that time. Several, in fact.

Indeed, Adam had heard it said that physical closeness was one of the things most lamented when one's husband or wife died. Not true in his case, of course; he and Fanny had not shared so much as a brief kiss from the moment he had learnt of her first infidelity just a month after their wedding.

But Elena Leighton was a young and beautiful woman, and she had already explained that she still wore her widow's attire for financial reasons rather than emotional ones. It was naïve on Adam's part to assume that she had not taken a lover. Quite when she met with that lover—perhaps on her one afternoon off a week?—he had no wish to know!

'We would only be gone for a week?' Her expression had brightened considerably.

Irritating Adam immensely. Which was in itself ridiculous; the woman's obvious eagerness not to be parted from her lover for any length of time was of absolutely no consequence or interest to him. 'Approximately,' he qualified. 'At the moment, the exact length of time I will need to stay in Cambridgeshire is undecided.' Mainly because Adam felt a certain inner discomfort about this departure for Cambridgeshire at all.

It was true that there were several matters there in need of his attention, but he had no doubts they were matters he could have settled by the sending of a letter to his man who managed the estate in his absence. His decision to visit the estate in person had more to do with his conversation with Royston last night, than any real urgency to deal with those matters himself.

Not because Adam was in any real fear of his grand-mother being successful in her endeavours to procure him a suitable wife—that, he had vowed long ago, would never happen!—but because, much as his grand-mother might irritate him on occasion, he did have a genuine affection for her, and as such he had no wish to hurt her. Like Royston, removing himself from London, far away from his relative's machinations, seemed the best way for him to avoid doing that.

However, he could not avoid having dinner at Lady Cecily's home this evening, when no doubt a suitable number of eligible young ladies would be produced for his approval—or otherwise, as he absolutely knew would be the case!—but as it would also give Adam the opportunity of telling his grandmother in person of his imminent departure for Cambridgeshire, he was willing to suffer through that particular inconvenience.

He frowned as he saw the look of consternation on the governess's face. 'I repeat, is there some objection to your travelling into Cambridgeshire with myself and Amanda?'

Elena drew herself up stiffly. 'No, of course there is not. And to answer your earlier question, I can have my own and Amanda's things packed and ready for departure in a matter of hours.'

Adam gave a tight smile. 'It is not necessary that you

be quite so hasty,' he drawled. 'I have a dinner engagement this evening. First thing tomorrow morning will be quite soon enough. I trust that will give you sufficient time in which to…inform any relatives and friends that you are to be absent from Town for the next week?'

'Approximately.'

'Indeed,' he conceded drily.

The only relative Elena had left in the world was Neville and the moment *he* learnt of her whereabouts he would no doubt call for her immediate arrest!

And Elena had decided at the onset that the less she involved her friends in her current unhappy situation—and she did have several who still believed in her innocence—the better it would be for them.

She necessarily had to accept a small amount of financial help from her closest friend, Lizzie Carlton, after fleeing the duke's estate in Yorkshire in late February, and she had also informed Lizzie by letter that she had safely reached London and secured suitable lodgings. But Elena could not, in all conscience, allow her friend to become embroiled in this situation any further than that.

Indeed, she had resolved to completely become the widowed Mrs Elena Leighton, a schooled young lady who had fallen on hard times since her husband's untimely death. As she must, if she were to be successful in her endeavour of hiding in full view of the populace of England's capital; it was sad, but true, that the *ton* rarely noticed the existence of the people whom they employed, let alone those employed by the other members of England's aristocracy.

'There is no one whom I would wish to inform, my lord,' she answered her employer coolly. 'If I might be allowed to return to the schoolroom now?'

'Of course.'

'Thank you, my lord.'

Adam tapped his cheek thoughtfully as he watched her quietly exit the study before closing the door behind her, irritated at the realisation that she had once again avoided revealing anything about herself or her connections. As she was perfectly entitled to do, he allowed; her family connections, or even her romantic ones, had been of no significance to him at the commencement of her employment with him, and they should not be of any import now.

Except he could not prevent himself from wondering—despite her denial of the need for her to inform anyone of her imminent departure for Cambridgeshire—as to which gentleman might currently be the lucky recipient of the ministrations of those full and sensuous lips…

Chapter Four

'She is merely ill from travelling in the carriage.'
Elena looked up at Adam apologetically as he opened
the door of the carriage just in time for Amanda to lean
out and be violently sick on his black, brown-topped
Hessians already covered in dust from where he had ridden on horseback all day beside the carriage. 'Oh, dear.'
Elena moved forwards on her seat to help her distressed
charge down the steps on to the cobbled courtyard of the
inn they were to stay in for the night, cuddling Amanda
against her before turning her attention to those now
ruined boots. 'Perhaps—'

'Perhaps if you had informed me of Amanda's discomfort earlier it would not have come to this.' Adam
glowered down at her.

Elena gasped her incredulity at an accusation she
believed completely unfair. 'Amanda was perfectly all
right until a short time ago and has only found this last
few bumpy miles something of a trial. Also, my lord,

as you had ridden on ahead I could not inform you of anything...'

'Yes. Yes,' Adam snapped, waving his hand impatiently. 'I suggest you take Amanda upstairs to our rooms while I speak to the innkeeper about organising some water to be brought up for her bath.'

Elena kept her arm about the now quietly sobbing Amanda. 'And some food, my lord. Some dry bread and fresh water will perhaps settle Amanda's stomach before bedtime.'

'Of course.' Adam turned his attention away from his ruined boots to instead look down at his distressed daughter. Amanda's face was a pasty white, her eyes dark and cloudy smudges of blue in that pallor, her usually lustrous gold hair damp about her face. Nor had her own clothing escaped being spattered, her little shoes and hose in as sorry a state as his boots. 'There, there, Amanda, it is not the end of the world— You are soiling your clothing now, Mrs Leighton,' he warned sharply as Elena ignored the results of Amanda's nausea, moving down on her haunches beside the little girl and gently wiping the tears from her face with her own lace-edged handkerchief.

'My clothes are of no importance at this moment, sir.' Her eyes flashed up at him in stormy warning, before she returned her attention to the cleansing of Amanda's face, murmuring soft assurances to the little girl.

Adam clamped down on his feelings of inadequacy. 'I was merely pointing out—'

'If you will excuse us?' She straightened, obvious

indignation rolling off her in waves. 'I should like to see to Amanda's needs before considering my own.'

A praiseworthy sentiment, Adam admitted as he stood in the courtyard and watched her walk away, her back ramrod straight as she entered the inn, her arms about Amanda.

Except for the fact that he knew that parting comment had been made as a deliberate set down for what she perceived as his lack of concern for his young daughter...

A totally erroneous assumption for her to have made; Adam knew his behaviour to be yet another example of his own lack of understanding in how to relate to a six-year-old girl, rather than the lack of concern Elena Leighton had assumed it to be. No excuse, of course, but Adam had no idea how to even go about healing the distance which seemed to yawn wider with each passing day between himself and Amanda.

Nor had the governess's anger towards him abated in the slightest, Adam realised an hour or so later when she joined him for dinner in the private parlour of the inn, as he had requested when the maid went to deliver food and drink to Amanda. Her eyes sparkled a deep and fiery green-blue as she swept into the room, with a deep flush to her cheeks and her whole demeanour, in yet another of those dratted black gowns, one of bristly disapproval and resentment—the former no doubt still on Amanda's behalf, the resentment possibly due to the peremptory instruction to join him for dinner.

'Would you care for a glass of Madeira, Mrs Leighton…?' Adam attempted civility. Bathed and dressed in clean clothes and a fresh pair of boots, he felt far more human; he tried not to think about the fact that his man Reynolds was probably upstairs even now, crying as he attempted to salvage the first pair!

'No, thank you.'

'Then perhaps you would prefer sherry or wine?'

She looked at him coolly. 'I do not care for strong liquor at all.'

Adam frowned. 'I do not believe any of the refreshments I offered can be referred to as "strong liquor".'

'Nevertheless…'

'Then perhaps we should just sit down and eat?' He could barely restrain his frustration with her frostiness as he moved forwards to politely pull back a chair for her.

'I had expected to dine in my bedchamber with Amanda,' she stated.

'And I would prefer that you dine here with me,' he countered, looking pointedly towards the chair.

She frowned as she stepped forwards. 'Thank you.' She sat rigidly in the chair, her body stiff and unyielding, ensuring that her spine did not come into contact with the back of the chair.

Adam gave a rueful grimace as he moved around the table and took his own seat opposite her, waiting until the innkeeper himself had served their food—a thick steaming stew accompanied by fresh crusty bread—before speaking again. 'Should I expect to be subjected to this wall of ice throughout the whole of dinner, or would you perhaps prefer to castigate me now and get it over with?' He quirked one dark brow enquiringly.

'Castigate you, my lord?' She kept her head bowed as she studiously arranged her napkin across her knees.

Adam gave a weary sigh. 'Mrs Leighton, I am a widower in my late twenties, with no previous experience of children, let alone six-year-old females. As such, I admit I know naught of how to deal with the day-to-day upsets of my young daughter.'

Elena slowly looked up to consider him across the table, ignoring his obvious handsomeness for the moment—difficult as that might be when he looked so very smart in a deep-blue superfine over a beige waistcoat — and instead trying to see the man he described. There was no disputing the fact that he was a widower in his late twenties. But Lord Adam Hawthorne was also a man whom senior politicians were reputed to hold in great regard, a man who ran his estates and a London household without so much as blinking an eye; it was impossible to think that such a man could find himself defeated by the needs of a six-year-old girl.

Or was it…?

He was a man who preferred to hold himself aloof from society. From all emotions. Why was it so impossible to believe he found it difficult to relate to his young daughter?

Some of the stiffness left Elena's spine. 'I think you will find that six-year-old young ladies have the same need to be loved as the older ones, my lord.'

He frowned. '"Older ones", Mrs Leighton…?'

She became slightly flustered under that icy gaze. 'I believe most ladies are desirous of that, yes, my lord.'

'I see.' His frown deepened. 'And are you questioning my ability to feel that emotion, Mrs Leighton?'

'Of course not.' Elena gasped softly.

'Then perhaps it is only my affection for my daughter you question…?'

Her cheeks felt warm. 'It is only the manner in which you choose to show that affection which—well, which—'

'Yes?'

'Could you not have hugged Amanda earlier rather than—' She broke off, suddenly not sure how far to continue with this.

'"Rather than…?"' he prompted softly.

She took hold of her courage and looked him straight in the eye. 'Amanda was upset and in need of comforting—preferably a physical demonstration of affection from her father.'

He looked obviously disconcerted with her candour.

Perhaps she had gone too far? After all, it was really none of her concern how Lord Hawthorne behaved towards his young daughter; she had briefly forgotten that she was no longer Miss Magdelena Matthews, the privileged and beloved granddaughter of a duke who was allowed to speak her mind, but was now an employee. And employees did not castigate their employers!

Elena lowered her gaze demurely. 'I apologise, my lord. I spoke out of turn.'

Now it was Adam's turn to feel discomforted. Elena Leighton's disapproval apart, he was fully aware that he had difficulty in demonstrating the deep affection he felt for Amanda; she had been only two years old when her mother died and had been attended to completely in the nursery until quite recently. Not that Fanny had ever been a particularly attentive mother when she was alive, but she had occasionally taken an interest and showered Amanda with gifts completely inappropriate to her age, whereas, perhaps partly because of his experiences with Fanny, Adam now found it difficult to show that deep affection he felt for his six-year-old daughter. Which he knew was not a fault of Amanda's, but due to his own emotional reserve as much as his lack of experience as a father.

He looked enquiringly at her. 'I thought it normal for men in society to spend only an hour or so a day in the company of their female offspring?'

'You do not strike me as the sort of gentleman who would be concerned as to how others might behave.'

'Possibly not,' he allowed slowly. 'But I am often at a loss as to know how I should behave. Perhaps you might endeavour to help guide me, as to how a father should behave towards his six-year-old daughter?'

Elena blinked. 'My lord…?'

Adam tried not to feel vexed at her surprise. 'I am suggesting, as Amanda's governess, that you might perhaps aid me in how best to take more of an interest in the happenings in my daughter's life.'

Her lips thinned so that they did not look in the least plump and inviting. 'Are you laughing at me, my lord?'

His top lip curled back derisively in response to that. 'I believe you will find, Mrs Leighton, that I rarely find reason to laugh at anything, so I very much doubt I will have made you the exception.' He eyed her closely, no longer sure he had any appetite for the rich and meaty-smelling stew that had been provided for them.

He had actually been anticipating the evening ahead when he dressed for dinner earlier, could not remember the last time he had dined alone with a beautiful woman—apart from Fanny, whom he had despised utterly, when those rare evenings they had dined at home together had been more a lesson in endurance than something to be enjoyed.

Just as his grandmother's dinner the evening before had been something to be endured rather than enjoyed!

Lady Cecily had totally outdone herself in that she had provided not one, not two, but four eligible young ladies for his approval. All of them young and beautiful—and all of them as empty-headed as Fanny!

He already knew that Elena Leighton was not of that ilk, that she was educated, learned and that he found her conversation stimulating. As he found her physically stimulating... Except on those occasions when she was determined to rebuke him for what she perceived as his lack of feeling for Amanda!

'Perhaps we should just eat our dinner before it cools any further.' He didn't wait for her response, but turned his attention to eating the food in front of him.

Elena ate her own stew more slowly, aware that she had displeased him. Was he justified to feel that? She was, after all, employed to attend to his daughter, not to comment on his behaviour and attitudes.

Disconcerted at being summoned to join him for dinner, and the two of them sitting down to eat their meal together alone in this private parlour, she had again forgotten the façade of being the widowed Mrs Elena Leighton and instead talked to him as an equal, forgetting that she no longer had the right to do so.

If Adam Hawthorne were ever to discover her true identity, then no doubt he would not hesitate to turn her over to the authorities himself!

She placed her spoon down carefully beside the bowl, her food untouched. 'I must apologise once again for speaking out of turn, my lord. It is not my place—'

'And exactly what do you consider to be "your place", Mrs Leighton?' he rasped irritably as he looked across at her with stormy-grey eyes.

Elena chewed on her bottom lip before answering, once again disconcerted, this time by the intensity of that deep-grey gaze. 'Well, It is certainly not to tell you how you should behave towards your own daughter.'

'And yet you have not hesitated to do so.'

She gave a wince. 'And for that I—'

'Do not apologise to me a second time in as many minutes, Mrs Leighton!' Adam pushed his chair back noisily as he stood up.

Elena looked up at him warily as he stood glowering down at her. 'I did not mean to displease you…'

'No…?' His expression softened. 'Then what did you mean to do to me, Mrs Leighton?'

Elena's pulse leapt at the sound of that huskiness, the lacing of sensuality she heard underlying his tone, his piercing grey gaze now appearing to be transfixed upon her mouth. Disturbing her with sensations she was unfamiliar with.

Elena ran the moistness of her tongue nervously across her lips before speaking. 'I do not believe I had any intent other than to apologise for speaking to you so frankly about what is a private matter.'

'No…?' He was far too overpowering in the smallness of the room. Too large. Too intense. Too overwhelmingly male!

She found herself unable to look away from him, her heart seeming to sputter and falter, before commencing to beat a wild tattoo in her chest. A fact he was well aware of, if the shifting of his gaze to the pulse in her throat was any indication. A gaze that slowly moved steadily downwards before then lingering on the ivory swell of her breasts as she continued to breathe shallowly.

As Miss Magdelena Matthews, she had of course attended assemblies and dinner parties in Yorkshire, as she had many other local social occasions. But her mother had unfortunately died shortly before her coming-out Season two years ago, and her grandfather had not been a man who particularly cared for town or London society, and his visits there had been few and far between, usually only on business or with the intention of attending the House of Lords.

As a consequence, even following her year of mourning for her mother, her grandfather's preference for the country meant that Magdelena had spent no time at all in London, and so had not learnt how to recognise or to deal with a gentleman's attentions. Indeed, Elena's only experience with a gentleman of the *ton* was of such a traumatic nature that she had feared ever becoming the focus of a male ever again.

Except Adam Hawthorne did not incite that same fear within her...

Rather the opposite.

The warmth she detected in the grey softness of his gaze, as he continued to watch the rise and fall of her bosom, filled her with unaccustomed heat. Her heart once again fluttered wildly and caused her pulse to do likewise, and her breasts—those same breasts he continued to regard so intently—seemed to swell and grow, the rose-coloured tips tingling with the same unaccustomed heat, making the fitted bodice of her gown feel uncomfortably tight.

It was an unexpected, and yet exhilarating, sensation, every inch of her skin hot and almost painfully sensitive, and she felt almost light-headed as she continued to shyly meet his gaze through the sweep of her dark lashes.

Adam had no idea what he was about!

The fact that he had anticipated enjoying Elena

Leighton's stimulating presence for a few hours, her obvious intelligence and sensitivity, did not mean he had to take their relationship any further than that. Indeed, he would be foolish to ever think of doing so.

Not only was she a splendid addition to his household, in that she appeared to have already developed a very caring relationship with his young daughter, but she *was* in his employ. And whilst some of the male members of the *ton* might feel few qualms in regard to taking advantage of their pretty and young female household staff, Adam had certainly never done so. Not even at the worst moments of his marriage to Fanny had he stooped to seeking comfort or solace from one of the young women working in any of his own households. Nor was it his intention to start now with this one.

He straightened abruptly. 'I suggest that we eat the rest of our meal before making an early night of it.' Adam gave a pained wince as her face became a flushed and fiery red. 'By that, I meant, of course, that we should then retire to our respective bedchambers.'

'I did not for a moment suppose you meant anything other, my lord,' she answered sharply.

Adam pulled his chair out noisily and resumed his seat. 'Good,' he growled, more than a little unsettled himself, both by their conversation, and the things which had not been said…

Thankfully Amanda seemed to have recovered fully the following day as they resumed the last part of their journey, the weather warm enough that Elena had been able to lower the windows and so allow some air into the carriage, and also making it possible for Amanda to poke her head out of the window when she saw something that interested her.

Lord Hawthorne had been noticeably absent when Elena and Amanda ate their breakfast earlier in the private parlour of the inn and he had again ridden on ahead once they resumed their journey, no doubt anxious to arrive at his estate so that he might begin to deal with whatever business had brought him to Cambridgeshire in the first place.

Elena sincerely hoped that it had nothing to do with his wishing to avoid her own outspoken company.

She had woken early this morning to the sounds of certain other inhabitants of the inn already being awake: the grooms chatting outside in the cobbled yard as they fed the horses prior to travel and the sounds of food being prepared for the guests in the kitchen below.

A quick glance at the neighbouring bed had shown that Amanda was still asleep, thus allowing Elena the luxury of remaining cosily beneath her own bedcovers for a few minutes longer, as she thought of the time she had spent alone with Adam Hawthorne yesterday evening.

It had taken only those few minutes' contemplation for Elena to convince herself she had imagined the intimate intensity of his gaze, both on her lips and breasts; her employer was not a man known for displaying desire for women of the *ton*, let alone the woman who was engaged to care for his daughter.

'Is it your intention to spend the evening, as well as all of the day, seated inside the carriage, Mrs Leighton?'

Elena's cheeks were flushed as she came back to an awareness of her present surroundings, looking out of the open carriage door to see Lord Hawthorne standing outside on the gravel looking in at her mockingly. While she'd been lost in contemplation, the carriage had come to a halt in the courtyard in front of two curved-stone staircases leading up from either side to the entrance of Hawthorne Hall. Amanda had already stepped down from the carriage and was even now skipping her way up the staircase on the left to where the huge oak door already stood open in readiness to welcome the master of the house and his entourage.

Elena stepped slowly down from the carriage to look up at the four-storeyed house; it was a grand greystone building, with a tall, pillared portico at the top of the two staircases, with two curved wings abutting the main house, dozens of windows gleaming in the late evening sunshine.

It was, Elena noted with some dismay, a house very like the one at her grandfather's estate in Yorkshire, where she and her mother had moved to live following the death of Elena's father, and where the late Duke of Sheffield had met his end so unexpectedly two months ago.

'Mrs Leighton…?'

She smiled politely as she turned to look at Hawthorne. 'You have a beautiful home, my lord.'

For some inexplicable reason Adam did not believe

her praise of Hawthorne Hall to be wholly sincere. Indeed, the strained look to her mouth and those expressive blue-green eyes convinced him of such.

He turned to look at the house with critical eyes, looking for flaws and finding none. All was completely in order. As it should be, considering the wages he paid his estate manager.

He turned back to Elena Leighton. 'Then do you suppose we might both be allowed to go inside it now?' he prompted drily.

'Of course.' She nodded distractedly, her smile still strained as she preceded him up the stairs, her dark curls hidden beneath another of those unbecoming black bonnets, her black gown reflective of that drabness.

A drabness that suddenly irritated Adam intensely. 'If I might be allowed to speak frankly, Mrs Leighton?' He fell into step beside her as they neared the top of the stairs.

She glanced up at him. 'My lord?'

'I intend to ask Mrs Standish to arrange for a local seamstress to call upon you at her earliest convenience.'

A frown appeared between the fineness of her eyes as she came to a halt at the top of the staircase. 'Mrs Standish, my lord?'

Adam had spent all of his adult life answering to that title —but it had never before irked him in the way it did when this woman addressed him so coolly!

Which was utterly ridiculous—what else should she call him? She was not his social equal, but a paid servant, and as such her form of address to him was perfectly correct. Should he expect her to call him Adam, as if the two of them were friends, or possibly more? Of course he should not!

He scowled his irrational annoyance. 'She is the housekeeper here and as such in charge of all the female staff, and consequently the clothing they are required to wear within the household.'

Elena's expression became wary. 'Yes, my lord...?'

Adam sighed. 'And I am tired of looking at you in these—these widow's weeds.' He indicated her appearance with a dismissive wave of his hand. 'I shall instruct Mrs Standish to see to it that you are supplied with more fitting apparel.'

She raised surprised dark brows. 'More fitting for what, my lord?'

Oh, to the devil with it! Another of those questions this particular woman seemed to ask and which took Adam into the realms of the unacceptable.

As it did now, as he instantly imagined Elena Leighton as his mistress, all of that glorious ebony hair loose about her shoulders, her naked body covered only by one of those delicate silk negligees Fanny had been so fond of parading about in. Not black as with Fanny, but rather white or the palest cream, in order to set off the almost luminous quality to this woman's ivory skin and allowing the tips of her breasts to poke invitingly and revealingly against that silky material. What colour would her nipples be? he wondered. A fresh peach, perhaps? Or, more likely, considering the colour of her lips, a deep and blushing rose—

His mouth tightened with self-disgust as he realised that he had once again allowed himself thoughts of this woman that were wholly inappropriate to the relationship that existed between the two of them. 'For spending so many hours a day with a six-year-girl who has already suffered the loss of her mother, without your own clothing reminding her of death on a daily basis,' he rasped harshly.

'Oh!' She gasped. 'I had not thought of that! And I should have done so. I am so sorry, my—'

'I believe I have already made clear my feelings regarding this constant and irritating need you feel to apologise to me for one reason or another.' Adam looked down the long length of his nose at her.

'But I should have thought—'

'Mrs Leighton…' He barely controlled his impatience at her continued self-condemnation. Damn it, he had thought only to get her out of those horrible clothes— Well, not exactly *out* of them— Oh, damn it to hell! 'Mrs Leighton, I am tired and I am irritable, furthermore I am in need of a decent glass of brandy, before sitting down to enjoy an even more decent dinner cooked by my excellent chef here, before then spending a night in my own bed!'

She blinked at his vehemence. 'I—please do not let me delay you any further.'

'If you will excuse me, then? Jeffries will see to it that you are shown the nursery and schoolroom as well as your own bedchamber.'

'As you wish, my lord.' Her lashes lowered with a demureness Adam viewed with suspicion.

'It is indeed as I wish.' He scowled, adding, as she made no further comment, 'Goodnight, Mrs Leighton.'

'My lord.' She nodded without so much as glancing up.

Adam gave her one last irritated glance before entering the house, pausing only long enough to hand his hat and cloak to the patiently waiting Jeffries, before striding down the hallway to his study without so much as a second glance.

Where, Adam sincerely hoped, he would not be haunted by any further lascivious thoughts about the widowed Mrs Elena Leighton.

Chapter Five

'I believe there has been some sort of mistake...' Elena viewed with consternation the brightly coloured materials the seamstress had laid out on the *chaise* in the bedchamber for her approval. They were predominantly green and blue, but there was also a cream silk and a lemon, all with matching lace.

Mrs Hepworth was aged perhaps thirty and prettily plump, that plumpness shown to advantage in a gown of sky blue in a high-waisted style that perfectly displayed her excellence as a seamstress. 'Mrs Standish was quite specific in her instructions concerning which materials I should bring with me for your approval, Mrs Leighton.'

'Are you sure?'

'Oh, yes, I am very sure of Mrs Standish's instructions, Mrs Leighton,' the seamstress confirmed cheerfully.

And Mrs Standish, as Elena knew, had received *her* instructions from the infuriating Lord Hawthorne...

* * *

'Come,' Adam instructed distractedly as he concentrated on the figures laid out in the ledger before him. The study door opened, then was softly closed again, followed by a lengthy silence. So lengthy that Adam was finally forced to look up beneath frowning brows, that frown easing slightly as he saw a flushed and obviously discomforted Elena Leighton standing in front of his wide mahogany desk. 'Yes…?'

She moistened her lips. 'I am not disturbing you, my lord?'

'I believe you have used the wrong tense, Mrs Leighton—you have obviously already interrupted me,' he drawled pointedly as he leant back in his chair to look across at her.

He had seen Amanda only briefly these past two days, and her governess not at all, having been kept busy dealing with the myriad of paperwork involved in running the estate. He frowned now as he saw the governess was still wearing one of those unbecoming black gowns that so infuriated him. 'Has Mrs Standish not yet engaged the services of a seamstress—?'

'That is the very reason I am here, my lord,' she rushed into speech. 'I fear there has been some sort of mistake. The seamstress brought with her materials that are more suited to—to being worn by a lady than a—a child's governess.'

Adam arched one dark brow. 'And is that child's governess not also a lady?'

'I—well, I would hope to be considered as such,

yes.' Elena looked more than a little flustered. 'But the materials are of the finest silks and of such an array of colours, when I had been expecting—I had expected—'

'Yes?'

She bit her lip. 'I had thought to be wearing service-able browns, with possibly a beige gown in which to attend church on Sundays.'

Adam gave a wince at the thought of this woman's ivory skin against such unbecoming shades. 'That would not do at all, Mrs Leighton.' His top lip curled with displeasure. 'Brighter colours, a deep rose, blues and greens, are more suited to your colouring, with per-haps a cream for Sundays.'

Exactly the colours, Elena realised, that the plump Mrs Hepworth had just laid out for her approval.

'And I am not a churchgoer,' Adam continued drily, 'but you may attend if you feel so inclined.'

'But is it not your duty to attend as—?' Elena broke off abruptly, aware she had once again almost been in-appropriately outspoken in this man's presence. Inap-propriate for the widowed Mrs Elena Leighton, that was. Which, considering she had not set sight on, nor heard sound of Adam Hawthorne these past two days, she probably should not have done.

'You were saying, madam?'

'Nothing, my lord.' It really was not her place to re-buke him for not attending church, even if she knew her grandfather had made it his habit to always attend the Sunday service. Not because he was particularly religious, but because he maintained that conversation afterwards was the best way to mingle with and learn about the people who lived and worked on his estate.

'This reticence is not what I have come to expect from you, Mrs Leighton,' he drawled mockingly.

'No. Well…' She pursed her lips as she thought of the past two days, the time that had elapsed since she had last irritated him with her outspokenness. 'Perhaps I am finally learning to practise long-overdue caution in my conversations with you, my lord.'

Adam stared at her in astonishment for several seconds before he suddenly burst out laughing. A low and rusty sound, he acknowledged self-derisively, but it was, none the less, laughter. 'Did you tend to be this outspoken when you were employed by the Bamburys?' He continued to smile ruefully.

'I do not understand.'

Adam knew Lord Geoffrey Bambury slightly, from their occasional clashes in the House in the past, and knew him as a man who believed totally in the superiority of the hierarchy that made up much of society; as such Adam did not see him as a man who would suffer being rebuked by a servant, which the other man would most certainly have considered Elena Leighton's role to be in his own household.

He shrugged. 'I merely wondered if I was the exception to the rule as the recipient of this…honesty of yours, or if it is your usual habit to say exactly what is on your mind?'

'Oh, I do not believe I would go as far as to say I

have done that, my lord—oh.' She grimaced. 'I meant, of course—'

'I believe I may guess what you meant, Mrs Leighton,' Adam said. 'And as such, I should probably applaud your efforts at exercising some discretion, at least.'

'Yes. Well.' Those blue-green eyes avoided meeting his amused gaze.

'You were about to tell me my religious duty, I believe?' he prompted softly.

Too softly, in Elena's opinion; she really did seem to have adopted the habit of speaking above her present station in life to this particular gentleman! Perhaps, on this occasion because she was still slightly disconcerted by the sound and sight of his laughter a few minutes ago...

He had informed her only three evenings ago that he found very little amusement in anything, and yet just now he had laughed outright. Even more startling was how much more handsome, almost boyish, he appeared when he gave in to that laughter,

She swallowed before speaking, 'Of course I was not, my lord. I just—I merely wondered if attending the local church would not be of real benefit to you, in terms of meeting and talking with the people living on your estate and the local village?'

'Indeed?' The suddenly steely edge to his tone was unmistakable.

Elena felt the colour warming her cheeks. 'Yes. I—I only remark upon it because I know it was Lord Bambury's habit to do so.' Her grandfather and Lord Bambury had discussed that very subject over dinner one evening at Sheffield Park…

Adam raised dark brows over cold grey eyes. 'And you are suggesting I might follow his example?'

Her cheeks burned at his icy derision. 'Perhaps we should return to the subject of the materials for my uniform, my lord?'

'What uniform?' He looked at her blankly.

Elena's eyes widened. 'Did you not say two days ago that it was your wish for me to wear a uniform whilst I am attending Amanda?'

He gave a slow shake of his head. 'I do not recall ever using the word "uniform" when I made the request for you to wear less sombre clothing in future.'

'But—' Elena frowned, thinking back to that conversation when they had arrived at Hawthorne Hall. 'I assumed…'

He gave a tight smile. 'It is never wise to make assumptions, Mrs Leighton.'

When it concerned this gentleman, obviously not. 'So it was your intention all along to supply me with new, prettier gowns, rather than simply a uniform?'

'Yes.' There was no mistaking the challenge in his monosyllabic reply.

Elena drew in a sharp breath. 'And is this—would this be your way of—of circumventing my earlier objections about this matter?'

'It would, yes.'

Elena clenched her fists tightly to rein in her frustration as Adam Hawthorne continued to look up at her calmly, one eyebrow raised in mocking—and infuriating!—query. 'In that case…perhaps I might ask something of you in return?'

That dark brow rose even higher. 'In return for what, madam?'

'In return for my making no further objections to the procuring of new gowns for me to wear.' In truth, Elena's heart had leapt in excitement earlier just at sight of those wonderful colours and delicious fabrics. True, she should out of respect for the recent death of her grandfather insist upon retaining her mourning clothes, but having already worn black for her mother for half a year, and then greys and dull purple for the rest of the year, with only a matter of months to enjoy wearing brighter colours, her youth and vivacity now chafed at thoughts of having to wear the sombre clothing any longer. Especially when she thought of those beautiful coloured silks and exquisite lace draped on the *chaise* in her bedchamber…

'In return for?' Adam felt incredulous. 'You make it sound as if you are the one doing me a service rather than the other way about?'

She arched a dark brow. 'And am I not?'

Adam's lids narrowed. Could this young woman possibly know how much he wished to see her in something other than those unbecoming black gowns she habitually wore? Or preferably in nothing at all!

He drew in a sharp breath. 'You are being presumptuous again, madam.'

'If that is so, then I apologise.' She looked flustered again. 'I am merely—I only wished to—' She broke off to gather herself and tried again, more calmly. 'Several days ago you asked for my help, for suggestions in how you might deal better with your daughter. It is Amanda's dearest wish to own her own pony and to learn to ride it, my lord.'

Adam stared at her, not sure that he had heard her correctly. Not sure he had ever met anyone quite like Elena Leighton before. 'Let me see if I understood your terms correctly?' he spoke slowly. 'You are willing to accept the new gowns, without fuss, if I agree to buying Amanda a pony and allowing her to learn to ride?'

'No.'

'No?' Adam looked perplexed as he sat forwards. 'But did you not just say exactly that?'

Elena's chin rose determinedly. 'I did say that it is Amanda's dearest wish to own her own pony and learn to ride, yes. It is also my suggestion that you should be the one to teach her.' The idea had come to her after those days of travelling into Cambridgeshire, when she had noticed that Amanda seemed the most attentive to the scenery outside when there were horses to be seen grazing in the fields. Several minutes' casual conversation with her charge had revealed Amanda's deep love of equines and her secret yearning to own a horse or pony of her own so that she might learn to ride.

The second part of Elena's suggestion—an inspired one, she had thought!—arose from her conversation with her employer in which he had asked for her help in finding ways of taking more of an interest in his young daughter's life. The stunned look on his face now would seem to suggest he had not meant that request to be taken quite so literally as this! 'Would it not be a perfect way for you to spend more time with Amanda, whilst also doing something she would enjoy?'

Adam was starting to wonder if he had not seriously underestimated this young woman, if he had not been fooled, both by her widow's weeds and her demur demeanour during those first few days in his employ, into thinking that she was both complacent and obliging.

Their last few conversations together had revealed her as being neither of those things!

He stood up to move around the desk until he was able to lean back against it, knowing a certain inner satisfaction as he noted her discomfort at his proximity. At the same time as he recognised, and appreciated, the way in which she remained standing exactly where she was, despite that discomfort, as testament to her spirited nature. 'Do you ride yourself, Mrs Leighton?'

She gave him a quick glance before as quickly glancing away again, a blush to her cheeks. 'Why do you ask?'

The reason Adam asked was because the more time he spent in this woman's company, the more convinced he became that there was something about her, an in-born ladylike elegance and a certain self-confidence, which did not sit well with her role as paid governess to a young girl.

She had also had no difficulty whatsoever in recognising that the seamstress had brought with her the finest silks for her approval, as Adam had instructed, rather than the inferior ones which might normally have been requested in such circumstances. Adam seriously doubted that most employers would ever buy expensive silks for a woman who was a member of their household staff. Unless that woman was also his mistress...

Of course he knew nothing of Elena Leighton's life before her employment with the Bamburys, so she could have been the daughter of an aristocrat, who had eloped with her soldier husband, for all Adam knew of that situation; he could certainly more easily believe that to be this elegantly lovely woman's history than he could see her as having been the daughter of an impoverished vicar or a shopkeeper!

He looked down the length of his nose at her. 'Do I need to give a reason in order to ask a question of one of my household staff?'

'No. Of course you do not.' The colour deepened in her cheeks—as if she had once again briefly forgotten that was now her place in life? he wondered. 'But to answer your question—yes, I have ridden since I was a child, my lord. I only thought this might be the perfect opportunity in which you might give pleasure to Amanda, whilst at the same time allowing you to spend more time with her.'

Adam's mouth twisted derisively. There was definitely something about this young woman—her background before she married Private Leighton?—which

Adam found himself becoming more and more interested in knowing.

That, in itself, was unexpected...

His brief marriage to Fanny had succeeded in revealing all too clearly the many vagaries of human nature to him—the lies, the greed, the utter selfishness—until his own character, out of self-protection perhaps, had become that of the true cynic, to the extent that Adam rarely saw good in people any more—most especially the female of the species.

For whatever reason, Elena Leighton remained a mystery to him, yet at the same time there was a burning honesty about her, a determination, a desire to right injustice—such as she perceived his own lack of interest in Amanda to be. It was so at odds with the selfishness Adam had come to believe to be the motivation behind every human action—even his own, to a great extent, an example being that he had dragged his daughter and her companion off to the wilds of Cambridgeshire, in the middle of the Season, with the intention of dealing with matters on the estate, but also for the purpose of escaping the matchmaking machinations of his own grandmother!

Yes, he had become both selfish and cynical these past six years. And yet... And yet this little governess had brought something to life in him that was neither of those things, a desire not to act in his own interest, but instead for the pleasure of others. A desire to please her that had nothing to do with the physical attraction he felt towards her...

Adam straightened abruptly before moving back round his desk and sitting down behind it, his tone cool and controlled when at last he spoke. 'The seamstress will think you have forgotten about her.'

In truth, Elena *had* forgotten that lady's presence upstairs in her bedchamber during this past few minutes' conversation. Indeed, she had forgotten everything but the disturbing gentleman who now looked across the desk at her so disdainfully. A gentleman who suddenly looked so very different to the handsomely boyish one who had burst into spontaneous laughter only minutes earlier…

'And Amanda's pony and riding lessons?'

His mouth thinned. 'I will see what can be arranged.'

Elena's heart sank in disappointment as she turned to leave, inwardly knowing that any 'arrangements' Adam Hawthorne chose to make about Amanda's riding lessons were unlikely to include him.

'And, Mrs Leighton…?'

She turned back slowly, her expression wary. 'Yes?'

He sighed his exasperation. 'You have a look on your face like that of a beast in fear of being whipped!'

Elena stiffened in outrage. 'I trust that is not the case?'

'It was not a personal threat, madam, but a figure of speech!' Adam scowled, knowing he had once again been wrong-footed by this exasperating woman.

'Then it was an exceedingly unpleasant one,' she protested.

Adam gritted his back teeth together so tightly he

feared they might snap out of his jaw, knowing he should not have delayed her departure from his study, but let her return upstairs to the attentions of the seamstress. And he would have done so, if not for the look of disappointment on her face after he had dismissed both her and her request that he be the one to teach Amanda to ride.

He took a steadying breath. 'I believe you take delight in misunderstanding me!'

She raised dark brows. 'I assure you, I take no delight at all in imagining you—or, indeed, anyone else—whipping an innocent beast of any kind.'

'I merely said—' Adam rose to his feet once again to round the desk with a sudden burst of frustrated energy before grasping her by the slenderness of her shoulders and shaking her slightly to emphasise his next words. 'I have never been a party to whipping a woman, man, nor beast, damn it!'

'I am glad to hear it.' Her voice had softened huskily.

Bringing Adam to an awareness of the fact that he still had hold of her by the shoulders, that he could feel the delicacy of her bones through the thin material of her black gown, the soft pads of his thumbs actually touching the silky softness of the flesh just above the ivory swell of her breasts...

And it was very silky skin, so soft and smooth as Adam lowered his gaze to watch as he gave in to the temptation to run the pads of his thumbs caressingly over that delectable flesh, his hands appearing dark and very big against that delicate and unblemished ivory.

Standing this close to Elena, he could once again smell lemons, and something lightly floral, the top of her dark head barely reaching his shoulders, her figure slender in any case, but appearing more so when measured against his own height and breadth. Even the firm swell of her breasts, above the scooped neckline of her gown, was delicately tempting rather than voluptuous.

Damn it, he should have stayed seated behind his desk, safely removed from that temptation! Should never have— His gaze became riveted on the full pout of Elena's mouth as she ran the moist tip of her tongue nervously across her lips whilst looking up at him from between silky dark lashes.

'My lord…?'

Adam drew in a deep, controlling breath even as he closed his eyes in an effort not to look at those now moist lips. Moist and utterly kissable lips. 'Do not— Elena…!' he groaned huskily in defeat as he opened his eyes and saw she had now caught her bottom lip between tiny, pearly-white teeth.

Her eyes widened slightly, those long, dark lashes framing those blue-green orbs, her throat moving when she swallowed as Adam slowly began to draw her closer towards him. 'My lord…?' she whispered again.

'Adam,' he encouraged gruffly.

Elena would have protested his request for such informality—if he had not chosen that moment to draw her closer still before lowering his head and she felt the gentle, intimate touch of his lips against the curve of her throat.

Surprisingly warm and sensuous lips, considering how cold and abrupt this man so often was. Instead of the fear and recoil that she might have been expected to feel, after Neville's harsh treatment of her, Elena relaxed into the safety of Adam Hawthorne's arms, safe in the knowledge that he was not a man to ever use force on any woman.

It was at once a surprise and yet the most thrilling experience of her lifetime, to be held by and touching Adam so intimately, and to feel the warmth of his breath heating her flesh, even as his lips tasted and caressed the slender column of her throat, the gentle bite of his teeth on her earlobe causing her to tremble as her breath hitched in her throat.

Her breasts became full, the tips full and sensitive, as those warm lips trailed along the line of her jaw before finally claiming her parted mouth in a deep and searching kiss that caused the heat to course through her, from the top of her head to the tips of her toes, settling at that secret, intimate place between her thighs. Elena's head was swirling, thought impossible, denial even more so as Adam's hands moved down from her shoulders to encircle her waist as he crushed her against him, his lips even more fiercely demanding against her own.

Then, just as suddenly, his mouth was wrenched away as he put her firmly apart from him before releasing her. Elena stumbled slightly as she attempted to regain her balance on legs that seemed to have all the substance of jelly, her lips feeling bruised and swollen, her cheeks flushed, breasts full and aching inside the bodice of her gown.

Elena blinked several times as she attempted to focus on Adam, only to step back in alarm as she found herself looking into the hard grey chips of ice that were his eyes.

'That was a mistake on more levels than I care to contemplate,' he rasped harshly, his face all sharp and disapproving angles, the tousled darkness of his hair the only indication that moments ago this man had kissed her, as Elena had kissed him back, and her fingers had become passionately entangled in his thick raven locks.

'A mistake…?' She felt a sharp tightening in her chest almost akin to pain, knowing that she felt the opposite, that kissing Adam had been the most wonderful of pleasures, more delicious than she had ever dared to hope a kiss ever could be. A kiss so unlike the ones her cousin had forced upon her—

No!

There were some things Elena could not—would not think about.

'On so many, many levels,' Adam repeated grimly as he saw the way in which her face had paled.

No doubt in reaction to the realisation that her employer had just kissed her with an intimacy and passion totally unacceptable to her, or the disparity in their social positions. Not that the raging of his libido cared one way or the other about that, but Adam must!

'For which you have my heartfelt apology,' he added,

mortified with himself. 'I do not know—it was not my intention—it will not happen again,' he vowed.

At least, Adam would do what he could to ensure that it did not happen again! In truth, he was not sure how it had happened a first time…

There had been perhaps a dozen or so women in his life since Fanny died, women he had spent a few hours of intimacy with and never seen again. Beautiful as Elena might be, for him to have stepped over that line, for him to not only have felt desire for one of his own servants, but to have acted upon it, was totally unacceptable to him. Quite how he was going to feel, to react to her, once she had ceased wearing these unbecoming gowns, he dare not think. With decency and restraint, it was to be hoped. But—

'You were about to say something earlier as I began to leave the room…?'

Adam scowled as he tried to remember what she was referring to, his mind and body both still dominated by only one thought: his desire for her.

Ah, yes… 'I believe I was about to suggest that a riding habit might also be a useful addition to your wardrobe.'

Her eyes widened dubiously. 'A riding habit, my lord?'

His jaw tightened. 'Yes. Perhaps in turquoise or blue?' he found himself adding —before instantly castigating himself for caring what the colour of her riding habit should be.

'Very well, my lord.' She looked at him for several

seconds longer, before giving a brief curtsy. 'If you will excuse me, I must return to the schoolroom.'

'And the seamstress.'

'Indeed.' She did not look at him again before leaving.

Adam frowned darkly once Elena had departed his study, knowing that he had made life decidedly uncomfortable for himself just now.

The throbbing ache in his groin spoke of his obvious physical discomfort, but it was the inner dissatisfaction, with his own completely uncharacteristic behaviour of making love to a female servant in his own household, and Elena's reaction to it once she had found the time and privacy in which to reflect, which caused Adam to continue to soundly castigate himself.

Elena might choose to believe that he did not take enough of an interest in his daughter or her life, but Adam knew enough to know that Amanda had been happier in recent weeks, more contented, since the advent of her new governess into her life.

His unacceptable behaviour just now might have put that in jeopardy if, on reflection, Elena should decide that she could not continue working for a man who attempted to take liberties with her.

There was another aspect to consider, Adam realised with a heavy heart, and that was his loss of control in kissing her at all. A loss of control he certainly did not welcome. Most especially with a woman he was fast beginning to suspect was much more than she seemed.

Chapter Six

'I thought your lessons would be over for the morning?'

'We are just finishing now.' Elena deliberately kept her gaze away from Adam and on the textbook she had been using to teach Amanda some basic arithmetic, but that did not stop the colour from warming her cheeks as she recalled— how would she ever be able to forget!— being kissed by him so passionately.

In fact, Elena had lain awake in her bed these past two nights unable to think of anything else.

Neville's brutality two months ago had been...shocking. Horrendous. Something Elena knew she would also never ever forget and not in a good way like Adam's kiss. She had been sure the experience would prevent her from ever allowing another man to so much as hold her, let alone kiss her, in future. And yet, not only had she allowed her handsome, charismatic employer to do so, but she knew she had kissed him back.

Because she felt safe with him? Could that be it? Yet how was it possible for her to feel safe with a man whom she also found so physically arousing? The feelings he'd created inside her still made her blush just to think of them.

'Papa?' Amanda looked at her father uncertainly as he stood in the doorway.

Elena's breath caught in her throat as she at last looked up and took in Adam's wide-shouldered appearance. He was pristinely attired in a deep-grey superfine, black waistcoat and pale-grey pantaloons tucked into black Hessians, with his dark hair brushed neatly back from his harshly handsome face. A face that looked every bit as remote as on the first occasion Elena had met him, grey eyes chillingly cold as he met her gaze unblinkingly. As warning, perhaps, that he deeply regretted the last time the two of them had been together? As if Elena had not already guessed that from the distance he had kept from her ever since then.

'What do you have in the basket, Papa?'

Elena, having also noted the wicker basket beside him in the doorway, had been wondering the same. Especially as it gave every appearance of being a picnic basket.

'Our picnic luncheon,' Adam confirmed that suspicion.

'A picnic, Papa…?' Amanda looked even more bewildered.

He nodded. 'It is the perfect day for it, if you two ladies would care to join me?'

Two ladies? Adam seriously expected Elena to join father and daughter for their picnic?

'Really, Papa?' For once Amanda completely forgot her usual reserve when in her father's company, as she instead jumped up and down excitedly. 'Oh, may we, Mrs Leighton? May we?' She looked up at Elena appealingly with those beguiling sapphire-blue eyes.

Much as Elena loved the thought of sitting on a blanket beneath one of the splendid oak trees in the garden, or possibly beside the huge lake beyond the gardens at the back of the house, and enjoying a leisurely alfresco luncheon, she was unsure of the wisdom of spending even that amount of time in close proximity with Adam, following the inappropriate behaviour between them, and her confusion, and his frosty demeanour towards her, ever since.

'Mrs Leighton?' Adam prompted when she didn't answer.

Elena deliberately kept her attention centred on Amanda. 'I am sure you do not need my permission to join your father for luncheon, Amanda,' she said with a smile. 'I, however, have some things in the schoolroom in need of my attention—'

'Such as...?' Adam challenged her coolly; he had initially been unsure of the wisdom of inviting Elena to join them in the first place, but now found, contrarily, that he was more than a little irritated at her reluctance to accept that invitation now he had made it, dash it all!

A frown appeared between those blue-green eyes. 'I have tomorrow's lessons to prepare—'

'And, as such, they can as easily be prepared this

evening,' he dismissed briskly. 'It is too fine a day to spend all of it shut indoors.'

'I would not wish to intrude.' Her smile was over-bright, her gaze not quite meeting his.

Adam's mouth tightened. It was as he had thought might be the case; after his appalling behaviour, she could barely stand to look at him, let alone spend any more time in his company than she had to. Perhaps if he tried to ease her nerves? 'It would be the ideal occasion on which to show off what I am presuming is one of your new gowns,' he cajoled, while allowing himself to inwardly admire the way in which her deep rose-coloured gown perfectly complemented her ivory complexion and the darkness of her hair.

She wore those dark tresses in a less-severe style today, too, several loose curls at her temples and nape giving her a much more youthful appearance, bringing about a sudden recollection of how she had not been altogether honest with him in regard to her true age when she had first applied for the job.

His mouth tightened as he privately wondered what other secrets the puzzling Elena Leighton might be keeping from him…

Her cheeks blushed the same becoming rose as her gown. 'Mrs Hepworth was able to finish and deliver this first gown early yesterday evening.'

'Her promptness is to be commended.' He turned away to look at his daughter. 'Now, I believe Amanda, for one, is eager for her luncheon.'

Amanda beamed up at him. 'We are really to have a picnic together, Papa?'

'I have said so, yes.'

Amanda did a happy little skip. 'I have never been on a picnic before.'

A frown appeared on Adam's brow as he looked at his young daughter's glowingly excited face. His marriage to Fanny had been a mistake, for which he had paid dearly, and he had always been grateful that Amanda had been far too young, when her mother died, to have ever witnessed the unhappiness that had existed between her mother and father.

But Adam had sincerely believed, until his conversations with Elena this past week, that he had been a good father to Amanda, given the circumstances, and his own lack of experience and knowledge in that regard. Amanda's excitement now, at the thought of such a simple pleasure as the sharing of a picnic together, once again led him to question that belief.

He forced the tension from his shoulders. 'Then it is for Mrs Leighton and me to do everything we can to ensure that you enjoy this, your very first one.'

Amanda reached out and wrapped both her arms about one of his as she gave him a hug. 'Thank you, Papa. Oh, thank you!'

'Mrs Leighton?'

Elena had watched the exchange between father and daughter with increasingly softening feelings; far from chastising Amanda for wrinkling his perfectly tailored superfine, as many gentlemen of the *ton* might have done, Adam had actually placed his hand on top of his daughter's in a gesture of affection. A gesture not lost on Amanda as she gazed up at him adoringly.

It took so little for Amanda to forget, for a time at least, to be that restrained little girl who normally spent only a very short time each day with her father; Amanda's eyes gleamed like sapphires, her face alight with anticipation at the prospect of such a treat.

'Mrs Leighton?' Adam repeated with unaccustomed patience at her continued silence.

Elena could not speak momentarily for the lump of emotion that had formed in her throat, her eyes having gone quite misty. She swallowed now to clear the dryness from her throat. 'If you are sure I will not be intruding…?'

'I would not have invited you if I had considered that to be a possibility,' he came back crisply.

No, of course he would not. Elena still continued to forget, on occasion, that she was now a governess rather than the beloved granddaughter of a duke. That same accomplished young woman who had once acted as mistress of her grandfather's estates, and as such, the person used to issuing the invitations, rather than the other way about. 'In that case, I should love to join you both, thank you.' She gave an almost regal inclination of her head— for she did not always have to forget she possessed the graciousness of extremely well-born manners!

'How are you liking Cambridgeshire, Mrs Leighton?'
Elena—sitting primly on the same blanket where

Adam, hat removed, lay in relaxed repose a short distance away, their picnic luncheon eaten—turned from watching Amanda scamper about the garden chasing elusive butterflies. 'I like it very much from the little I saw of it on the drive here.'

He raised dark brows. 'Is that a complaint regarding the lack of any outings since your arrival?'

Elena's cheeks felt once again as if they had flushed the same deep rose as her new gown. Why did he constantly put her on the back foot? 'It is not my place to complain, my lord,' she murmured.

He snorted in patent disbelief. 'I seem to recall you telling me it is "not your place" to advise me how to bring up my own daughter—and yet you have done so, on several occasions. I believe you also claimed it is "not your place" to tell me how and when I should deal with the tenants on my estate, whilst at the same time pointing out that it is my duty to attend church on a Sunday, in order that I might converse with them.' One dark teasing brow flicked up to gently mock her. 'Tell me, madam, why should I now believe you when you say it is "not your place" to complain about the lack of entertainment provided since your arrival here?'

Elena's cheeks had grown hotter and hotter with each word that he spoke. Each damning, *truthful* word. For she had done those things. Out of a sense of rightness. The first for Amanda's benefit, the second out of consideration for the workers and tenants of Adam's estate. But Elena felt sure that the real Mrs Leighton would never have forgotten 'her place' as to be so forward, or so outspoken, in her views.

She winced. 'I was merely commenting on the fact that I cannot make an educated judgement as to the attractions or otherwise of Cambridgeshire when I have seen so little of it—have I said something to amuse you, my lord?'

Adam exploded into full-throated laughter at the look of indignation on Elena's beautiful face. Indeed, he had laughed more in this woman's company than he had for—in fact, he could not remember how long it had been since he had last laughed with such spontaneity!

Admittedly, he was laughing at her this time rather than with her, but it nevertheless felt good to once again experience that lightness of humour and heart, to truly enjoy a woman's company. 'Do not look so indignant.' He was tempted to lift his hand to reach up and smooth the frown from Elena's brow with his fingertips, and at the same time enjoy touching her smooth and velvet-soft skin. His laughter slowly faded as he strongly resisted that temptation. 'Perhaps I should consider organising a dinner party so that you might meet some of my neighbours?'

Elena looked more than a little alarmed. 'Even if you were to do so, the governess of your young daughter could not possibly be one of the guests at your dinner table.'

Adam raised an arrogant brow. 'I believe it is for me to say who may or may not be seated at my dinner table.'

She gave a sharp shake of her head. 'And, as such,

you know it would not be fitting for me to be present, my lord.'

Yes, Adam knew better than most the dictates of society—he should do, Fanny had broken them often enough! Which was why he always took care to do the opposite, mainly by absenting himself from society completely.

What was it Royston had called him several evenings ago? Besides a prickly bastard? Ah, yes, Royston had accused him of being a recluse. Not completely accurate, but close enough; removing himself from inclusion in society was by far the easiest way of ensuring that Adam broke none of society's rigid rules. As a widower, his invitation for the beautiful governess of his young daughter to join his other guests for dinner would certainly cause every bit of that gossip and speculation he had managed to avoid since Fanny's death.

Adam frowned. 'You are far too beautiful to want to hide away in the schoolroom forever.'

'I am content there,' she insisted softly.

'You have no ambition in life other than to be a governess to a six-year-old girl?'

She blinked long dark lashes. 'Amanda will not always be aged six.'

He gave a tight smile. 'I believe you are being deliberately obtuse.'

Elena had no idea what she was being, what she was thinking. How could she, when Adam was looking up at her with eyes as soft and dark a grey as a pigeon's wing? 'What—what else should I be if not governess to Amanda, or someone like her?'

The black of Adam's pupils seemed to expand so that they almost encompassed that soft velvet grey even as he moved closer. 'Have you never considered—?'

'Papa, come and see the tiny kitten I have found!' Amanda, totally relaxed in her father's company following their picnic, called excitedly to him from across the garden.

Elena continued to be caught in the spell of those velvet grey-eyes for several long seconds more before she made a deliberate effort to break away, turning and looking across to where Amanda held a black kitten cradled gently in her arms. 'Careful it is not feral!' She gathered her skirts before rising quickly to her feet. 'My lord…!'

She looked at Adam imploringly as he rose to his booted feet beside her.

Adam cursed himself for being a fool even as he hurriedly crossed the garden to Amanda and quickly relieved her of the tiny black kitten, knowing he had been about to make a scandalous suggestion to Elena that would have resulted in her either accepting that offer or slapping his face for daring to voice it. Neither of which he wanted.

He did not want nor need a mistress.

Not even one he found as amusing and desirable as Elena Leighton. Most especially one he found as amusing and desirable as Elena Leighton!

And if she had slapped his face, for daring to make

her such a reprehensible offer, then she would no doubt
have given him notice only seconds later, too. For they
could not continue in the way they had been if he were
ever to make such an offer and she were to refuse it.

Leaving Amanda without a governess she liked and
Adam without the unexpected source of pleasure, and
amusement, the brief times he spent with Elena were
becoming to him. It was an unpalatable thought and
one he swiftly pushed out of his head.

'It is all right, is it not, Papa…?' His daughter looked
up at him uncertainly.

Adam focused on the tiny kitten in his hand, knowing by the healthy glow to its grey-green eyes, as it
looked up at him so trustingly, that it was not diseased.
The soft rumbling purr that shook its little body was in-
dicative of it not being feral, either. 'Perfectly all right.'
Adam nodded as he gently replaced the kitten back into
Amanda's waiting arms. 'But it is not wise to pick up
stray animals, pet.'

'Where do you think it came from, Papa?' Amanda
stroked the kitten even as she looked about the otherwise deserted garden.

His expression softened as he appreciated how pretty
his daughter looked today in her yellow gown, a ribbon
of the same colour tied about her golden curls. Tall for
her age, and already giving indications of the beauty she
would possess when she was older, Adam had no doubts
that he would one day be beating his daughter's beaus
away from his door. 'I suggest you try looking in the

stables for its mother and siblings,' he murmured indulgently. 'There is usually a litter or two hiding in there.'

'You are not hurt, Amanda?' A slightly breathless Elena prompted huskily.

Adam's expression tightened as he looked down at the woman he had moment ago considered asking to become his mistress, damn it!

Admittedly, Elena looked very beautiful today, in that rose-coloured gown and with her hair in that softer style. And, yes, she had once again succeeded in amusing him, in making him laugh, in a way no other woman ever had, but he could not and would not lower his guard by inviting any woman to become his permanent mistress. Most especially he could not ask it of the widowed Elena Leighton. If she accepted, he would no doubt be provided with amusement for a matter of days or possibly weeks, but ultimately it would deprive Amanda of her governess forever.

Much better if he were to remove himself from this situation, if only briefly, and find some other woman—a woman who offered far fewer complications—to scratch the sexual itch that presently demanded satisfaction!

He looked over at his daughter. 'Perhaps Mrs Leighton would care to accompany you to the stables?' He turned to address Elena. 'I have some business to attend to this afternoon before my departure later this evening.'

Elena looked at him sharply. 'You are going back to London?' There had not even been so much as the suggestion of it whilst they were eating their picnic luncheon, or of him going anywhere else today. Not, she acknowledged ruefully, that he owed her any explanation as to his movements.

A sentiment he completely echoed, if the expression of arrogant disdain on the haughty handsomeness of his face was any indication. 'As it happens, I am not returning to London, but have a business appointment elsewhere—'

'You are going away, Papa?' Amanda, momentarily distracted from where she now sat on the grass playing with the kitten, looked up at him in pouting disappointment. 'How long will you be gone?'

'Two, perhaps three days—'

'Do you have to go?' Amanda cut in pleadingly. 'I have so enjoyed our picnic today that I thought we might have another one tomorrow?'

Her father smiled slightly. 'Picnics can only be considered fun if they are a treat rather than an everyday occurrence.'

'But —'

'Amanda,' he reproved softly.

'But I so wanted another picnic tomorrow!' Amanda stated mutinously—a mutiny that Elena, at least, recognised as a precursor to one of the little girl's rare temper tantrums.

He shook his head. 'There is urgent business in need of my attention.'

'There is always urgent business in need of your attention!'

'Possibly because my estates do not run themselves—'

'Go away, then!' Amanda jumped to her feet, two bright spots of angry colour in her cheeks as she stamped one slippered foot on the grass in temper. 'You always do!' She gave a sob before turning and running across the lawns, then disappearing inside the house with a flourish of golden curls.

'Do you see where your interference has led?' Adam accused as he continued to look across at the house with narrowed and disapproving eyes.

Elena's own eyes widened indignantly. '*My* interference…?'

He shot her an impatient glance. 'I have never, before today, needed to explain my movements or actions to my six-year-old child!'

She gasped. 'And you believe *I* am to blame for that?'

'I believe your suggestion that I needed to "spend more time with my daughter" is to blame for that, madam,' he bit out. 'In the past Amanda has always been content with the time we spend together each day. Now I've spent more time with her, she's suddenly not satisfied.'

Elena frowned at the unfairness of these accusations. 'She has perhaps *seemed* content with only a half hour, perhaps—'

'She *was* content, damn it!'

'In *your* opinion.'

He turned to look down at her with chill grey eyes. 'Yes, in my opinion. Which, unless you have forgotten, is not only the opinion of Amanda's father, but also that of your employer.'

Elena's gaze lowered at this timely reminder of her position in this gentleman's household; she was becoming far too fond of forgetting that fact. 'I will go and talk to her.'

'Does she often throw such tantrums?' Adam asked grimly. He realised he was probably overreacting, but Amanda's display of temper just now had been far too much like that of her late mother for him to be able to address the matter in his usual calm manner.

Fanny had been wont to throw such tempers, in public as well as privately, whenever she could not get her own way, but Adam had never before witnessed such a display from his young daughter. Perhaps because he had spent so little time in her company in the past? If that should be the case, then it was perhaps as well that he had discovered Amanda's temper before it was too late to be rectified, for there was no way, absolutely no way that he would tolerate the same selfish wilfulness in her as he had experienced so often in his late wife.

'No, she does not,' Elena assured him firmly. 'And I am sure it has only happened on this occasion because Amanda is a little upset at your imminent departure, after having enjoyed such a lovely afternoon in your company.'

Adam's gaze narrowed ominously. 'Do you think to humour me, madam?'

Warmth entered her cheeks. 'I was only—'

'I am well aware of what you were doing, Mrs Leighton.' He grimaced. 'Nor was there anything "little" about Amanda's display of bad manners.' Adam's frown didn't bode well for the child. 'It was a spoilt and wilful display which cannot be overlooked.'

Elena looked dismayed. 'Oh, but—'

'No, Mrs Leighton, it is my belief that it is my having listened to you which has brought about this unpleasantness in the first place,' he insisted.

She looked up at him pleadingly. 'If you will only allow me to talk with Amanda—'

'I advise that, whilst you are doing so, you are sure to convey my deep displeasure in her behaviour just now,' Adam said as he crossed to the blanket to pick up his hat before placing it upon his head. 'I will speak to her on the matter upon my return.'

'And when might we expect that to be?' Elena dared to venture, only to rear back slightly as she now found herself the focus of his displeasure. 'I should not have asked,' she acknowledged quickly.

A nerve pulsed in his rigidly clenched jaw. 'I trust that your inclusion in our picnic today has not caused you to once again misunderstand your "place" in my household, madam!' He gave her one last dismissive glance before striding forcefully across the lawn towards the house.

Elena had felt the colour drain from her cheeks as she was very firmly—and with a touch of deliberate cruelty, perhaps?—reminded that her 'place' in Adam Hawthorne's household was only that of a servant.

Chapter Seven

'Why didn't you let us know you were to be here this evening, my lord?'

Adam kept his gaze guarded as he looked up at the blousily beautiful woman currently pouring the red wine the same ruby colour as her painted lips, which he had ordered to be served with his late evening meal at the coaching inn he was to stay at for the night, situated thirty miles or so from his estate in Cambridgeshire.

Josie was the widow of the late innkeeper and a woman whose favours Adam had accepted a time or two when he had travelled through to Cambridgeshire in the past. A woman with auburn hair and come-hither brown eyes, her low-necked red gown doing very little to hide the voluptuous swell—and nor was it intended to do so!—of her considerable charms.

Charms that, unfortunately, were of absolutely no interest to Adam this evening. Nor were those of any other woman but the one he could not, should not, even think of wanting... 'Do not fret, Josie,' he drawled drily,

'I am well aware that some other lucky gentleman has already beaten me into sharing your bed tonight.' Josie was as generous with her invitations as she was warm in her bed.

She gave him a saucy grin. 'None that I wouldn't see off in a minute if'n you was to say the word…?'

'I fear I am too exhausted tonight to do you justice, Josie.' Adam smiled to take the sting out of his refusal, knowing the fault lay with his desire for another woman rather than any diminishing of the charms of this woman's warm invitation for him to enjoy her plump and alluring curves.

She returned his smile to show she had taken no offence at that refusal. 'In that case, I hope it's because ye've found yourself a decent woman to satisfy ya needs.'

Adam's smile grew rueful. 'Is that not a contradiction in terms?' He frowned as he realised how pompous he had just sounded. Incomprehensible, perhaps, to a woman who felt no qualms whatsoever in admitting she could neither read nor write, but could count any amount of money accurately and quickly. He shook his head. 'What I meant to say—'

'I knows as what ye meant, my lord,' Josie dismissed unconcernedly. 'Even so, I would've expected a good-looking gent, and an expert and satisfying lover such as yerself, to 'ave found a suitable lady and remarried afore now.'

'I thank you for the compliment, Josie.' Adam smiled.

'Ain't no compliment when it's the truth,' she insisted.

Gratified as he was for Josie's praise, it was nevertheless a little difficult for him to completely accept the second part of Josie's compliment, when his own wife had admitted to being adulterous with another man only a month after their wedding!

Not that he had ever heard any complaints from any of the women he had taken to his bed before he married Fanny, as those liaisons had always resulted in the enjoyment of mutual pleasure. Since Fanny had died, however, he had preferred to pay for that pleasure, so he supposed it was not in the best interest of any of those women to show dissatisfaction in his performance, was it?

Josie gave him a shrewd narrow-eyed glance. 'I hope you'll excuse me for being so bold, my lord, but that wife o' your'n didn't know 'ow to appreciate a good thing when she were married to it!'

Adam let out a bark of laughter as he leant back in his chair. 'You are very good for a man's ego, Josie.' He raised his glass to her in a toast before taking a sip of the ruby-red wine.

'But the answer's still no, I'm guessing...?' She quirked an auburn brow knowingly.

'I am afraid so, yes.' Adam frowned his inner irritation as he slowly placed his glass back down onto the table, knowing that he had lied just now when he claimed to be too tired to do this lady justice in her bed; the reason for his uninterest lay much closer to home. *His* home.

Out of sheer contrariness—or perhaps desperation!—he had been away from Hawthorne Park for a total of four days now, tomorrow, the day he expected to return there, being the fifth day. And not one of those days had passed without his having thought more of the beautiful Elena Leighton than he ought to have done. Dear Lord, a single moment's thought, given to a young woman in his employ, beautiful or otherwise, was one moment too many!

And yet…

Her beauty had continued to haunt and beguile him. Her air of inborn elegance intrigued and bedevilled him, as well as her ability to puzzle and tempt him, to amuse him, to the extent that he actually laughed in her company—all despite his previous decision not to give in to the weakness of this unexpected and unwanted attraction!

They had parted badly four days ago. Very badly. He had been both cold and condescending towards her. Attitudes which should not have been directed at Elena at all, but towards his young daughter. Amanda's temper tantrum that day, even the words she had used as to his 'always being busy with estate affairs', had been far too reminiscent of the accusations her mother would fling at him in her fits of pique or temper.

As a result, Adam had responded to Amanda's wilfulness instinctively, but unfortunately his own anger had rained down on Elena's innocent head rather than his absent daughter's. Something that had continued to bother him in the four days that had passed since, along with his ever-weakening determination to withstand the deep attraction Elena held for him.

While his libido had been totally uninterested in any other woman the last few days, he only had to think of Elena to become aroused. He imagined her now, perhaps in her bedchamber getting ready for bed, with her long ebony hair loose about her sweetly swelling, rose-tinted breasts, the slenderness of her waist above the gentle swell of her hips—

'I hope she appreciates her good fortune,' Josie said, unwittingly breaking into his pleasant thoughts.

'Sorry?' Adam looked up to raise a questioning brow.

Josie gave another of her saucy grins. 'Whoever the lady was you was just thinking about 'as brought a devilish gleam to your eyes and a hardness to your thighs!'

It was true, damn it!

Obviously he could not speak for the 'devilish gleam' in his eyes, but the other part, at least, was without a doubt true, that hot and throbbing arousal evident in the obvious bulge pressing against the front of his breeches. An arousal he would probably have to deal with himself when he retired to his bedchamber later this evening. As he'd had to do this past four nights. Unless…

'Best bring me another flagon of this wine, Josie,' he advised ruefully as he refilled his glass; inebriation was another way of banishing these intruding thoughts of the delightful governess from his mind. And quelling the raging desire of his shaft!

Josie gave a throaty chuckle. 'Just say the word and I'll shimmy 'neath the table and see 'e's settled quick as a wink.' She gave a slow and pointed lick of painted ruby red lips as she looked down at the bulge in his breeches.

'Tempting…but let me try the wine first, hmm,' Adam murmured evasively.

'You knows where I am if'n ye should change ya mind.' She shrugged her shoulders good-naturedly, jiggling her ample breasts temptingly, before leaving the parlour to collect a second flagon of wine.

Adam sat back with a sigh, knowing he had to find a suitable solution to this dilemma, of desiring a woman he had no right to desire, that he could not go on living in this physical and mental purgatory indefinitely; both he, and his estates, would suffer if he did not soon find some way of putting an end to what had become a hellish situation.

This past four days' absence from Hawthorne Hall, of thinking constantly of Elena Leighton rather than the business he should be dealing with, had more than proved that point. And it provided him with only two solutions going forwards.

Elena must either leave his household forthwith, and so be removed from both his sight and temptation, or Adam must give in to his desire and offer her the role of his mistress and hope—or fear—that she would accept…

'Do you think Papa will be cross about Samson…?' Amanda looked at Elena anxiously as she stroked the soft black fur of the rapidly growing kitten currently purring in her lap.

In truth, Elena had absolutely no idea how Adam would react to his daughter having adopted the black kitten they had found after the picnic. He had left in his carriage for his business appointment later that very same day, without so much as saying goodbye to Amanda or leaving instructions for Elena.

Elena did know that Amanda had been sobbing inconsolably when she had sought out the little girl in her bedchamber that day, Amanda's disappointment at her father's imminent departure having been replaced with regret and remorse for having behaved so badly. A regret Amanda had unfortunately not had the opportunity to voice to her father before he'd left.

And ever since he'd been gone, Elena had tried but failed in her attempts to forgive the dratted man as she witnessed her young charge's misery.

Amanda was aged only six, Adam Hawthorne was eight or possibly nine and twenty, and that disparity in years between father and daughter should have carried a similar disparity in their maturity. Unfortunately, in this case, that did not appear to have been the case.

Consequently Elena was very angry with Adam. More angry than she could remember being for a long, long time—if ever. As a result, when it transpired that the black kitten was a stray, unaccepted by any of the mothering she-cats in the stables, Elena had taken it upon herself to give her permission when Amanda had asked if she might have the kitten for her own. And if

Lord Adam Hawthorne did not like that decision, then Elena would tell him exactly why she had made it!

'Not at all,' she assured Amanda briskly. 'I have every reason to believe your father is a fair and reasonable gentleman—'

'I am glad to hear it,' that very same 'gentleman' drawled from the schoolroom doorway. 'Just as I would dearly love to hear what I have done to be deserving of such an accolade…?'

'Papa!' Amanda's previous anxiety disappeared like a summer mist as she ran across the schoolroom to launch herself into his arms.

'Careful, pet,' her father advised gently as the kitten looked in danger of being squashed between them. 'What do we have here?'

He gently took the kitten and held it up for his inspection.

'I have given Amanda permission to keep the kitten,' Elena, sensing another crisis looming on the horizon, rushed in to claim decisively.

'Indeed?' Adam spared her only a cursory glance before turning his attention back to his daughter. 'What do you call him?'

'Samson,' Amanda supplied almost shyly.

He smiled. 'You called this little fellow Samson…?'

'He will grow into his name, I am sure,' Elena defended briskly, feeling slightly indignant on behalf of both Amanda and the tiny kitten. Admittedly the kitten was probably the runt of whatever litter he had come from, which was perhaps why he had been cast out, but he had huge paws that must surely one day support an equally as large body.

Her employer gave her another enigmatic glance before smiling down at Amanda as he gave the kitten back into her care. 'He is a fine little fellow.'

'And I may keep him, Papa?' Amanda prompted.

'How can I possibly decide anything else when Mrs Leighton herself has declared me to be such a fair and reasonable gentleman?'

The underlying sarcasm of that comment was completely lost on the now-beaming Amanda. Not so on Elena, who was only too well aware that he had to be mocking her.

'It is so good to have you home again, Papa.' Amanda's pleasure shone in her sapphire-blue eyes.

'It is very good to be home again, pet,' he assured gruffly. 'I have missed you.'

Elena eyed him sceptically; if he truly had missed the company of his young daughter then he should have returned sooner, rather than leaving Amanda in an agony of anxiety for the past five days over their strained parting.

'As a special celebration of my return, perhaps you and Mrs Leighton would care to join me downstairs for dinner this evening?'

'Really, Papa?' Amanda's eyes were wide with disbelief at the offered treat.

Elena, on the other hand, was still too irritated and annoyed by his long absence to be able to contemplate spending the evening in his company, or to enjoy how

dashingly handsome he looked now in a deep-green superfine and buff-coloured pantaloons and black Hessians. 'You will have to excuse me, I am afraid, Lord
Hawthorne.'

'Indeed?'

Elena ignored the coolness of his tone. 'My evenings
are my own to do with as I wish, I believe, and I have
several other, personal and more important things in
need of my attention this evening.'

Adam eyed her mockingly. 'Such as?'

She gave him a reproving frown. 'Such as my ironing and washing my hair, sir!'

So now he knew where he stood in Elena Leighton's
list of considerations, Adam acknowledged ruefully—
obviously placed after her ironing and hair-washing!

Her manner had been more than a little frosty since
he first entered the schoolroom, Adam acknowledged
ruefully, and also defensive in regard to Amanda and
the kitten. The latter might be attributed to the protec-
tive role she held in Amanda's young life and the manner in which father and daughter had parted five days
ago. Yet he sensed there was more to it than that, that
whether she was aware of it or not, the indignation was
also on her own behalf.

Because of the way in which he had spoken to her
before his departure?

No doubt about it.

Amanda had obviously already forgiven him for
going away so suddenly and remaining away longer

than he had anticipated. Elena Leighton, apparently, was of a less forgiving nature altogether...

'Both of those chores might wait another day, I am sure,' Adam briskly dismissed her excuse. 'Perhaps it would help if you were to look on this evening as a lesson to Amanda in manners and etiquette,' he added persuasively as he saw Elena was about to refuse his dinner invitation a second—or was it a third?—time.

She arched dark brows. 'In that case, might I expect to be allowed another afternoon off this month in lieu?'

His mouth thinned at the stubborn defiance she made little or no attempt to disguise. 'And what would you do with that second free afternoon, when, by your own admission, you do not know the Cambridgeshire area well?'

She looked at him coolly. 'I could use that free afternoon in which to know it better.'

Adam bit back his instinctive reply, knowing that it would suffice nothing, change nothing, except to make her more determined not to dine with him rather than the opposite. 'Then perhaps I might offer to be your guide?' he came back with a good attempt at that reasonableness she had attributed to him earlier.

She looked more alarmed than pleased at the suggestion. 'You are such a busy man, my lord, I could not possibly ask or expect that you waste any of it on showing me Cambridgeshire.'

'Or you to Cambridgeshire?'

'I very much doubt, my lord, that the county has feelings one way or the other about meeting the governess of your young daughter!'

Yes, whether she acknowledged it or not, she was indeed frostily indignant on her own behalf, as much as Amanda's!

It was an indignation totally at odds with her role of governess, an indignation that had given a flush to her ivory cheeks that was slowly moving down over the plump slope of her breasts visible above the low neckline of the turquoise gown she wore. Another of Mrs Hepworth's creations, no doubt, Adam mused, approving of this gown even more than he had the rose-coloured one, admiring the way in which it deepened the colour of Elena's eyes as they met his gaze unblinkingly and gave a soft glow to the ivory texture of her skin.

Adam continued to hold that gaze with his as he spoke to his daughter. 'Amanda, should you not consider taking Samson outside for a short time?'

'Oh, yes.' She gave a little giggle. 'May I be excused, Mrs Leighton?'

Those blue-green eyes narrowed slightly on Adam. 'Yes, of course you may, Amanda. With your father's agreement, I believe our lessons are over for today.'

'Papa?'

He smiled down at her approvingly. 'I will see you at dinner, Amanda.' Adam waited until his daughter had left the room before speaking again. 'I believe, Elena, that I owe you an apology for my…brusqueness the last time we spoke together.'

She raised haughty brows. 'Is it now my turn to dismiss the repetitiveness of your own apologies, my lord?'

'Adam.'

She blinked. 'I beg your pardon…?'

'I believe I once asked that you call me Adam,' he reminded her.

Her cheeks warmed with colour as she obviously recalled the occasion on which he had made that request and the exact circumstances under which he had made it. 'And I believe that I declined that invitation.'

His mouth tightened. 'Do you decline it still?'

She gave a gracious inclination of her head. 'As I must.'

'Why must you?'

Elena was unsure of how he came to be standing only inches away from her. She had not seen or heard him move, yet here he was, so close to her that she could see that black circle about the deep-grey iris as she looked up into his eyes and smell the sandalwood cologne he wore. The darkness of his hair looked slightly damp, seeming to imply he had bathed and changed before coming to the schoolroom.

She lowered her lashes to hide the expression in her eyes. 'It is not fitting for me to address you so informally.'

'Elena—'

'Do not!' She stepped back in alarm as he would have reached out and taken hold of her arms.

He released a heavy sigh even as his hands fell back to his side. 'Will you at least allow me to explain—to try to explain—why I was so ill-humoured on the last occasion we spoke together?'

She clasped her hands tightly together. 'I am sure there is no reason for you to either apologise or explain your moods to me, my lord.'

'In this instance I should like to do so,' he insisted huskily.

Elena continued to avoid meeting that soft grey gaze, so unlike that chilling coldness of five days ago. 'I am fully aware that Amanda's loss of temper had angered you—'

'Would you not like to know the reason why it did so…?'

Would she? Did Elena want to know anything more about the dynamics of this small family than she already did? To have Adam's emotions explained to her?

Elena had believed, when she fled Sheffield Park as if the hounds of hell were at her heels, that her future was bleak, her only course of action to cease being the fugitive Miss Magdelena Matthews and instead become a woman whom no one noticed, a servant in the household of one of the very people who believed her guilty of murder and theft.

And for a short while she had succeeded in doing exactly that, quietly going about her business as Amanda Hawthorne's governess and seemingly invisible to Lord Adam Hawthorne. Quite when, or why, that had changed, she was not quite sure—she only knew that for some inexplicable reason he had indeed noticed her, that he had actually sought out her company on several occasions. To the point that he had kissed her the previous week! A kiss, which although surprising, she had been unable to forget. Or her unexpected response to it.

Making her position here untenable?

She was very much afraid that was exactly what was happening...

If it had not already done so!

The fact that she knew her cousin would never give up his search for her meant she could not allow Adam to see her as anything more than his daughter's governess, that to do so would place her in a position of danger and vulnerability.

To her loss of freedom.

As well as her heart...

Because she was becoming attached to this family in spite of herself. Amanda, although given to those occasional tempers, was on the whole adorable, and as for Lord Adam Hawthorne—Elena found herself thinking about that gentleman far more often than was wise. Admittedly it had been mainly in annoyance most recently, and a certain sense of injustice at becoming the focus of his displeasure following Amanda's outburst, but even so she had still found herself thinking of him often. Of how much she admired his handsome looks. Of how charming he could be when he relaxed his guard and appeared to forget to be coldly reserved. She also found herself thinking of that kiss far more often than she ought...

Everything came back to that kiss. The surprise of it, the unsuitability of it, and the unexpected *pleasure* of it, when Neville's brutality to her two months ago should have caused her to feel only nausea.

The same pleasure still caused Elena to tremble every time she thought of those chiselled and yet softly questing, lips pressed so intimately against her own…

She straightened her spine. 'As I have said, it is not necessary, my lord.'

'Damn whether or not you think it necessary—!' Adam broke off his angry retort, fully aware that it was caused by the tension of awaiting her reply rather than any real anger he felt towards her. A tense wait that had been rewarded by another of her cool set-downs. 'Look at me, Elena.' He raised his hand beneath her chin and lifted her face up towards his when she did not obey him. 'I reacted in the way that I did because—'

'Adam, I—am I interrupting something…?'

Adam stiffened with shock, his hand dropping back to his side as he turned sharply at the sound of that familiar voice. A familiar voice, which by rights, should have been many miles away from here. 'Grand-mama…?'

Chapter Eight

Lady Cicely stepped into the schoolroom, grey brows raised in query. 'You look surprised to see me, Adam.'

That surely had to be the understatement of the Season! Adam was not only surprised to see his grandmother here, but he was less than happy about it too, bearing in mind his recent suspicions concerning her matrimonial machinations in regard to himself.

Adam turned briefly to give Elena a censorious frown. 'Why did you not inform me immediately of my grandmother's arrival here?' If he had known his grandmother was in the house, he would most certainly have delayed his conversation with her. Delayed, but not dismissed it completely...

How could he dismiss it, when just to look at her again, to briefly touch her, had caused a bulge in his pantaloons he was forced to cover with the fall of his jacket!

Her eyes widened. 'It was my assumption that Jeffries would have informed you on your arrival of Lady Cicely's presence, your lordship.'

A perfectly logical assumption to have made—except that Adam, having made up his mind as to his future relations with this woman, had been more intent on bathing and going to the schoolroom rather than listening to anything Jeffries might wish to impart to him. 'Obviously not,' Adam muttered.

'I fail to see what all the fuss is about concerning who did or did not tell you of my arrival?' his grandmother said querulously. 'I am here, as you can clearly see.'

And Adam's instant reaction to that was 'and for how long do you intend staying?' Which was not only rude of him, but also less than familial, considering he and Amanda were Lady Cicely's closest relatives.

His mouth quirked and he forced the tension to ease from his shoulders. 'I am merely surprised at seeing you so far from London, and your dear friends there, in the middle of the Season, Grandmama.'

'I missed you and Amanda so.'

His brows rose. 'We have only been gone a few days…'

'If you will excuse me, my lord, Lady Cicely, I believe I must go and check on Amanda and the kitten.' Elena gave a brief curtsy, her head remaining bowed as she crossed and then departed from the room.

Adam's mood was one of pure frustration as he watched her leave. Not only had he been unable to talk privately to Elena, but he also apparently now had to deal with having his grandmother visit for goodness knew how long.

'There is…something about that young lady, which does not quite…sit right, with the role of a governess, my dear…'

Adam scowled darkly as he turned to look at his grandmother, a scowl completely lost on her as she continued to look in the direction of the doorway through which Elena had just passed. But he couldn't ignore the fact that his grandmother echoed some of his own doubts about Elena Leighton's suitability as a governess; she was very ladylike and elegant in her manner, and she often, but not always, appeared to forget to treat him with the deference of his other servants. Of course, a governess was an occupation slightly above that of the maids or footmen, but surely no more so than Jeffries or the housekeeper, neither of which ever forgot either that Adam was Lord Hawthorne, or that he was their employer.

Nevertheless, they were doubts which Adam had no intention of sharing with his grandmother. 'I believe it is time we both had tea and then you can explain to me exactly why it is you have chosen to leave London in order to visit me here.' He offered her his arm.

Lady Cicely gave him a sideways glance as she placed her gloved hand on that arm. 'Is that your polite way of saying that the subject of Mrs Leighton is at an end?'

Adam could not prevent a burst of laughter escaping him. 'I do believe you have been spending far too much time in the company of the forceful and forthright Dowager Duchess of Royston, my dear!'

She gave him a coquettish smile as she preceded him through the doorway, waiting outside for him to join her before they strolled down the hallway together towards the wide staircase. 'In that case, you will not be at all surprised if I also comment on your reluctance to discuss your newest, rather beautiful employee?'

Adam's mouth tightened. 'Because there is nothing to discuss. Mrs Leighton was employed as governess to Amanda, and I can find no fault with her in that regard.'

'But what do you know of her background? Her family? Her connections?'

He controlled his impatience. 'Not a thing above her widowhood—nor is it necessary for me to know anything else about her, Grandmama,' he added firmly as he saw how the curiosity had deepened in his grandmother's expression.

Lady Cicely frowned slightly. 'She has a look about her, seems to remind me of someone that I know, or have known, in the past...'

Adam glanced at her sharply. 'Do you have any idea who that someone might be?'

'It escapes me for the moment.' His grandmother gave a vague shake of her head. 'Perhaps she is some gentleman of the *ton*'s illegitimate daughter—'

'Grandmother!'

She raised a grey brow. 'I am not too old to be unaware of these things, Adam.'

'I was not for a moment suggesting that you were, but still—'

'It is the elegant tilt of her head, and possibly that

abundance of silky dark hair, which seem so familiar.'
Lady Cicely continued to muse softly. 'And, of course,
her eyes are quite magnificent.'

Considering that Adam inwardly echoed that sentiment he wisely kept silent, knowing that to comment
at all on the fineness of Elena's eyes would only result
in deepening his grandmother's curiosity, if that were
even possible. Much better if he were to appear uninterested in the whole subject.

'I am certain I have seen eyes of that unusual
colour before.' Lady Cicely gave a pained moue as she
searched for the memory that continued to elude her.
'Never mind.' She shook her head as she straightened.
'I am sure it will come back to me at some later date…'

Adam was unsure as to whether or not he wished his
grandmother to recall that knowledge, his curiosity to
know more of Elena Leighton warring with the possibility of his learning that she was not who she claimed
at all, but some other man's runaway wife.

Elena, having gone briefly to her bedchamber, in
order to collect her bonnet and gloves before going outside in search of her small charge, had emerged out into
the hallway behind her employer and his grandmother,
just in time to hear their conversation.

And now trembled at the significance of it.

For she knew who it was that Lady Cicely had pre-
viously met with these same unusual blue-green eyes:
Elena's father, the late Lord David Matthews, youngest
son of the previous Duke of Sheffield. He had caused

many a female heart to swoon over the years with eyes of such an unusual blue-green. He would have been at least twenty or so years younger than Lady Cicely, of course, but her parents had been much a part of society before her father's death, an occurrence that would have ensured Lady Cicely saw them both even if she did not know them intimately. And Elena's mother, Lady Maria Matthews, had been the lady with an 'abundance of silky dark hair' so similar to Elena's own.

'It really is too bad of my grandson to have dragged you away from London in the middle of the Season.' Lady Cicely smiled at Elena sympathetically as the two of them sat in the green salon together, where they had retired to drink tea following a sumptuous dinner, after leaving Adam alone in the dining room to enjoy his brandy and cigars.

Adam had kept to his invitation for Amanda and Elena to join him for dinner, an invitation which also included his grandmother. And if Lady Cicely found it strange to find herself sitting down to dine with her great-granddaughter and her governess, then she did not show it by word or deed, her conversation pleasant and kept to subjects that both Amanda and Elena could contribute to, if they wished.

On several occasions Elena had felt she had no choice but to do so, when Adam, magnificent in his black evening clothes and snowy white linen, remained broodingly silent at the head of the table for the most part, eating little but enjoying several glasses of ruby-red wine.

Elena had left the room for a short time following dessert, when it was decided that Amanda had stayed up quite long enough for one evening, and Elena had gratefully risen to her feet in order to take the little girl to her bedchamber. Only to feel her heart sink again when Lady Cicely had expressed a wish for Elena to return downstairs and join her for tea once she had seen that Amanda was safely abed.

'As I am not part of society it is of little significance to me whether I am here or in London, Lady Cicely,' she answered smoothly now.

'But it is always so much more…lively, in London, during the Season. And I see you are no longer in mourning…' The older woman smiled approval of Elena's cream gown, delivered yesterday by Mrs Hepworth, in plenty of time for attending church tomorrow, and the only gown Elena had which was suitable for wearing to a formal dinner such as this evening's had been.

Elena sat stiffly in the armchair facing Lady Cicely as she sat on the green-velvet sofa. 'Lord Hawthorne did not think my black gowns suitable attire for when I am in Amanda's company.'

'No?'

'He feared it was too much of a reminder to Amanda of her deceased mother.'

The older woman's smile faded as she nodded slowly. 'And I am sure none of us needs to be reminded of the absence of Amanda's mother from this household.'

It was, Elena decided, a strange way to refer to the death of Adam's wife. 'No,' she answered slowly; she knew from Adam that he had been a widower for some years, but she had no idea of the happiness or otherwise of that marriage before Fanny Hawthorne's death.

Strangely, there had been no talk below stairs in regard to Adam's brief marriage, at Hawthorne House in London or since their arrival in Cambridgeshire. Which was unusual in itself; most household servants took delight in discussing the private lives of the family for whom they worked. But perhaps in this case the marriage had been of such short duration that no lasting impression had been made in regard to her ladyship?

Whatever the reason for that silence, Elena found that she was becoming increasingly more curious about Fanny Hawthorne. To wonder what manner of woman she had been that she had managed to ensnare the heart of a man as cold and arrogant as Adam could be. Or perhaps he had not been quite so cold and arrogant all those years ago? He could only have been in his early twenties when he married, hardly old enough for his true nature to have emerged and become quite so set in stone. Literally. For there was no doubt that, apart from his obvious affection for his daughter and grandmother, Adam Hawthorne now possessed a heart as cold as ice.

'Do you have any children of your own, Mrs Leighton…?'

Elena's attention sharpened as she realised she had allowed her thoughts to wander into conjecture regarding her employer's marriage. A serious lapse in attention, when, despite all outward appearances to the contrary, Lady Cicely was far more sharply astute than she gave the impression of being. 'Sadly, no.' Elena smiled briefly.

'I should have loved to have been blessed with a daughter, but unfortunately it was not to be. Nor a granddaughter, either.' The older woman sighed wistfully.

'But you have a great-granddaughter now,' she consoled the elderly lady.

'So I do.' Lady Cicely brightened briefly before that smile faded once again. 'Which is all well and good, of course, but it is a male heir that is needed if we are to keep the title within the family—'

'The last I heard, Cousin Wilfred was still a member of this family?' came a cool voice Elena knew only too well.

She gave a guilty start as she turned in the armchair to face Adam, knowing that guilt was reflected in the flush that also warmed her cheeks as those cold grey eyes raked over both women. Rightly so, perhaps, when it was obvious they had been gossiping about his succession.

'Being your third cousin, he is not a Hawthorne by name and is currently employed as a lawyer.' Lady Cicely showed no outward sign of apology at being caught discussing her grandson in his absence, or to hide her distaste for her distant relative's occupation. 'Furthermore, he has a shrew for a wife and at least half-a-dozen unruly children.' She wrinkled her nose delicately. 'I cannot even bear to think of him and his family being invited here on a visit, let alone imagine them all residing here!'

Adam had delayed joining the ladies for as long as he had felt able, not wishing to appear too eager, but at the same time only too well aware of how artfully his innocuous-looking grandmother could draw information from people when she chose to do so. And despite having claimed earlier that she had decided to come to Cambridgeshire on a whim, that she had missed the company of both himself and Amanda, she had also made her interest in learning more about Elena Leighton only too obvious during their earlier conversation.

He entered the salon and quietly closed the door behind him before answering his grandmother. 'If it is any consolation, I very much doubt that you will still be alive when the time comes for Cousin Wilfred and his family to reside here!'

Lady Cicely gave a grimace. 'No, Adam, I do not believe that to be of any consolation to me whatsoever!'

Adam lowered hooded lids as he saw that Elena was doing her best to hold back a smile at their conversation. 'I thought only to cheer you.'

'Then you failed utterly.' His grandmother gave him a knowing look before turning to Elena once more. 'As you may have gathered, my grandson finds the discussion of his heir to be a disagreeable subject,' she confided ruefully.

Adam's mouth tightened. 'Your grandson finds it a ridiculous subject, because I have stated, on more than one occasion, that it is not my intention to ever remarry, so leaving Cousin Wilfred in possession of the title when I die, whether that is what the rest of the family wants or not.' He looked arrogantly down the length of his nose.

Lady Cicely rose gracefully to her feet, very slight and delicate in a gown of pale grey. 'And on that cheerful note I believe it is time I retired for the night…'

Elena matched her action, equally as elegantly. 'I believe I might also retire, my lord.'

Adam studied her beneath lowered lids, the cream gown she wore seeming to give a moon-glow to the ivory of her skin. With an ebony sheen to the dark arrangement of her hair and her cheeks a pale rose, she was a vision of loveliness that had taunted and tempted Adam all the evening, her every move increasing the throb of his desire, to a degree that he had grown more and more silent and surly as the time passed.

'I, too, am fatigued from my long journey today,' he made his own excuses, only to then find himself irritated by the expression of relief Elena was not quick enough to mask as she quickly turned away. 'Unless Mrs Leighton finds the hour too early for sleeping?' Adam gave an internal grin of satisfaction as she stiffened. 'In which case, I will, of course, offer to act as her escort if she wishes to take a stroll outside before bedtime?'

'Is it not a little cold and late for strolling outside, Adam?' His grandmother glanced out into the darkened garden.

Adam kept his gaze firmly fixed on the tense and still Elena. 'I will happily wait here while Mrs Leighton goes upstairs to collect her bonnet and cloak.'

Elena was totally at a loss to know how to deal with a conversation that seemed to have progressed to the acceptance of her strolling outside in the moonlight with Adam Hawthorne, without the inclusion of so much as a single word of encouragement or agreement from her!

A totally inappropriate and improper stroll… 'I really would prefer to go straight to my bedchamber,' she refused primly. 'But I thank you for the offer, my lord,' she added awkwardly.

'I will do my best to bear the disappointment, Mrs Leighton,' he drawled, a derisive smile tilting his lips as those dark-grey eyes met hers mockingly.

Telling Elena more clearly than anything else could have done that he had not been serious in his offer, but simply playing with her all along. A part of her longed to wipe that mocking smile from his lips by telling him that she had changed her mind, and would, after all, like to go for a stroll outside. But another part of her, the more sensible part, warned that she would be playing with fire by daring to challenge this gentleman when he was in this dangerously unpredictable mood.

'Shall we go upstairs together then, Mrs Leighton?' Lady Cicely linked her arm with Elena's. 'Adam?' She offered her cheek to her grandson.

As a consequence Elena was standing far too close when he bent down to pay his respects to his grandmother. So close that she could not mistake the challenge in those dark-grey eyes when he continued to look down at her as he lingered over kissing Lady Cicely's powdered cheek.

'Darling boy.' His grandmother patted his own cheek affectionately when he finally straightened. 'I am so glad I decided to visit you.'

'As are we, Grandmama,' Adam replied noncommittally.

'Am I not the most blessed of grandmothers, Mrs Leighton?' Lady Cicely turned to beam at Elena as the two of them crossed the room together to where the door was even now being opened by the attentive Jeffries.

Adam could almost have laughed out loud as he witnessed the way in which Elena's natural frankness warred with the politeness expected of her as a member of his household staff; those blue-green eyes glittered at him briefly with that scathing honesty as she stepped aside to allow his grandmother to walk out into the hallway first. 'You are indeed blessed in many ways, Lady Cicely,' Adam heard her murmur ambiguously as the door was closed softly behind them both.

An answer that had no doubt pleased his grandmother, but did not fool Adam for a moment; Elena obviously did not number *him* amongst Lady Cicely's many blessings.

Adam sighed deeply as he turned to stare sightlessly out at the moonlight gardens beyond the windows, becoming lost in thought as the silence of the night covered him like a shroud.

He would have to talk to Elena in private, and at the

earliest opportunity. Not necessarily with a view to asking her to become his mistress—not only because, as things stood between the two of them, she would no doubt deliver a sharp and painful blow to his cheek for even daring to voice such a suggestion—but because Adam now felt that he should ask Elena to tell him more about herself before thinking in such terms, as well as attempt to clear the air between them.

For Amanda's sake, nothing more, Adam assured himself briskly as he moved to the window to stare out at the dark starlit sky. It would not do for Amanda's father and her governess to be constantly at odds with each other—

Adam turned sharply as he heard the door softly open behind him, his eyes widening as he saw that Elena had returned.

Alone…

Chapter Nine

'Oh!' Elena felt consternation as she stepped back into the green salon and found herself face to face with Adam. 'I did not mean to interrupt, my lord—I thought you would have retired to your rooms by now,' she hurried to excuse.

'As you can clearly see, I have not,' he drawled softly in reply, arms behind his back.

'Yes.' Elena avoided looking at the man whose very presence disturbed and yet somehow excited her. 'I believe I may have dropped my handkerchief earlier.' She began to look about the furniture and floor for the missing scrap of silk and lace, given to her as a gift by her late grandfather, with her initials, *MM*, damningly sewn into one of the corners—a realisation which had thrown her into something of a panic once she reached her bedchamber and noticed it was missing from the pocket concealed in her gown.

She should never have kept the scrap of silk and lace, of course, should have left that behind with all the other personal effects which identified her as Lady Magdelena Matthews. But she had wanted to keep something with her which had been given to her by her grandfather, and it was such a tiny piece of silk and lace...

'Ah.' Adam rocked back on his heels. 'Perhaps I might be of assistance—'

'No! No, I have found it now.' She straightened swiftly, the handkerchief crushed in her hand before being pushed into the pocket of her gown.

'Perhaps—' he broke off to look enquiringly towards the door.

Jeffries entered the room. 'May I get you anything further this evening, my lord?'

'No, that will be all for tonight, thank you, Jeffries.' Adam Hawthorne nodded dismissal of the other man.

Elena felt the jolt of alarm in her chest as she looked across at him sharply even as Jeffries bowed out of the room, leaving her alone with him, the very air between them seeming to crackle and dance in a manner that made her tremble. She cleared her throat before speaking. 'I am sorry for disturbing you—'

'Are you?'

'Of course.' Elena eyed him warily, not sure they were talking on the same subject. 'If you will excuse me, my lord, it has been a very long day.'

'Then a few minutes more should make little difference.' He eyed her calmly. 'I wish to speak with you, Elena,' he added huskily as she stared at him uncomprehendingly.

Elena's gaze dropped under the intensity of that unblinking grey one. 'Yes, my lord.'

Adam took a calming breath. 'You may safely dispense with your air of deference, Elena, when my grandmother is no longer present to witness it.'

She regarded him warily. 'My lord…?'

Adam had spent the past two hours or more, sitting at the head of his dining table, as he broodingly contemplated this woman from between narrowed lids. Had watched as she ate very little of the food placed before her. Listened as she added only the odd comment to the conversation between his grandmother and Amanda. Noted the way in which she rarely glanced in his direction.

And he had drawn but one conclusion from those observations. 'I have no idea how it may have occurred, but I am nevertheless of the opinion that you somehow overheard at least part of my grandmother's remarks to me earlier this evening concerning yourself?'

Her chin rose slightly. 'I don't know what you mean, my lord.'

Adam gave an impatient snort. 'Do not insult my intelligence by attempting to pretend otherwise!'

Those blue-green eyes snapped with her own impatience before she lowered dark lashes to veil those enticing orbs. 'I would not be so presumptuous, my lord.'

'Hah, every demure word you speak only confirms my suspicions!' he pronounced triumphantly.

A frown appeared on her brow. 'Just because I am being mindful of my manners —'

'Just because you are behaving in a most un-Elena-like manner,' he corrected derisively. 'The Elena Leighton I have come to know was not the woman who sat calmly silent during dinner this evening, her gaze lowered as much as it was a few minutes ago, adding very little to the conversation, and offering not a single opinion, despite the fact that I know she has many.'

Elena frowned her irritation with this summing up of her character. 'You make me sound like an unpleasant cross between a harridan and a blue-stocking!'

Better, Adam noted with satisfaction, deciding that he liked this indignantly flushed Elena much better than the beautiful but mainly silent statue which had sat at his dinner table this evening. 'Whatever you may have decided to the contrary, I assure you that my grandmother was merely expressing her curiosity and did not mean to be in the least derogatory towards you in our conversation earlier.'

Elena raised dark brows. 'And I can assure both of you that far from being illegitimate my mother and my father had been married—to each other!—for almost two years on the day that I was born.'

'And in which part of England might that have been, Elena?' he prompted curiously.

'Subtlety is not your forte, is it, my lord?' she commented ruefully, the tension leaving her shoulders.

'Apparently not,' Adam muttered before he chuckled throatily. 'I have no idea how it is you always manage to do that…' He gave a slightly dazed shake of his head as he looked at her admiringly.

'Do what, my lord?'

He spread his hands. 'I can be in the blackest mood possible, feel beleaguered on all sides, by my family and other circumstances, and yet you nevertheless manage to say or do something which succeeds in making me smile or openly laugh. It is…a gift I had not expected.'

She moistened her lips with the tip of her tongue before answering him, not in artful invitation, Adam realised, but more in the way of a nervous gesture. 'It is a gift I had not known I possessed either until now, but if it has succeeded in lightening your lot in life then— then I am glad of it.'

Adam stared across at her for long, timeless seconds, aware that the very air seemed to have stilled between them. 'Will you stay and join me in a glass of brandy before retiring, Elena?' he finally requested. 'It would be pleasant to…linger together here awhile longer.'

Elena looked at him searchingly, knowing she should say no and straight away go upstairs to her bedchamber. Far away from the temptation of this gentleman's compelling handsomeness. And yet… 'Perhaps a very small glass, my lord.'

He smiled, not in triumph but in pleasure as he strolled across to the where the decanter and glasses sat upon a silver tray. 'My grandmother really did not mean any insult to you by her remarks earlier,' he assured as he poured the brandy into the glasses before carrying them across the room and offering one to Elena. 'She was merely voicing the fact that she finds you a woman of unexplainable contrasts. A puzzle, in fact. As do I,' he added softly.

Elena tensed warily, careful not to let her gloved fingers come into contact with his as she took the glass he offered. 'I am no puzzle, my lord, just a widow fallen on hard times who is in need of work in order to support myself.'

'You are a lady who has fallen upon hard times,' he corrected huskily.

She eyed him. 'I am not sure I care for that description, my lord. It sounds…somehow indecent.'

It was the perfect opportunity for Adam to put forward his offer, the ideal opening for him to ask this woman if she would consider becoming his mistress.

And yet he found he could not do so. Oh, he assured himself that it was because he now wished—needed—to find out all there was to know about her, before he considered entering into a relationship of intimacy with her. He told himself that. But the truth of the matter was, he did not wish to spoil the delicate ease that currently existed between the two of them…at the same time as he hungered to taste once again the perfect bow of her lips!

So much for his earlier concerns regarding the effect this woman had upon his self-control, the caution he had earlier decided he should practise with regard to her. If this was a lack of control, a weakness, then for the moment he knew he had no guard against it!

The top of Elena's silky black curls barely reached his shoulder, a delicate blush adding rose to her cheeks as she looked up at him with those luminous blue-green eyes through sooty dark lashes, her pulse pounding rapidly at the base of her long and slender throat, her breasts—oh lord, her breasts!

All of Adam's good intentions, all of those inner warnings for caution seemed to evaporate into mist as he gazed upon the wonderful swell of her breasts.

Besides which, there was a distinct possibility that Elena would turn down such an offer from him and that she might then leave his home altogether. Something which Adam currently found he did not even wish to contemplate.

'I toast you, Elena.' He touched his brandy glass gently against hers. 'You have worked wonders with Amanda,' he explained as she looked a little confused.

Elena made no effort to sip the brandy. 'She was very upset after you had departed last week.'

'And I, as a consequence, was just as upset when I departed,' he returned.

'You were?' She looked surprised.

Adam sighed. 'Contrary to what you so obviously believe, I do not enjoy being at odds with my daughter. But, conversely—' his mouth firmed '—I will not allow myself to be manipulated by emotional blackmail of the kind Amanda demonstrated that day. That sort of behaviour is too much like her mother's to be tolerated.'

Elena's curiosity quickened at Adam's mention of his wife. A lapse he already regretted if the bleakness of his expression was an indication. 'Amanda never mentions her mother—is it possible that she has memories of her?' she asked gently.

'Lord, I hope not!' A scowl darkened Adam's wide brow. 'No, I am sure not. She was not quite two when her mother died, could not possibly remember how Fanny screamed and ranted when she could not get her own way by persuasion or trickery.'

'My lord...?' Elena quietly gasped her shock.

Adam focused on her with effort—almost as if he had forgotten for a moment that she was there—before his jaw tightened. 'I do not believe it has ever been a secret in society that my marriage was far from a happy one.'

It had been to Elena because she had never had the chance to be a part of London society. Indeed, she had found herself wondering these past few weeks if Adam might have remained a bachelor after his wife died because he was still in love with her.

Elena admitted to feeling curious at the lack of conversation in the household, above or below stairs, in regard to the late Lady Fanny, as well as Lady Cicely's enigmatic comment earlier this evening, but there was no escaping the fact that Adam was a compellingly handsome gentleman of wealth and title, a gentleman in need of a male heir, who might take his pick of any of the young and beautiful single ladies of society as his second wife.

His remark just now would seem to imply his reason for not marrying again was not because he was still in love with his first wife, but because that marriage had been such an unhappy one he had no desire to repeat the experience.

'That is regrettable, my lord,' she murmured, only to open her eyes wide as Adam, after remaining silent for several seconds, now gave a loud shout of laughter.

Despite her confusion, she could not stop herself from once again appreciating how much younger, how much more compellingly attractive this man looked when he laughed or smiled.

Adam's shoulders shook as he took her brandy glass from her gloved fingers and placed it on the table with his own. He turned back to her, clasping both her hands in his own as he continued to grin widely. 'Do not look so offended, Elena,' he said as he saw her expression. 'It is only that "regrettable" does not even begin to describe my disastrous marriage to Fanny.' He could never remember finding that marriage a subject of mirth until Elena's understatement had made him see it as such. His fingers tightened about hers. 'For you see, Fanny, I am ashamed to say, was already two months along with my child when we married.'

'Are you sure you should be confiding any of this to me, my lord?' Elena looked alarmed as she tried to pull her fingers free of his.

Adam refused to release her. 'It is not a matter of should I tell you, but whether or not you wish to hear it?'

Did she wish to hear it? Miss Magdelena Matthews, granddaughter of a duke, and therefore Lord Hawthorne's equal, very much wished to know more of what had made him into the reserved gentleman he now was.

But Elena Leighton, young and widowed governess of his young daughter, surely should not be made privy to such personal information as to the reason for her employer's hasty marriage and Amanda's subsequent birth seven months later.

Those two personalities warred inside Elena for several long seconds. But after all, she had been Miss Magdelena Matthews for far longer than she had been Mrs Elena Leighton… 'If you wish to tell me, then I will, of course, listen.'

He quirked a teasing brow. 'And not comment?'

A smile curved her lips. 'Oh I could not promise that, I am afraid.'

'I did not think so!' Adam eyed her ruefully. 'Nor do I think you a woman who is afraid of anything.'

In that he would be wrong, Elena acknowledged sadly. For she had been frightened in the past, and still was. Very frightened. Her cousin's forced attentions upon her had sickened her. His coercion, and then threats, when she had refused him, had terrified her. And hardly a moment had passed since that time when she was not afraid of Neville, still. Of someone discovering who she really was, then finding herself returned to Neville to pay for the crimes of which she was innocent, but which he had accused her of publicly as a cover to his own crimes against her.

She gave a shiver of revulsion. 'Everyone is afraid of something, my lord.'

He eyed her searchingly. 'Elena, what is it…?'

Elena gave herself a mental shake; Adam was a man

of deep sensitivity as well as sharp intelligence—it would not do to alert his suspicions. She attempted a reassuring smile. 'I, for example, do not care for spiders.'

'Spiders...?' Adam echoed doubtfully.

She met his gaze unblinkingly. 'Yes, my lord, spiders.'

He gave her a wicked look. 'Does that mean that you might call upon my services one night so that I might rescue you from such a creature?'

Elena felt hot inside at the very thought of Adam entering her bedchamber, for whatever reason. 'I am not *that* afraid of them, my lord,' she assured huskily.

'Pity,' he drawled.

She swallowed before speaking. 'If we could resume our earlier conversation...?'

'Of course.' He straightened. 'You will try not to judge me too harshly?' He looked down at her searchingly.

Elena met that gaze openly, 'I do not believe I could ever think too badly of you, my lord,' she finally murmured. Truthfully. The man Adam kept hidden behind that mask of coldness and reserve was a gentleman Elena knew she was coming to like, and most of all to trust—to be attracted to!—far too much for comfort.

Adam's fingers tightened about hers momentarily before he released her to step away, his expression having turned grim once more. 'I was only young myself when I was first introduced to Fanny Worthington, who was the débutante of the Season that year. She was—' He drew in a deep breath. 'Her golden-haired, blue-eyed beauty was such that I thought her an angel fallen to earth to dazzle and bewitch unsuspecting humans.'

Amanda's colouring and prettiness were already showing the promise of such dazzling beauty herself when she was older, and so easily allowing Elena to imagine the exquisite beauty of her mother.

She also felt a slight jolt of something—jealousy, perhaps?—at hearing how besotted Adam had been with the beauty of his wife. A beauty so unlike her own dark hair, and eyes that were neither blue nor green…

His mouth had become a firm, flat line. 'I was both dazzled and bewitched to such a degree that I did not notice the mercenary intent towards my fortune in the depths of those blue eyes, or realise that the marked preference Fanny showed towards my company was for that reason alone rather than a return of the love I believed I felt for her.'

'I think you underestimate your own…attractions, my lord,' Elena protested.

'Not where Fanny was concerned,' he insisted harshly. 'Although it is kind of you to say so,' he added.

Elena dare not look at Adam now, for fear that he might see the expression in her own eyes was far from innocent. 'I was not meaning to be kind, only truthful.'

'As you invariably are.' Adam smiled.

Elena felt a clenching in her chest, very aware that she had not been truthful with him at all about what was most important about her, namely her true identity and the circumstances that led her to come here.

An oversight that she doubted Adam, with his obvious loathing for deceit of any kind, would willingly forgive.

'You are grown very quiet, Elena…?'

She kept her lashes lowered. 'I am merely waiting for you to continue.'

He sighed heavily. 'It is such an unpleasant tale.'

'Then do not tell it, if it makes you so uncomfortable.'

'I am more concerned that I may be making *you* feel uncomfortable?'

Elena's own emotions were in such confusion she did not know how she felt about these ridiculous feelings of jealousy, while at the same time she had a desire—a yearning—to know about Adam's marriage to the beautiful Fanny. 'I am not discomforted, only sorry that your marriage was such an unhappy one.'

'I was young. And very foolish. To a degree I allowed myself to be seduced into Fanny's bed—I think perhaps this is not a fit conversation for one such as you, after all!' he muttered as he heard her gasp.

'"One such as me"…?'

Adam saw the way her little chin had risen defensively, as if Elena imagined he somehow meant to insult her. 'I now realise that it is both a sordid and unpleasant tale, and not for the ears of a lady.' And he knew, innately, that Elena was far more of a lady than Fanny had ever been, for all that she had been the daughter of a baron.

Also, strangely, despite the fact that she was a widow, Adam found he was uncomfortable talking to Elena of the physical intimacies he and Fanny had obviously shared before their marriage—and for a very short time after it!

There was an innocence to Elena which he found he had no wish to besmirch with the sordid details of the reason for his marriage to Fanny, or the hell that marriage had become just a short month after their wedding day.

He smiled tightly. 'I am sure I have already told you enough that you realise my marriage to Fanny was not a love match.' He grimaced. 'By the time she died I believe we heartily despised one another.'

'Surely not…?' Elena looked dismayed. 'You shared Amanda, if nothing else.'

Adam shrugged. 'Fanny saw my love for my baby daughter as nothing more than a weakness which she could, and did, exploit in her constant attempts to emotionally blackmail me into doing exactly as she wished.'

'Is that the reason—?' She broke off with a self-conscious moue.

'"Is that the reason"…?' He quirked dark brows.

'I wondered if that was the reason you were now… occasionally aloof towards Amanda?' A heated blush warmed her cheeks. 'Because in the past your love for her was exploited and used against you?'

He gave her a shocked look. 'I had not thought of it as being so, but perhaps you are partly right… But only partly, I am afraid.' He frowned. 'The rest of my fatherly bungling really is due to a complete lack of experience in dealing with six-year-old children.'

'But which you are now attempting to rectify.'

'But which I am now attempting to rectify,' Adam agreed.

'What happened on the occasions when your wife's attempts to emotionally blackmail you failed?' Elena prompted curiously.

He smiled thinly. 'Ah, then she would have fits of temper which occasionally resulted in my sporting physical evidence of her displeasure!'

'She was violent towards you?' Elena gasped.

He grimaced. 'Her attacks were usually of a verbal variety, but I do recall suffering three scratches down my cheek from her fingernails on one occasion, and a bite on my bottom lip on another,' he recounted grimly. 'I very quickly grew to dislike such excessive displays of emotional temperament, and even all these years later, I still shy away from them.'

'Ah.' Elena breathed. 'Which is no doubt the reason you were so displeased when Amanda appeared to have a temper tantrum of a similar nature last week.'

'Yes...'

Elena realised now exactly why this man gave the appearance of being so cold and haughty, when she now had good reason to believe he was neither of those things. Well...perhaps Adam was naturally haughty, she allowed ruefully. But, after the things he had chosen to reveal to her, she now believed that coldness to be a barrier, one that he had deliberately erected in order to keep from suffering the same hurt as he had time and time again during his ill-fated marriage to the volatile

Fanny; no doubt it also served to warn others to keep their distance.

Except Elena, standing but inches away from him, was not at a safe distance.

She moistened her lips with the tip of her tongue. 'I am…honoured that you have chosen to share this information with me, but—but perhaps it is time I now retired for the night.' It was a question as much as a statement.

One that caused Adam's eyes to darken with an emotion she could not fathom. 'Is that what you want?'

'It is very late.'

He smiled slightly. 'That is not what I asked, Elena.'

The tension between them was palpable. 'I— Surely that would be for the best?'

'Again, that is not what I asked. Is it what you *really* want to do?' He pressed as he reached out to grasp both her gloved hands in his.

Elena's fingers trembled within the firmness of that grasp.

Because it was not what she wanted at all. What she *wanted* was to remain here with Adam awhile longer, drinking the brandy in her glass as the two of them sat quietly together and talked some more, of pleasanter things than his unhappy marriage to Fanny, and then— then she would like it very much if Adam were to take her in his arms and kiss her again!

The memory of the last kiss they had shared, a kiss of warmth and pleasure, had helped to wipe away some of the nightmare of the memory of Neville's brutality.

To a degree that Elena had thought of that kiss often this past few days: while she was teaching Amanda, eating her meals, strolling about the garden, or alone in her bed at night, but most of all when she was alone in her bed at night. Instead of the revulsion and nausea she might have expected, Elena had instead felt warm and satisfied just at the delicious memory of Adam's gentleness and passion.

She had only to think of that kiss to once again feel Adam's lips against her own, to remember how wonderful, how utterly safe, it had felt to be held in his arms, to feel the hardness of his body pressed against hers, that sensuous mouth moving softly, assuredly, over her own, wiping out those other horrific memories and instead igniting a passion, a desire, within Elena that she had never realised existed.

A passion and desire she had longed to feel again.

Adam's breath caught in his throat, as he now saw the emotions he'd been waiting for burning in Elena's beautiful blue-green eyes as she gazed at him silently.

Emotions— and a woman—Adam knew he did not have the strength to resist as all doubts and caution fled his brain, along with those fears for the tight control he had held over his life for so long, the blood swiftly travelling from his brain and going southwards. 'Elena…!' He released her hands only long enough to take her into his arms, the intentness of his gaze locked with hers, his lips parting as he slowly lowered his head to claim the delicious softness of hers.

Chapter Ten

She tasted of honey and brandy, her lips warm and compliant as they moved shyly beneath his, and her skin smelt of the strawberries and cream which had been their dessert at dinner earlier. A heady combination that Adam could not, did not, want to resist and one that all too quickly took him to a height of desire he had not felt in a very long time.

Too long, Adam realised with a groan as he very quickly became completely engorged inside his breeches, thickening and lengthening to an almost painful degree as he continued to kiss and taste, to tenderly nibble on the fullness of Elena's bottom lip. His tongue ventured into the moist and heated cavern of her mouth, seeking out each sensitive and secret place as he heard her breath catch in her throat and felt her gloved fingers reach up to cling to the broad width of his shoulders.

His arms tightened about her and his lips continued to devour and claim hers as he pressed his burgeoning thighs against Elena's much softer ones, as he sought, craved, to find some relief for the fierce ache of his pulsing erection.

A relief he could not, should not, press upon the woman who had borne so much of his temper these past few weeks, only to then be ignored, before becoming a willing listener this evening to his torments, both past and present!

A woman Adam employed as governess to his daughter.

And a woman who could not afford, quite literally, to deny the liberties he was taking, for fear that he might dismiss her.

He knew that his disastrous marriage to Fanny had made him cold and occasionally cruel, but was he now guilty of also becoming a man one who took advantage of unprotected females? That thought did what nothing else could and threw a bucket of ice-cold water on his libido.

Elena stumbled as Adam suddenly wrenched his mouth from hers before holding her at arm's length, those grey eyes blazing darkly in the fierceness of his face. She blinked in an effort to clear her muddled brain, having been totally swept away by the rage of passion created by the taste and feel of Adam's mouth possessing hers. 'I do not understand. Did I do something wrong?'

His expression was harsh as he released her to step back. 'It is I who am the one in the wrong,' he rasped harshly. 'I should not have—I apologise for—' He gave a self-disgusted shake of his head. 'You have my permission to slap my face, without fear of reprisals.'

Elena noted the tension in his shoulders and spine, the nerve pulsing in his tightly clenched jaw and the fierce glitter of those dark-grey eyes, his hands once against clasped tightly behind his back. She also recognised that he had just invited her to inflict physical retribution upon him in the same way that his wife had once taken such pleasure in doing.

'I could not possibly do that. But perhaps you regret what just happened?' she queried gently.

He gave a humourless smile. 'How could I possibly do that when I obviously enjoyed it so much?'

Some of the tension eased from Elena's own shoulders. 'As did I,' she admitted, knowing it was true. She trusted Adam not to hurt her. Physically, at least…

He drew in a deep, controlling breath. 'It is not right for me to take unfair advantage of you or force my attentions upon you.'

She gave a frown of confusion. 'Did I give the impression that I felt forced or taken advantage of?'

'No… But you must feel as if you have been—'

'Adam.'

'—and as such I—' He broke off his explanation to stare at her. 'That is the first time that you have voluntarily called me by my given name.'

'Yes.'

'Why now?'

The softness of her gaze met his levelly. 'Possibly because I enjoyed being kissed by you, as much as you enjoyed kissing me, and that I now think of you as Adam.'

The strong column of his throat moved as he swallowed before speaking. 'Did you enjoy it enough to re-peat the experience?'

Elena knew that she should refuse him. That if she didn't, it would irrevocably change their relationship. Except…after the things Adam had just told her about his marriage, and after being held in his arms and kissed by him again, she accepted that it was already irrevo-cably changed.

She might only have that one nightmare experience with Neville with which to compare Adam, but even so she recognised that his kisses were nothing like her cousin's, that Adam had kissed her as a starving man newly arrived at a feast, or a man dying of thirst in a desert, a man who longed to eat and drink until that hunger was sated.

Elena knew she should be frightened of such an in-tensity of passion, that she should resist—should not want or crave the compelling and irresistible attractions of her employer. Yet she found she did, that she needed to erase those memories of Neville's attack upon her once and for all with Adam's gentleness.

It had also been months since she had felt anyone wanted so much as her company, let alone desired her with the intensity of passion Adam had just displayed so readily; Neville did not, could not, count. Indeed, Elena wanted another memory, a much pleasanter one, to put in its place!

'I believe I might, yes,' she whispered, then stepped forwards until she was once again pressed up against the lean and muscled length of his body, her gaze clear and steady as she raised her face invitingly to his.

It was an invitation that Adam did not, could not, refuse. He swept Elena up in his arms and once again claimed those full and pouting lips with his own, the kiss questioning and yet fiercely demanding at the same time as he moulded her slender curves to his much harder ones.

But, as Adam had already knew only too well, it was not enough, not with this particular woman. He wanted more, so much more of Elena than the taste of her lips or the feel of the soft skin of her throat as his own lips sought out each and every sensitive dip and hollow with teeth and tongue, as the insistent pulse of his desire told him only too clearly!

As it must also be telling her!

Elena was not an innocent young miss, but a widow, a woman, not a girl, who would recognise the depths of Adam's desire for her when his arousal pressed so insistently against her.

Adam's teeth closed on the lobe of her ear as he murmured. 'I have been dreaming, imagining, wondering…'

'Yes?' she breathed softly, her neck arched as she leant into him.

'While I was away I thought endlessly of your breasts…'

Her breath caught sharply. 'You did?'

He nodded. 'And I have wondered…are they tipped with rose or peach?'

The breasts Adam spoke of so candidly suddenly felt

hot and swollen inside the bodice of Elena's gown, the tips now swelling, tingling, becoming painfully sensitive against the material of her chemise.

It was at once shocking and yet strangely exciting to imagine Adam thinking so intently about her breasts and the colour of her nipples. Should she be so bold as to respond to that? 'They are rose,' Elena answered him huskily. 'A deep rose.'

'Ah,' he moaned, his lips a trail of fire across the full swell of her breasts. 'May I touch you, Elena?' Adam raised his head to look at her, his eyes an intense glittering grey, a dark flush across the sculptured planes of his cheekbones. 'May I look at you there, touch you and then kiss you?'

Elena could no longer breathe, felt as if she were drowning in the unfathomable depths of his eyes, finally dragging her own gaze away to instead look at his lips. Sensuously soft lips. Lips that he'd asked if he might kiss her with. Not on her own lips, but on her breasts. As he would perhaps wish to kiss that other, even more intimate place between her thighs, too?

Elena felt a sudden warm rush of moistness just at the thought of Adam touching her there. With his hands. With his lips. With his tongue, perhaps?

Did men and woman do that to each other? Would Adam expect her to touch and kiss him with the same shocking level of intimacy?

Elena thought that he might.

Because Adam believed her to be a widow. A woman who had been married, and was therefore perfectly familiar with the physical intimacies that took place between a man and a woman. He thought she would not be shocked by the things he was saying to her, the things he was describing he wished to do to and with her.

She trembled with longing, but had to be prudent. 'We cannot—I could not permit—' She gave an embarrassed shake of her head even as she straightened her shoulders, determined to get her point across. 'I could not permit full intimacy.' There, she had said it! And surely, now that she was aware of the reason for Adam's hasty marriage to Fanny Worthington, he would not want to take the risk of impregnating her, either?

'I would not ask for it,' Adam reassured her immediately.

'Then…yes, you may.' Elena's stomach gave a sickening lurch of anticipation even as her heart skipped several beats. 'But—is it not overly bright in here?' She glanced self-consciously about the candlelit room.

Adam gave her an understanding look. 'Would you feel more relaxed if I were to blow out some of the candles?'

'Or all of them,' she suggested ruefully.

He made a throaty sound of protest. 'Then I would not be able to see you at all!'

Of course he would not. And Elena knew she should not allow him to see her. Except her breasts now ached so as they pressed and throbbed against the confines of her gown, bursting to be free, as if they at least knew, and ached, for the pleasures of Adam's hands and mouth.

If Adam had been in the least rough with her, or demanding, or seemed in the least arrogantly triumphant about her obvious responses to him, then Elena knew she would not have hesitated to refuse him. It was Adam's very gentleness— his gentlemanliness, his regard for her own comfort and pleasure—which now piqued Elena's curiosity to know, to experience the desire of a man not intent upon hurting her.

'A few less candles alight would be…preferable,' she conceded.

'Then fewer candles you shall have.' He reached up to cup her chin, the soft pad of his thumb a caress against her bottom lip as he looked down at her searchingly. 'I will not do anything you do not wish for, Elena.'

Her eyes widened. 'I never thought that you would.'

'No?' Adam was sure he was not mistaken about the trepidation he had seen in the depths of her eyes. As if she feared he might somehow hurt her. As someone else—her husband, perhaps?—had once hurt her? Adam had never been able to understand why a man, any man, would ever wish to hurt a woman rather than give her pleasure.

Even in the depths of the despair over his awful marriage with Fanny, despite several times suffering the painful provocation of her scratching and biting, Adam had never once felt a desire to instigate physical retribution of his own. Partly, perhaps, because Fanny seemed to want, even crave him to lose control and strike her, before taking her in a sexually violent manner, which Adam had refused to do. He'd found it totally abhorrent and against his very nature to dominate a woman in that way.

He already knew Elena well enough to know she was Fanny's complete opposite, in looks as well as temperament. A woman of dignity and elegance, gentleness, and yet at the same time deeply hidden passions. A quietly self-contained woman, who did not need to be constantly reckless in her efforts to prove her feminine power over men. Over him.

As if sensing some of the unpleasantness of his thoughts, Elena reached up to gently smooth the frown from between his eyes. 'I fear we have both been hurt in the past.'

'Yes...'

She nodded. 'I will make myself comfortable on the *chaise* and unbutton my gown whilst you blow out some of the candles.'

Adam looked down at her intently for several more seconds before nodding his satisfaction with the trust he could see in her eyes. 'I should like that very much.' He released her before turning away, primarily to give her the privacy to unfasten the back of her gown, but also so that he might move about the room extinguishing half a dozen of the eight lit candles.

The room was thrown into golden shadow by the time Adam crossed the room to join Elena on the *chaise*, his eyes glittering even more brightly in the soft glow of the dimmed candlelight as he looked down at her. 'It hardly seems fair if I remain fully dressed.'

She blinked those long dark lashes. 'And if Jeffries should decide to return, after all?'

'He will not.'

Elena paused for a second to think before speaking. 'I—is Jeffries accustomed to your bringing women here and making love to them—?' She fell silent as Adam placed his fingertips against her lips.

'No, he is not, he merely knows when he is dismissed for the evening,' Adam answered firmly, evenly, knowing it was a fair question for Elena to ask, but resenting it all the same. 'I never bring the women I…take to my bed, to my estates, Elena. Nor would I ever think of doing so now, when my grandmother and daughter are both abed upstairs.'

Her smile was strained once he had removed his fingertips. 'Perhaps, then, it is nothing more than a convenience that I am already here?'

Adam closed his eyes briefly. 'My desire for you is not in the least "convenient",' he assured ruefully. 'Indeed, it is most *inconvenient*. It is just—I can no longer resist wanting to kiss and touch you, Elena,' he admitted gruffly.

Her cheeks coloured warmly. 'I apologise. I—' She moistened her lips, unknowingly drawing the heat of Adam's gaze to that provocative movement. 'I am only—I have never—this is not something I have ever done—allowed —before.'

He knew that, had been aware of her shyness when she asked for most of the candles in the room to be extinguished before she allowed him to look upon her breasts.

Elena might be a widow, but Adam knew beyond any shadow of a doubt that she had not become promiscuous after her husband died, and her very youth, and the brief duration of her marriage, implied that she could not been so beforehand, either. Nor did that marriage itself appear to have given her the physical satisfaction she deserved and that Adam wished to share with her, if her continued shyness was any indication.

His gaze continued to hold hers as he stepped back slightly. 'I believe it only fair that I join you in partially disrobing.' His hands moved up to remove his superfine and untie his neckcloth, before putting them both aside, his waistcoat joining them seconds later. He unfastened the three buttons of his shirt and then pulled it free from the waistband of his breeches to leave it hanging free about his thighs.

Elena sat unmoving as she watched Adam between thick dark lashes, her heart beating a wild tattoo in her chest as she looked at the gold smoothness of his skin revealed at this throat, the fine dusting of hair on his chest also just visible. She was barely breathing as she waited to see if he would remove the shirt completely.

She had taken off her gloves so that she could unfasten the buttons at the back of her gown, the release having somewhat lessened the pressure against the fullness of her breasts, but that very freedom of movement serving to heighten the full and tingling sensation at their tips.

Quite what happened next, Elena had no idea, but she was happy—indeed, she quivered with eagerness!—at the thought of putting herself into Adam's gentle and more experienced hands. And lips. And tongue. And teeth…

Adam did not remove his shirt, but sat down beside her on the *chaise*, the warmth of his thigh resting against the length of hers. He reached out and slowly slid the loosened material of her gown from her shoulders and down the length of her bare arms before slipping the bodice down completely, her breasts only covered by the thin material of her chemise now. 'You have beautiful hands…' he murmured even as he raised one of those hands to his lips to kiss each individual finger before once again looking up into her eyes. 'I should very much like to feel them against the bareness of my chest, so if you will help me to remove my shirt…?'

Elena was moved beyond words by Adam's continued tenderness, knew that most men—how that past memory was still burned within!—would have simply made an eager grab at her breasts rather than take the time to kiss her fingers, totally uncaring as to whether or not she enjoyed the experience. Which, with Neville, she most certainly had not.

'Do not think of the past, love.' Adam reached out to gently touch Elena's cheek as he saw the shadows that had once more entered her eyes. 'This is you and me. Adam and Elena. And there is no room for anyone else here, not between the two of us.'

Tears glittered in those blue-green depths. 'Why are you being so kind to me?'

How could he not be kind to her? How could any man not wish to show kindness to this beautiful and entrancing woman? 'Help me off with my shirt, love?'

Instead of continuing to sit beside him as she reached up to help him, as Adam had expected she would, Elena now stood up, causing her unfastened gown to fall to the carpet at her slippered feet, and leaving her clothed only in that revealing white chemise over her drawers, and delicate white stockings held in place at her thighs by white garters adorned with rosebuds.

Drawing Adam's gaze unerringly to those other rosebuds now visible through the thin material of her chemise, full and delicious red berries that were clearly and temptingly outlined against that gauzy material.

Adam continued to gaze hungrily at those pouting red berries as Elena slowly raised his shirt up his chest and then over his head before discarding it completely, only looking up into her face as he heard her gasp softly. 'What is it, love?'

'You will think me silly.' Her cheeks had flushed a fiery red, her eyes overbright.

'I am currently sitting half-naked in the salon where I usually receive guests, and I will think *you* are the silly one?' he teased huskily.

'I am standing here half-naked in that very same salon,' she came back ruefully. 'And the reason for my shock was that you are very beautiful, Adam,' she said shyly.

His own breath caught in his throat at her unaffected candidness, then he ceased to breathe altogether as those long and slender hands moved tentatively to the nakedness of his chest, fingers tracing a delicate and seductive path across the muscled width of his shoulders before moving down to touch the silky dark hair covering his chest. Adam let out a hoarse exclamation of pleasure as her fingernails rasped lightly across the flat nubbins hidden there. His arousal surged and leapt inside his breeches to the same rhythm as those caressing fingers, causing him to shift uncomfortably.

Elena flattened her fingers against those hardened nubbins. 'Am I hurting you?'

'Only with pleasure,' Adam acknowledged throatily.

Her eyes widened. 'You enjoy being touched?'

'By you, yes, very much so.' Adam reached up to slide the thin shoulder straps of her chemise down to her elbows, finally baring those breasts to the avidness of his heated gaze.

Surprisingly full breasts, considering the slenderness of her body. They were round and pert, and tipped with delectable rosy-red nipples that seemed to swell and deepen in colour the longer he continued to look at them hungrily.

'May I?' Adam moistened his lips in anticipation of the taste of those ripe berries as he slipped the straps down completely, allowing her chemise to fall down to her waist.

'Please…!' Elena stepped forwards to stand between

his parted thighs, her bared breasts swinging temptingly close to his mouth.

Adam placed his hands on her hips to steady her as he leant forwards and gently kissed each rosy-red nipple, one after the other, before lingering to lave one engorged berry with his tongue, around and around, urged on by her softly keening cries. She reached out to cling to the bareness of his shoulders as he slowly, skilfully drew that sensitive nubbin fully into the heat of his mouth.

Elena's knees threatened to fold completely and she knew she would have fallen, if Adam had not tightened his grip on her hips to hold her in place. Her throat arched, head thrown back. She became totally consumed with the pleasure he gave with his lips and tongue—ah, yes, his teeth!—as he laved and suckled and nibbled upon that engorged berry.

This was nothing like that terrible memory of her cousin's touch, Adam's causing her drawers to become wet with moisture, her folds there swollen and aching, and a throbbing between her thighs that she could not explain.

She whimpered as Adam ceased his ministrations to her breasts and turned his attention to its twin, no longer gentle as he drew deeply on that nubbin, his breathing laboured as he suckled hard and long until it grew bigger still, elongating as he rasped his tongue across the tip over and over again until Elena thought she might go mad with the pleasure. The ache inside her was now so great that it caused her to thrust her thighs forwards, her movements restless as she burned, ached, begged for a release from the torment, at the same time as she never wanted this pleasure to stop.

Her back arched as she leant into him, pleading, asking, needing—for what she did not know. She groaned in protest as Adam released her nipple with a loud popping sound, that berry red and moist as Elena looked down at him with dark and sultry blue-green eyes.

'Part your legs, love,' Adam encouraged throatily as he pushed her chemise up her thighs to her waist. 'I want to touch you here, too,' he breathed, looking at her long and deeply before once again slowly, deliberately, latching on to the engorged pout of her nipple. Her legs slowly parted, allowing his hand to seek out the slit in her drawers.

Elena felt his fingers part her silky curls to seek out her swollen folds, dipping those fingers into the moisture there before parting those folds and moving higher, circling, caressing, moistening her there but not quite touching the part of her that throbbed, ached for his touch. 'Please, Adam..!' She moved her thighs restlessly against those caressing fingers, seeking, wanting— 'Yesss!' Elena cried out at the first touch of those fingers against that ache, fingers that now alternately stroked and circled that swollen and moistened nubbin to the same rhythm that he suckled deeply on her nipple. His free hand moved from her hip to cup her other breast, finger and thumb tweaking, pulling on that second nipple.

The triple assault upon her senses was too much. Too

many different sensations at once. Too much pleasure. Too much, too much, too much—

That pleasure released, climaxed so suddenly, that it took Elena's breath away as it rippled and surged, then exploded in a cascade of overwhelming sensations, the moisture rushing freely between her thighs, wetting Adam as he thrust one finger deep inside her even as he continued to stroke her into ecstasy.

On and on it went, as the tears coursed hotly, unknowingly, down Elena's cheeks.

Chapter Eleven

'We are not finished yet,' Adam said as Elena, flushed and obviously self-conscious after her loss of control, turned her face away and would have moved out of his reach. Instead he continued to hold her lightly with one arm about her waist as he reached up to release the pins from her hair, so that he might admire those long silky dark curls as they cascaded down the length of her spine and fell softly about her flushed face. 'You are a very beautiful woman, Elena…'

She moistened full and swollen lips, those blue-green eyes slightly unfocused from her recent climax. 'I— thank you.'

Adam chuckled softly at the obvious absence of her usual calm and composure—he was feeling less than calm or composed himself! Nor had he had his fill of her beautiful body. 'Come, lie here beside me, love,' he encouraged as he turned with her in his arms to place her down gently upon the *chaise*.

His gaze darkened appreciatively at the totally wanton picture she presented as he sat back to look at her, those dark curls falling wildly about her shoulders and breasts, breasts swollen from his ministrations, the nipples tight red buds, becoming even more so as Adam's gaze lingered there before moving down to the slenderness of her waist where her chemise was gathered.

'These need to come off.' He suited his actions to his words as he rolled both her chemise and her drawers down over her thighs and legs before discarding them completely, Elena now wearing only those white stockings held up by rosebud-adorned garters. 'Please do not.' Adam reached out to clasp Elena's hand in his as she would have self-consciously covered the curls between her legs, dark and silky curls that he could see were slightly damp from her recent release. 'Will you allow me to kiss you here?' He allowed his fingers to tangle lightly with those silky dark curls as he raised his soft grey gaze to hers.

Elena's eyes widened. Adam wished to—he wanted to place his mouth against her *there*?

She had not known what to expect from Adam's lovemaking, her past experience with Neville—both painful and terrifying, and one she had tried in vain to erase from her memory—having in no way prepared her for the pleasure she had just known. He had been so gentle with her, so careful not to hurt her, as he showed her that lovemaking could be a pleasurable and caring experience. With him, at least.

Even so, could she—dare she—allow him to kiss

her *there*, to feel those sensual lips against her most intimate place?

'Your husband did not deserve you, love!' Adam rasped as he obviously saw, and understood, the uncertainty in her expression, though he did not know the correct person to blame for it. 'Lovemaking is for the enjoyment of both parties, Elena,' he continued gently. 'And it would give me as much pleasure to kiss you here as I believe it would for you to be kissed. But I appreciate that some ladies do not even like the thought of such intimacy. Do you trust me, Elena?'

She looked up at him. 'I trust you, Adam.'

His eyes darkened. 'Thank you.'

She nodded. 'You have been very kind and gentle and I have enjoyed our time together up to this point.'

'I promise I will stop if you decide you do not like what I do to you now.' His caressing fingers gently parted her legs so that he might separate the dark curls and stroke against that already swelling nubbin between her thighs as he draped the leg nearest to him across the muscled hardness of his own thighs before his head began its slow descent. 'I so badly wish to taste you!'

Elena swallowed the saliva that had gathered in her mouth, that swallow turning to a breathless sigh, her lids closing, at the first touch of Adam's lips against her swollen folds, pleasure coursing through her anew as she felt the rasp of his tongue against her most sensitive place.

'You taste divine, Elena.' The warmth of his breath

moved lightly, arousingly, against her moist heat. 'So sweet and creamy,' he murmured.

Elena's hands seemed to move of their own volition as her fingers became entangled in the darkness of Adam's hair. Her back arched as her hips began to undulate in the same rhythm as the almost unbearable rasp of his tongue, his fingers moving to stroke the little nubbin, causing Elena to shift restlessly.

He raised his head only slightly. 'Do you wish me to stop?'

'Heavens, no!' Elena's husky laugh caught on a sob—she wished him to do the opposite!—as she glanced down into those dark-grey eyes rimmed by black, allowing her to see lips damp from her. 'Unless… Do you wish to stop?'

His gaze continued to hold hers as he once again lowered his head and resumed that skilful flicking of his tongue, at the same time as both his hands moved up to cup her breasts, capturing the nipples between thumb and index finger and pinching gently. This combined assault upon her senses was altogether too much for Elena as she felt the burn of that pleasure coursing through her once again, hotly, frantically, until she exploded a second time, even more fiercely than the first, her back arched up as wave after wave of pleasure consumed her.

'Does that answer your question, love?' Adam asked as he lay his head against her bare thighs. 'I would kiss and caress you here all night long if you allowed it,' he assured her. 'You are as beautiful here as you are everywhere else.' His gaze lowered as the gentleness of his fingers stroked against her sensitive flesh. 'So, so beautiful, Elena.'

She chewed lightly on her bottom lips before answering him shyly, 'And you...you really enjoy performing such...such intimacies?'

'Any man would, love.' A smile curved those sensual lips as he looked up at her. 'To give you pleasure is to give myself pleasure also.'

'Would you not enjoy it more if I—if I were to touch you now?' She looked at him anxiously, unsure if she had gone too far as she saw his eyes widen. Except... she ached to touch Adam, to explore the hardness of his arms and chest, the flatness of his abdomen, and perhaps lower still?

'You do not have to do so,' Adam said gruffly, that reassurance belied by the heated glitter that had entered his eyes and the deepening flush in his cheeks, the bulge in his breeches seeming to grow larger still.

Elena had only seen a man's rampant rod once before in her life, seconds before it was pushed painfully inside her, ripping through her innocence and causing her immeasurable pain. What had followed had been even more excruciating and unpleasant.

But this, here and now with Adam, was so unlike that last time, both the man and the experience. Adam was intent only on giving her pleasure, to a degree that he had asked nothing of her in return. She *wanted* to give something back to him, to perhaps be able to give him the same release he had given her—twice.

Well, perhaps she should not expect it to happen

twice for Adam, for Elena had overheard two of the maids gossiping once at Sheffield Park, in regard to one of the footmen, a gentleman with whom it seemed that both young ladies occasionally engaged in love-play, and there had been much giggling between them over that gentleman's need to rest for several hours before he could 'perform' a second time.

She looked up at Adam shyly once again. 'And if I should wish to?'

His throat moved as he swallowed before answering. 'Then I would like that very much indeed. You are sure, love?'

She nodded as she tucked her legs beneath her before moving up on her knees and placing her hands upon his bare shoulders as she knelt in front of him. 'If you will help to instruct me as to what I may do, how to touch you, so as best to please you?'

Adam's breath caught in his throat as he gazed at her unashamed nudity: those firm, uptilting breasts, reddened now from his ministrations as they peeped through the ebony waves of the long hair cascading over her shoulders and down her spine, the curve of her waist, her legs slender and shapely, slightly parted so as to reveal the dampness of the curls between her thighs.

'You would perhaps find such intimacies…unpleasant.'

She gave him a calm, trusting look. 'I do not believe that I should. Not with you.'

Something welled up in Adam's chest. Something too fleeting to be recognised. Something he had no time or inclination to analyse, as Elena reached down and began to unfasten the buttons at the sides of his breeches.

His shaft, already a painful throb, surged to even greater heights as those slender fingers brushed lightly against his heat, a small amount of liquid moistening his smalls as it eagerly escaped.

'I believe you will have to be the one who now lies down.'

Adam dragged his gaze away from Elena's flushed face to glance down and see that she had his breeches completely unbuttoned and pulled down to his thighs, along with his smalls, his manhood bobbing free and far longer and thicker than Adam could ever remember seeing it before. 'I believe he is pleased to see you,' he murmured ruefully as he lay down on the *chaise* in order to completely divest himself of his clothing.

'"He"?' She gave an uncharacteristic giggle as she moved to kneel between his parted thighs.

'All men call that part of their anatomy "he", love,' he teased

'As if "he" is an entity apart from yourself?'

'Sometimes I believe he is,' Adam drawled ruefully. 'Certainly, men have allowed themselves to be led about by it. Myself included—' He broke off as once again Elena smoothed the frown from between his brows caused by memories of the past.

'We will not talk of anything but the here and now,' she spoke firmly, as if she too had memories she would rather not dwell on. As no doubt she had. 'My instinct is to curl my fingers about him, is that correct?'

'Your instinct is perfectly correct.' Adam nodded, watching between narrowed lids as Elena moved her hand to allow her fingers to curl about his girth. Well, almost to curl about his girth, for it was now so thick and throbbing that her fingers were too tiny to span him completely. 'Perhaps you should use both hands?' he teased, only to catch his breath in a gasp as she did exactly that, those fingers tightening and relaxing at the same time as she began to pump lightly and rhythmically.

Elena was obviously completely enthralled by what she was doing and Adam was more aroused by her wonder in his response than he had ever been aroused by anything, or anyone, in his life before. It was almost as if she were seeing a man's responses to her for the first time—and perhaps she was? Her surprise earlier, when she had reached her first climax, would seem to imply that whatever manner of man her husband had been, he had not seen to Elena's physical needs before his own. That he had not seen to her needs at all, or shown her how to please him!

Not so unusual, in any marriage. Indeed, the marriages of the *ton* especially tended to be arranged or loveless affairs, forged only to produce an heir and a spare, before the gentlemen returned to their mistresses and the woman very often took a lover of her own. Why should he have assumed it would be any different between men and women of the lower classes? Elena's lack of experience in what pleased her or the man in her bed made a complete nonsense of any such assumption. He—

'Dear God…!' Adam groaned low in his throat as he felt Elena's tongue against him, trailing up the velvety side, seconds before she parted her lips wide and took the sensitive tip fully inside the hot cavern of her mouth. 'Elena!' His fingers became entangled in her hair as she took him deeper still, at the same time as her fingers tightened about him and her other hand moved to cup him beneath.

At which time Adam knew he was never going to hold!

Elena had never seen or felt anything as beautiful as the shapely length of Adam's rod: long and thick and hard, the skin surprisingly soft to the touch. It was no longer enough for her to merely hold him; she needed to taste him fully, in the same way he had tasted her.

Instinct had told her to part her lips and take him into her mouth. The same instinct that told her to pump her fingers lightly along the shaft as Adam began to thrust his rod into her mouth, slowly at first, and then faster, his breathing laboured.

'It is all over for me, Elena,' he cried out in a strangulated voice. 'I cannot hold any longer. I am going to— oh, dear God…!' The last was a low and husky cry as hot and creamy spurts of Adam's release poured out of him like molten lava.

* * *

'We should both dress and go upstairs to bed.'

'Yes.'

'The candles have both burnt out.'

'Yes.'

'The fire will soon have burnt down, too.'

'Yes.'

'Elena…?'

'Yes?'

He chuckled softly and glanced down at her as she lay in his arms upon the *chaise*, the darkness of her hair a silky curtain across his bare chest. 'I believe you would make that same reply to anything I were to say to you at this moment!'

'Possibly.'

'Ah, a different reply, after all.'

'I would not wish to become boring.' There was a smile in her voice.

'I doubt you could ever be that, Elena,' Adam murmured, and, to his surprise, meant it.

Women had become a necessary inconvenience to him before and since Fanny had died, something Adam had need of every now and then in order to assuage his physical needs, but none of those women had been for conversation, certainly not for lying in each other's arms once he had found his release, or sharing a conversation which did not appear to be conversation at all but what he believed to be lovers' nonsense.

Was that what Elena was to him now? His lover?

Had he taken her as his mistress, after all, without so much as even asking her?

Without any of the finer details of that relationship having been discussed and agreed upon?

That very much appeared as if it might be the case.

An occurrence he should have thought of sooner.

Adam scowled the following morning as he walked through the capacious entrance hall and through to the breakfast room. He paused only long enough to bestow a kiss upon his grandmother's powdered cheek, as she sat at the table drinking the herbal tea she favoured in the mornings, before turning his attention to where the array of breakfast foods were laid out in covered silver dishes and plates for his selection. Jeffries had already disappeared to the kitchen to collect the pot of strong tea he knew Adam preferred with his breakfast. His stomach gave a sickening lurch as his nostrils were assailed with the smell of the breakfast foods.

'No appetite this morning, Adam?' his grandmother prompted as he sat down opposite her at the table.

'None whatsoever,' he muttered gruffly.

His grandmother nodded. 'You did not sleep well?'

Adam was uncertain as to whether or not he had slept at all after being assailed with the worst feelings of guilt once alone in his bedchamber. Guilt. And uncertainty as to what the future held, if anything, in regard to his relationship with Elena. The latter emotion was due, he knew, to his feeling out of control whenever he was with her. An iron control he had maintained over all of his emotions since shortly after his wedding to Fanny. For his own protection. A protection that he could not, dared not, allow to be pierced. Even by a woman as sweetly responsive as Elena. *Especially* by a woman as sweetly responsive as Elena!

'Obviously not,' his grandmother said drily. 'Perhaps that is because you did not sleep alone?'

Adam stiffened. 'Grandmama!'

'Adam,' she bit back with uncharacteristic firmness. 'I am not so old that I am unaware of a man's desire for a woman. And my insomnia is such that I heard you and Mrs Leighton talking softly together as you passed my bedchamber late last night. Very late last night. Had the two of you arranged an assignation after I had retired?' She arched questioning brows.

Adam and Elena had parted outside Elena's bedchamber, a long and lingering goodnight, neither of them in any hurry to bring the night to an end. Except Adam's euphoria, his physical satisfaction, had ended the moment he entered his own bedchamber and realised the enormity of what he had done.

He had not realised she had heard them and would not have wished for his grandmother to have done so if he could have helped it. 'I do not—'

'Ah, thank you, Jeffries.' Lady Cicely turned to bestow a smile on the butler as he entered with Adam's pot of tea.

'That will be all, thank you, Jeffries,' Adam dismissed distractedly.

'Shall I pour?' his grandmother offered once the two of them were once again alone.

Adam scowled darkly. 'I am quite capable of pouring my own tea, thank you, Grandmama.'

'As you wish.' She gave him a nod before continuing to sip her own cooling brew.

Adam poured his own steaming tea from the fresh pot, his thoughts in turmoil as he contemplated his grandmother guessing what had taken place between himself and Elena the night before. It was not only embarrassing, for any man of eight and twenty to be 'caught out' by his own grandmother, it was also damned inconvenient.

'Oh, do stop looking so po-faced, Adam,' Lady Cicely said briskly. 'I only mentioned the subject at all because I wished, if you intend to continue the relationship with Mrs Leighton, to offer a few words of warning.'

Adam's spine stiffened even further. 'This really is not a fit conversation for the breakfast table.'

Grey eyes twinkled at him merrily over her teacup. 'Would you prefer I wait until luncheon?'

'I would prefer that we not discuss the subject at all!' He glared at her down the length of his nose.

'I feel I must, my dear.' She placed a hand upon his. 'I have no wish to see you hurt or disappointed again—'

'I shall not be.'

'How can you be so sure?' she asked gently. 'Mrs Leighton is a beautiful young woman. And one whom you obviously desire. But there can be no future in such a relationship. None that would not see both of you hurt—'

'There is not a relationship to continue!'

'I sincerely hope not, my dear.' His grandmother patted his hand. 'Because not only do I seriously doubt that really is her name, but I have other reservations, too.'

'Do you know something about Elena that I do not?' He eyed his grandmother suspiciously.

'Nothing definite, no.' She sighed. 'Only the doubts I expressed to you yesterday. But whether or not that really is her name, or she really is a governess, I am sure I do not have to remind you, of all people, to have a care. For I have no doubt that somewhere in the world, as was the case with Fanny, Elena Leighton will have a father, or a brother, or perhaps even a husband still alive, who will be just as desirous that their daughter or sister, or wife, was not debauched and disgraced by Lord Adam Hawthorne!'

'I do not believe a mutual passion can be called debauching, Grandmother!' Adam's expression had turned icy again.

'If that is the case, then Mrs Leighton must now have some idea of her value.'

Adam stilled. 'Value…?'

Lady Cicely nodded. 'You may be lucky, of course; she does not seem like a particularly grasping sort of gel to me.' His grandmother smoothed the already-smooth skirt of her gown. 'A pretty piece of jewellery and a suitable reference will perhaps suffice.'

'Reference?' he echoed again, sharply.

'Really, Adam—' she sounded exasperated '—whether you choose to continue the relationship or otherwise, you cannot be so naïve as to think that the gel can continue to be employed by you and live in the same household as your own daughter?' Lady Cicely arched disapproving brows.

No, he was not that naïve. Just as his grandmother's comment had also reminded him, all too forcibly, of his own earlier doubts and suspicions about Elena's background and identity.

Doubts and suspicions which he had chosen to ignore, or simply forget the night before, in his desire, his eagerness, to make love to her.

But which he could ignore no longer.

Chapter Twelve

Elena found herself smiling inwardly and often as she spent the following morning in the schoolroom with Amanda. She hugged memories to her of being with Adam the night before, her thoughts drifting time and time again to the wonders of his lovemaking even as she distractedly attempted to teach Amanda her lessons.

Adam had been so gentle with her, so solicitous of Elena's needs, that there had been no thoughts of denial inside her. Nor had there been any reminder of horror and pain to mar the experience. Rather, she had responded eagerly to each new pleasure Adam gave and shared with her. Shy and inexperienced though her own caresses had been, she also believed that she had given him that same pleasure back tenfold.

Even now, Elena felt a moist and burning heat between her thighs every time she so much as thought of having Adam's mouth upon her there. And the warmth of colour entered her cheeks at the memory of how wonderful it had been to kiss and touch him just as intimately, to taste and hold him as he lost his normally icy control to pleasure.

Those long precious minutes of being in his arms afterwards had been almost as rewarding, a time of shared contentment, when their conversation had been of little import in comparison to their physical closeness. And they had laughed with the lightness of children when they had thought themselves discovered going up the stairs together. She could still feel his long and lingering goodnight kisses upon her lips.

Elena had not seen him as yet this morning, having breakfasted in the nursery with Amanda, as was her habit, before the two of them had then gone through to the schoolroom. But Elena very much hoped that they might see each other again at luncheon now that Lady Cicely had joined the family.

And if they did, how would they greet each other? Elena wondered dreamily. With Amanda and Lady Cicely present, Elena knew she and Adam would not be able to reveal, by word or deed, the intimacies they had shared the night before, or the closeness that had followed. But surely he would be able to give some indication, some small gesture that only she would know and understand, to acknowledge the change in their relationship?

The hours until luncheon, until she saw him again, could not pass quickly enough for Elena...

Adam was aware of the exact moment that Elena entered the salon where the family gathered before luncheon, could feel her presence behind him as much as he could hear Amanda's excited chatter at being allowed to join the adults.

It had not been Adam's suggestion for them to do so, but his grandmother's, with the added comment that he 'would have to face Mrs Leighton at some time today, so he may as well get it over with at luncheon'.

'Getting it over with' was not paramount in Adam's mind at this moment—finding the right way in which he might do that was his greatest concern!

He had been too aroused, and then too satiated after making love to Elena, to give much thought as to how they would proceed from there. It had only been later, alone in his bedchamber, that the full import of his actions had struck him.

Indeed, it would seem his impetuous behaviour the previous night had placed Elena in a position of power, one that now required Adam to either offer her monetary or similar recompense for last night, or, if Elena were agreeable to continuing the relationship, then he would be expected to set her up in a household of her own until such time as that relationship ended, before again offering her monetary or similar recompense.

Either way, it seemed that Elena could not remain as a member of his household.

Either way it would seem that last night Adam had behaved just as foolishly as he had with Fanny all those years ago, in that he had allowed his physical attraction to a woman to influence his actions rather than the cold logic that had stood him in such good stead in the years since Fanny died. And that lapse, enjoyable as it might have been at the time, had once again placed a woman in the position of dictating the tenure of their future relationship.

An unpleasantly familiar feeling, which he found totally unacceptable…

Whatever Elena had secretly hoped would be Adam's response to her today, she was doomed to be disappointed as the luncheon progressed without his so much as glancing at her, let alone addressing a word to her directly!

Not only was his behaviour bewildering, but it was hurtful in the extreme.

Elena could come to only one conclusion: the time which had passed since they were together had given Adam the opportunity to reflect, and regret, the closeness they had shared yesterday evening.

'—a little distracted today, Mrs Leighton…?'

Elena gave a start as she realised that, while she had been lost in her misery, Lady Cicely had addressed a remark down the table to her. Had her misery been noted? As well as the surreptitious glances Elena had occasionally given Adam beneath the sweep of her dark lashes? Elena hoped not; it would not do for Adam's grandmother to become suspicious of the tension that now existed between her grandson and the governess of his young and motherless daughter.

She forced a smile to her lips. 'I was merely enjoying this delicious dessert.'

'Really?' Lady Cicely gave the barely touched mousse in front of Elena a pointed glance.

Embarrassed colour warmed her cheeks as she acknowledged she had, in fact, eaten very little of the luncheon. But how could she possibly eat, when she felt so nauseous?

'I was remarking upon the pleasantness of the weather for the beginning of May.' Lady Cicely appeared to take pity on her confused state.

Goodness, yes, today was the first day of the new month. And the sun, as Lady Cicely had observed, was shining brightly. Elena only wished that her own feelings of inner turmoil allowed her to appreciate that warmth. 'It is very pleasant, yes,' she instead answered noncommittally.

Lady Cicely turned to her grandson as he sat stonyfaced and silent at the head of the table, his own dessert as untouched as Elena's. 'Perhaps we might all take a stroll outside in the sunshine after luncheon?'

His eyes were flinty between narrowed lids. 'You must do as you please, Grandmama, as must Mrs Leighton and Amanda; I am far too occupied with estate business for such frivolity.'

'All work and no play makes for a very dull fellow,' Lady Cicely came back drily.

'Then I must remain dull,' her grandson ground out, 'for I have neither the time, nor the inclination, for walks in the sunshine.'

His grandmother gave him a long and measured look before turning to Amanda. 'If you have finished your meal, dear, shall we go upstairs together and collect our bonnets? No, do not trouble yourself, Mrs Leighton.' She smiled gently at Elena as she would have risen too. 'You obviously have not finished eating as yet and I am sure that Amanda is perfectly capable of collecting a bonnet for you, too.'

And Lady Cicely and Amanda's departure would leave Elena alone at the table with Adam…

It was an occurrence which obviously pleased him as little as it did Elena, if the chilling gaze Adam swept over her, as he stood politely to his feet when the ladies of his family rose to leave, was an indication of his feelings on the matter. 'If you will excuse me, there is work in my study urgently in need of my attention.'

A frown creased Lady Cicely's brow as she paused in her own departure. 'Perhaps you might accompany Amanda upstairs after all, Mrs Leighton?'

'Of course.' Elena was only too relieved to have this opportunity to absent herself from Adam's icily unapproachable company.

That he deeply regretted their closeness of the evening before had become painfully obvious. So painfully obvious that Elena had to force herself not to run from the dining room.

'I advise you not to interfere in this matter, Grandmama,' Adam warned as he guessed that was exactly what she was about to do now that they were alone in the dining room.

'When the icy demeanour you have shown that poor woman all through luncheon is already working so well, you mean?' She eyed him with gentle reproof.

'I would hardly refer to her in those terms,' he said.

'Perhaps that is because you appear to be completely impervious to the obvious distress you are causing her?' his grandmother accused.

Of course Adam was not so unfeeling as to be completely unmoved by her response to his recent attitude. But what else was he to do? Any warmth or kindness on his part would surely be seen as an encouragement, after the events of yesterday evening, and Adam could not, would not, allow any woman to lead him about by his libido ever again!

His mouth thinned. 'This is a turnaround, isn't it? After all, you were the one to point out to me earlier on the unsuitability of such a…relationship.'

'I believe I advised caution, not cruelty, my dear.'

'I do not consider it a cruelty to make clear my regret for my previous actions.'

A frown marred his grandmother's creamy brow. 'Am I to understand, then, that your present behaviour is somewhat in the form of being cruel to be kind?'

'Exactly,' he confirmed tersely.

Lady Cicely looked exasperated. 'It is one way of doing things, I suppose…'

'It is the only way I know how to deal with this delicate matter.' Adam turned away to stare sightlessly out of one of the dining-room windows. 'I freely admit I made a mistake last night. A mistake that can only be rectified by Mrs Leighton's immediate removal from my household. In the circumstances, I believe it would be better, for all concerned, if she were to be the one to make that decision.'

'I am not disputing that decision, but I am sure there must be a kinder way of going about it.'

Adam's top lip curled back with self-derision as he continued to stare out of the window before him. 'Kindness has never been my forte—'

'If you are ready to go outside, Lady Cicely? Amanda is even now awaiting us in the entrance hall.'

Adam swung round at the first sound of Elena's brisk tone, a single glance at her unwavering blue-green gaze in the pallor of her face beneath the straw bonnet she now wore enough to tell him that she had once again overheard the last part of his conversation with his grandmother, at least.

Despite those remarks to his grandmother, cruelty was not a natural part of Adam's nature, but something he'd had necessarily to learn during his marriage to Fanny, out of a sense of self-preservation. Nor, whatever decisions he might have made regarding Elena, was this the manner in which he would have chosen to make her aware of them.

He turned to his grandmother. 'If you would care to take Amanda outside whilst I talk briefly to Mrs Leighton, my dear?'

'Of course—'

'I assure you, it is unnecessary for us to talk on this

matter any further,' Elena burst out, colour warming her cheeks as she recognised her own rudeness in doing so.

But she was not herself. How could she be, when she had just overheard Adam, the gentleman to whom she had felt closer than any other, not only discussing the events of last night with his grandmother, but also how best to now rid himself of her embarrassing presence from his household!

And Elena had believed herself to be half in love with him. Had thought that Adam felt some measure of affection for her in return. His remarks to Lady Cicely just now had served to show her just how foolish she had been in that regard. Lord Adam Hawthorne had taken what he wanted from her last night and now he just wanted to be rid of her embarrassing presence. And the sooner the better, as far as he was concerned.

Her chin rose proudly. 'I shall pack my things and make my arrangements to leave here first thing tomorrow morning.'

'You will leave when I give you permission to leave,' Adam bit out harshly.

Elena gave him a stony stare. 'I was under the impression that you had already done that, my lord.'

'It was my intention to return to London tomorrow,' Lady Cicely put in softly. 'There is a ball I must attend on Saturday evening,' she turned to inform her stony-faced grandson. 'You are more than welcome to accompany me in my carriage to London, if that is where you wish to go, Mrs Leighton?' she added gently.

It was a gentleness that brought tears to Elena's eyes;

no matter what Lady Cicely's private thoughts might be, as to the relationship that now existed between her grandson and his young daughter's governess, the elderly lady was not so disgusted with her that she did not show compassion for her present dilemma. And Elena now wished to be as far away from Adam Hawthorne as he wished for her to be from him!

'Thank you,' she accepted politely, her gratitude for the older woman's compassion shining in her eyes. Alongside the tears…

But Elena would not cry. Refused to allow herself to cry in front of Adam. The tears could come later, once she was alone in her bedchamber. For now she would maintain a calm demeanour—along with her dignity.

Adam did not at all appreciate the arrangements for Elena's departure tomorrow being made without any input from him. 'And what do you intend saying to Amanda in regard to your hasty departure?'

Lowered long dark lashes hid the expression in Elena's eyes as she answered him drily, 'Obviously not the truth.'

Adam felt the warmth of colour enter his cheeks at the obvious rebuke. 'If you would leave us now, Grandmama…?'

'Of course.' She moved forwards to briefly to place her hand gently on Elena's arm in obvious sympathy before leaving the room and closing the door softly behind her.

Damn it, his bungling of this affair had his own

grandmother believing him to be not only cruel, but heartless, too! A belief so far from the truth as to be ludicrous…

Those hours Adam had spent with Elena last night had been some of the happiest he had ever known. Free of artifice and pretence, he had believed. Just two people enjoying each other's bodies and company.

Before he'd had the time to realise the consequences of their actions, that is.

But the thought of her leaving as early as tomorrow morning, of never seeing her again, was just as unacceptable to him. 'There is no need for leaving in such haste—'

'There is every need, my lord.' She did not look at him, but kept her beautiful blue-green gaze fixed on the unlit fireplace.

Allowing Adam to admire the alabaster perfection of her face in profile, similar to the beauty of a cameo brooch once owned and worn by his mother… He drew in a sharp breath. 'I regret that you obviously overheard at least some of my conversation with my grandmother—'

'Do you?' Elena turned slowly to look at him with cool blue-green eyes.

Adam gave a small frown at that unwelcome coolness. 'Of course I regret it. It was not the way in which I wished for you to hear of my concerns about the change that recently occurred in our relationship.'

Elena choked back a bitter laugh at this major understatement. As she saw it, Adam's only 'concern' amounted to nothing more than a desire to have her removed from his sight, and his home, as quickly as was humanly possible! So that was what she was going to do.

Her mouth firmed. 'Perhaps, after all, it was for the best that I overheard. It has achieved what you wished it to achieve, in that I am now leaving your household tomorrow morning, without any further embarrassment, or for the need for you to tell me to go.'

He stepped forwards quickly. 'Have you considered that we might perhaps come to some other sort of arrangement agreeable to both of us? A discreet house in London, perhaps, paid for by me, of course,' he added hastily. 'Where we might meet when I am in town—'

'No!' Elena gasped her shock.

And her outrage.

She had believed this man cared for her—had truly thought last night to be beautiful and sincere.

How foolish of her. How utterly, utterly foolish of her to have ever thought their lovemaking last night meant anything to him at all; he might just as well have called her a whore just now, with his insulting suggestion of setting her up in a house in London. His own personal whore, whose bed he proposed visiting whenever he was in London.

How strange it was, that the man who had raped her had wished to make her his wife, and the man who had made love to her only wished to make her his mistress . .

'No, my lord,' she repeated flatly.

'Why the hell not?' He glared his irritation at her intransigence to what he could see was an ideal solution to their dilemma.

Elena gave him a pitying glance. 'I am sure I must have made many mistakes in my life, my lord, but I would hope that they are mistakes I will have learnt from. And never repeated,' she added stingingly.

A nerve pulsed in his tightly clenched jaw. 'You consider last night to be one of those mistakes?'

She nodded distantly. 'I am sure that we both do.'

'You will not even try to understand the awkwardness of this situation from my point of view—'

'If I might be permitted to interrupt, my lord…?'

Adam turned fiercely to face his butler as Jeffries stood in the doorway. 'What is it, man? Whatever it is, can it not wait until I have finished speaking with Mrs Leighton?'

Jeffries looked unruffled by Adam's aggression. 'There is a person outside, wishing to speak with you, my lord. He says you are expecting him.'

Adam scowled. 'Who is he?' The condescending tone of his butler's voice clearly implied that Jeffries did not consider the visitor to be of any note at all.

'A groom, my lord. He says he is—'

'I know who he is,' Adam cut in wearily; he knew exactly who the other man was, and why he was here, but the events of these past few hours had put the matter completely from his mind. 'Ask him to go round to the stables and inform him I will join him there shortly.'

'Yes, my lord.' Jeffries remained stoic as he quietly left the room.

Elena waited only long enough for the door to close behind the butler before turning to look coolly at Adam. 'I really should go and begin my packing—'

'You will remain exactly where you are!' he instructed succinctly, halting Elena's escape as she came to an abrupt halt, her back stiffly unyielding as she continued to face away from him.

'Elena…' his voice gentled '…we need to discuss this situation without allowing emotion, either yours or my own, to cloud the situation—'

'Emotions?' Her eyes glittered as she whirled to face him, angry colour in her otherwise pale cheeks. 'I confess, I no longer believe you to be capable of such frivolity as experiencing genuine emotions!'

'Just a minute—'

'I do not intend to waste so much as another second of my time on a man such as you, my lord, let alone a minute.' Elena gave a scathing snort.

'What do you mean, a man such as me?' he exclaimed indignantly.

Elena spread her hands. 'What sort of man is it that would discuss one woman's virtue so openly with another? Moreover, a kind and gentle woman whose respect and liking I valued?' Her voice broke emotionally. 'You have humiliated me in the worst way possible, have allowed Lady Cicely to believe you have ruined me. I shall never forgive you for that. Never!' She turned on her heel and almost ran to the door.

'Elena!'

'Leave me alone, Adam.' She wrenched the door

open before glancing at him over her shoulder. 'I shall accept your grandmother's offer to share her carriage when she leaves tomorrow for London. After which you will never have to see or hear from me again.'

'Damn it, I want—'

'I have heard what it is you want from me, my lord.' Elena fought to contain the tears, refusing to allow the final humiliation of actually crying in front of him. 'And I have informed *you* that such an arrangement is completely unacceptable to me. Now, if you will excuse me—I advise that you remove your hand from my arm this instant, sir!' she instructed levelly as, having crossed the room in pursuit, Adam had his fingers now curled about her upper arm. She was not at all sure how much longer she could hold back those tears, or be forced to employ some other method of expressing her anger and disappointment.

She had believed Adam to be a better man that this. Had thought him so much *more*. And instead he was no better than Neville Matthews. Worse, in fact, because Neville had at least offered her marriage. Or the asylum...

Those had been the choices Neville had offered to Elena two months ago. A loveless marriage to him, her cruel and sadistic cousin, or for Neville, as her closest male relative and guardian, to have her placed in an asylum for the rest of her life.

Elena had searched for and found a third option, which was to assume another identity and run away, as far and as fast as she could, from Yorkshire. From Neville.

Only to now find herself the victim of her own heart. A heart that had cried out for love, for protection, only to learn that she had instead found a desire equally as selfish as Neville's had been.

Her chin rose proudly. 'I do not believe we have anything more to say to each other, on this subject, or any other, my lord.'

Adam continued to grasp her arm as he stared down at her in frustration. He freely admitted he had handled this situation badly, from start to finish. For it was the finish, he could see that clearly in Elena's contemptuous gaze as she looked up at him unblinkingly, and leaving him in no doubt that she now utterly despised him.

He had been expecting cajoling or threats, a demand in one form or another, that Adam must now provide for her. Instead Elena had turned down his suggestion—a suggestion Adam could still not believe he had made, considering his earlier decision to remove her from his household as soon as possible—that he set her up in a discreet house in London.

He frowned in bewilderment. 'What is it you want from me?'

She blinked long lashes at last. 'I have told you, I wish for you to release me—'

'I do not mean this exact moment!' He scowled.

'If it is not too much trouble, I would appreciate it if you would give me a reference so that I might find another situation.'

'I meant, what is it you want from me as recompense?' he grated impatiently. 'For last night?'

Elena did not wait any longer for Adam to release her, but instead wrenched her arm out of his grasp, no doubt bruising herself in the process, although she did not seem concerned by this, her face now as pale as snow, her eyes dark unreadable pools as she shook her head violently. 'You are without doubt the most *despicable*—'

'Papa? Papa!' Amanda burst into the room unannounced, her face alight with excitement as she ran to him. 'Papa there is a man come into the stables leading the most beautiful pony you ever saw!' She bounced up and down on her heels in her excitement. 'Come and see, Papa! Oh, Mrs Leighton…' she turned to grasp Elena by the hand '…do come and see!'

Elena's expression softened at the complete lack of the reserve Amanda had so often shown in her father's presence in the past. 'I am sure your father would love to come and see the pony, but I have something else I need to do—'

'You must come, Mrs Leighton…' Some of Amanda's excitement faded as she now looked up appealingly at Elena.

'Yes, do come and see the pony, Mrs Leighton,' Adam drawled, feeling stung, both by Elena's dismissal of his ability to feel emotion, as well as the tirade of names she had obviously been about to inflict upon him before Amanda interrupted them.

He freely admitted—to himself, at least—that he

appeared to have seriously misjudged Elena; despite what he had assumed, she appeared to want nothing from him. Except never to see him again once she had departed from here tomorrow...

Which made absolutely no sense to him. He shouldn't have made love to a woman employed in his household and it was a mistake Adam had fully expected to be made to pay for, in one way or another. As he had learnt the hard way, no woman gave of herself without expectation of payment, of some kind. Admittedly Elena was not a member of the highest society, but she was a respectable widow and the wife of a dead soldier. Yet she maintained she wanted nothing from him except a reference before she left so that she might seek other employment.

She perplexed Adam totally.

He straightened. 'Yes, Mrs Leighton, as you had a hand in its appearance, you must certainly come and see Amanda's pony.'

'*My* pony, Papa?' Amanda was the one to answer him in awed breathlessness. 'Is it really mine?'

Adam's expression softened as he looked down at his daughter. 'It is really yours, pet,' he confirmed tenderly.

Elena took the opportunity of Amanda's launching herself into her father's arms, amidst squeals of excitement, in which to edge closer towards the doorway.

Only to have that progress halted as Adam reached out to once again grasp the top of her arm to prevent her from going any further. 'You will accompany us to

the stables, Mrs Leighton,' he commanded in a voice
that brooked no further argument.

No argument that Elena could put forwards in front
of Amanda, at least. And so, with Adam's fingers still
curled firmly about her arm, as he carried Amanda in
his other arm, Elena was left with no other choice but
to accompany father and daughter out of the house and
round to the stables where Lady Cicely stood in conversation with the head groom, and another man who
was holding the leading rein of the pony.

Elena was pleased for Amanda that her father had
obviously acquired a pony for the little girl during the
days he had been away from the estate. It truly was a
beautiful little mare, with a gleaming coat of golden
honey and a mane and tail of pale cream, its eyes the
softest brown as it gazed down adoringly at Amanda
as, having squirmed to be put down by her father, she
hurried forwards to pet its silky soft nose.

'Ah, there you are, Adam.' Lady Cicely turned towards them, allowing a better view of the two men she
had been conversing with—and at the same time allowing the two men to have a better view of Elena…

Adam's visitor, the man holding the leading rein of
the pony, stared at her in disbelief and recognition.

Elena gasped with horror. Darkness eclipsed the sun
and the world went completely black.

Chapter Thirteen

'I appreciate you catching Mrs Leighton as she fell and carrying her up to her bedchamber, Adam, but you really cannot continue to remain in the room now!'

'I can and damn well will! I apologise for swearing, Grandmama.' There was the sound of a heavy sigh. 'But I am sure you will admit, it has been something of a trying day.'

'I realise that. And I am sure we are all anxious to know why Mrs Leighton fainted, but I really do feel it is best if I am the one to continue to sit with her rather than you. As you instructed, Bristol is giving Amanda her first riding lesson and Jeffries has taken the visiting groom to the servants' hall for some tea, but I am sure the young man will wish to be on his way soon.'

'Not until after I have questioned him.'

Elena had been awake for the past several minutes, but had continued to keep her lids firmly closed, so as not to alert grandmother and grandson to the fact that she was no longer lying unconscious upon the bed. In truth, also in an effort to delay having to face the questions which were sure to be asked of her.

She had fainted because she had recognised the 'visiting groom' and, despite the changes in her appearance and circumstances, she knew that Jeremiah had recognised her, too, as Magdelena Matthews.

What was she going to do? What *could* she do to avert further disaster? And disaster it most certainly would be, once Adam Hawthorne and Lady Cicely learnt she was the runaway granddaughter of the Duke of Sheffield. The same young woman accused by her own cousin of murder and theft. A claim Elena could not disprove, and which had given Neville the leverage to threaten her with the choice of marrying him or being sent to an asylum. Needless to say, she had chosen to escape than suffer either of those horrors.

Jeremiah's appearance at Hawthorne Park would seem to have put an end to that escape...

There was another sigh, from Lady Cicely this time. 'I did try to talk to the groom myself before coming upstairs, but the poor man refused to answer any of my questions. I do believe he may be suffering from some sort of shock.'

'I shall shake the answers out of him if I have to!'

Elena had heard enough. 'There will be no need for any physical violence towards Jeremiah,' she murmured huskily, opening her eyes at the same time as she moved up the bed to sit back against the pillows; thankfully someone had removed her bonnet. 'I fear that poor young man will have thought he was seeing a ghost, Lady Cicely,' she added as she looked up at the older woman, not feeling strong enough as yet to face the cold accusation she knew would be in Adam's haughtily aristocratic face.

'A ghost...?' the older lady repeated uncertainly.

Elena nodded. 'Until he saw me here, no doubt Jeremiah believed me either dead or, as so many others were also led to believe, that I had gone abroad somewhere I would never be found.'

Lady Cicely frowned her confusion. 'You and the young groom are acquainted, then?'

Elena would hardly call Jeremiah young, at aged thirty or so, but no doubt he seemed so to the much older Lady Cicely. 'Yes,' she confirmed.

Adam gave a disgusted snort. 'What eclectic taste you appear to have in your choice of male friends, Elena! First a groom and now a lord—will a duke be the next to share your bed, I wonder?'

'Adam!' His grandmother widened scandalised eyes even as Elena felt her face go even paler.

These past few minutes since Elena had fainted had been decidedly unpleasant ones for Adam as his imagination had run amok and he speculated wildly as to the nature of the acquaintance between her and the young man she had just referred to so familiarly as Jeremiah.

A familiarity Adam found less than pleasing following the intimacies they had shared the previous evening. 'Then perhaps Mrs Leighton would care to explain how it is that she and Lord Stapleton's groom come to be so well acquainted that she refers to him by his first name?'

Elena blinked. 'I beg your pardon?'

Adam gave her a confused look. 'It was from his estate in Warwick that I purchased the pony for Amanda, which his own daughter had outgrown.'

She stared at him with puzzled blue-green eyes. 'Jeremiah now works for Lord Stapleton?'

'Have I not just said so?' Adam snapped his impatience with what to him seemed merely a delaying tactic in answering his previous question.

She frowned. 'When I knew him before he worked for—' She broke off abruptly, her lips clamping firmly together.

'Who? Who did he work for?' Adam prompted, still unaccountably jealous that she'd known the good-looking groom at all.

'Someone else.' That blue-green gaze no longer met his as she stared down at the coverlet her fingers were nervously plucking. 'I—I should like the opportunity to talk with him before he leaves, if that is permitted?'

'What the—!' Adam broke off his angry tirade to glare down at her in disbelieving exasperation. 'If you are expecting me to allow that young man to come up to your bedchamber then you are sorely mistaken.' He looked down the length of his nose at her. 'You may talk with whom you wish, where you wish, once you have left my household, but until that time you will behave in a manner befitting that of my daughter's governess.'

She gave him an exasperated glare. 'I do not believe

that I either requested or implied that I wished to speak to Jeremiah here in my bedchamber.'

'No, I do not believe that she did either, Adam,' his grandmother joined in the conversation. 'Now, might I suggest that we all calm down,' she added soothingly, 'so that Mrs Leighton may explain to us why seeing the groom Jeremiah—what a charmingly old-fashioned name that is!—should have such an effect upon her that she fainted dead away?'

Elena almost laughed at the disgusted expression on Adam's face at his grandmother's aside concerning the charm of the groom's name. Almost. Because there really was nothing in the least amusing about her present situation...

She would have liked nothing better than to be able to just continue to lie here with her eyes closed until all of this just went away. All of it. The love-making of last night. The scene with Adam earlier. Her dismissal and departure tomorrow. Jeremiah's unexpected arrival. The disclosure as to who she really was that must surely follow...

Most of all Elena wished that she did not have to witness the disgust in Adam and Lady Cicely's expression and demeanours once they learnt the truth about her.

But she knew it was unavoidable. Just as Adam's actions, following that disclosure, would be just as unavoidable...in that he would have no choice but to call the local authority and have her arrested. After which, she would surely find herself transported to the gaol closest to her grandfather's estate, where she would then be accused and tried by the local magistrate. Who just so happened to be Neville Matthews, the evil eleventh Duke of Sheffield.

Elena feared being at Neville's mercy as much as she dreaded seeing the disgust and dislike in Adam's face once it was made known to him who she really was.

'Well?'

Elena blinked as she glanced up at Adam, her breath catching in her throat as she saw the bleak expression in his unyielding grey eyes, assuring her that she should expect no mercy there! She moistened the dryness of her lips before speaking. 'Once Jeremiah has had chance to drink his tea and recover from his shock, then he will no doubt tell you that—that my name is not, and never has been, Mrs Elena Leighton.' She inwardly trembled even as she forced herself not to flinch under the sudden fierceness of his gaze.

'Not Mrs Elena Leighton…?' Adam's tone was dangerously soft.

She swallowed hard. 'No.'

'You are not the widow of Corporal Leighton, late of his Majesty's Royal Dragoons?'

'No.'

Adam breathed deeply in an effort to hold on to his rapidly rising temper. A temper he had not truly lost in all the years since Fanny died. 'Then perhaps you would care to tell us what your real name is and exactly who you are?'

The slenderness of her throat moved as she swallowed, her face now as pale as alabaster. 'Once I have told you my name, I doubt there will be any need for me to tell you who I am.'

'Adam—'

'Leave this to me, Grandmama,' he instructed tautly, his gaze remaining fixed on Elena.

'But—'

'Grandmother!' He turned sharply to glare her into silence. 'Please allow Mrs—this person to tell us who she is and exactly what she is doing in my household masquerading as someone else!' Adam's voice rose on those last two words, as he could no longer hold his anger in check. He turned to scowl that displeasure down at the woman on the bed. 'Are you even a governess?'

'No.'

'I do not see what difference it makes as to whether or not she is a governess,' his grandmother put in mildly.

'It makes a difference to me!'

'I do not see why, Adam,' Lady Cicely soothed. 'When Mrs—this young lady has obviously done such a wonders for Amanda's education and social demeanour.' She beamed at Elena approvingly.

An approval, Elena recognised heavily, which must surely turn to the same anger and suspicion with which Adam now viewed her once Lady Cicely knew the truth.

'It will make a great deal of difference if this young woman is someone less than suited to being companion to my daughter,' Adam insisted stiffly.

Elena noted that he'd said 'woman' rather than 'lady' as Lady Cicely had.

'Perhaps you should leave me to talk with Mrs—er—the young lady?' Lady Cicely suggested lightly. 'I have always considered myself a good judge of character, and I believe that Elena—is that your real name, dear?' She looked down kindly at Elena.

'Yes…well, sort of.'

The older woman nodded before turning back to her grandson. 'I am sure that this is all just a misunderstanding, Adam.'

'The only misunderstanding made was by this person, when she came into my household falsely masquerading as the governess she is not.' He looked down his aristocratic nose at Elena. 'Now, madam, you will tell me exactly who you are and what your association is with this Jeremiah.'

Elena gave a start. 'I do not have an "association", as such, with Jeremiah—'

'So you would have me believe that you fainted at the sight of him because he is merely a past and casual acquaintance, then?' he scorned.

Elena frowned; if anything, Adam seemed more angry about Jeremiah than he was about her working for him under a false identity. 'I only know Jeremiah because he worked for—he worked for my—'

'I do believe that Mrs—Elena is in danger of fainting again, Adam; perhaps you should go and get some of your best brandy to revive her?' Lady Cicely gently pushed her grandson aside so that she might sit on the side of the bed before taking one of Elena's hands into both of hers.

Elena gave the older woman a searching glance, sure she detected something more than casual concern in Lady Cicely's gently lined face—sympathy for her plight in those faded grey eyes, perhaps?

A suspicion that seemed to be borne out as the other woman gave Elena's fingers a reassuring squeeze before she looked up at her grandson. 'Adam?'

He crossed his arms across his muscled chest. 'I am not going anywhere until El—this young woman has answered my questions to my satisfaction.'

'I admit to feeling a little in need of a restorative myself, after all this upset,' his grandmother murmured weakly.

'And I repeat, I am going nowhere, Grandmama, until this puzzle has been solved,' Adam repeated firmly, his gaze remaining stubbornly fixed on Elena.

In truth, his imagination was once again running amok at Elena's obvious reluctance to reveal her identity. Who, or what, was she that she had lied in order to obtain a position in his household?

If she was merely a woman left alone in the world and desperate to find a way of supporting herself, then it should not have been necessary for her to lie about her name. Unless she was, after all, that runaway wife Adam had once suspected her of being?

The mere thought that she was another man's wife was enough to drive him completely insane.

Adam needed to know—*now*—exactly who she was and what she was doing here! 'Well?' he demanded.

Her lashes lowered. 'If I might be allowed to sit up, Lady Cicely…?'

'Of course.' The older woman stood up so that Elena might sit up on the side of the bed.

Her face was a pale oval against her dark and dishevelled hair as she looked up at Adam. 'My name is Magdelena Matthews.'

Adam's face remained a blank following Elena's announcement, but she heard a slight gasp of recognition from Lady Cicely's direction. Needing every ounce of courage she possessed, in order to continue, Elena did not so much as glance in the direction of that lady, but continued to look up at the stony-faced man standing in front of her. 'My grandfather was—' Her voice broke emotionally as she talked of her grandfather in the past tense. 'He was George Matthews, the late Duke of Sheffield.'

Adam recoiled away from her as realisation of her identity finally dawned on him. 'You are the same granddaughter suspected of murdering that gentleman and robbing his home?'

Elena's vision blurred as the tears came readily to her eyes. 'Yes.'

'Good God…!' Adam exclaimed in horror; this was worse, so much worse than he had even imagined. He had been harbouring a murderess in his household! A young woman who had cold-bloodedly done away with her own grandfather before then stripping his home bare of every jewel she could carry.

Good God, she might have murdered them all in their beds this past month before robbing them too!

'*That* is why— You have your father's eyes, my dear,' Lady Cicely murmured.

'Yes.'

Adam turned to his grandmother incredulously. 'How can you stand there and talk of the colour of her eyes when she is nothing more than a murderess—?'

'I believe you just stated she was a suspected murderess,' his grandmother reproached him. 'Personally, I have always had my suspicions as to the validity of that claim—'

'The only reason she is not presently in a prison cell awaiting sentence is because she ran away before the authorities could charge her with such!' Adam growled, pinning her to the bed with his piercing gaze. 'You were about to tell us who the man Jeremiah is?'

She drew in a deep breath. 'He is one of the grooms who worked on my grandfather's estate—'

'You were romantically involved with one of your grandfather's grooms?' he barked incredulously.

'No, of course I was not.' Irritation flickered in those blue-green eyes. 'Jeremiah merely recognised me as being the Duke of Sheffield's granddaughter.'

Another thought occurred to Adam at the full import of this statement. Rather than making love to his daughter's governess yesterday evening, as he had thought, he'd dallied with the granddaughter of a duke. An occurrence that would, in normal circumstances, have resulted in his being forced by the dictates of society into offering marriage to that same person.

His mouth thinned. 'You realise that this disclosure means I shall have to call in the authorities and have you taken into custody?'

Her face paled to the colour and stiffness of white parchment. 'Yes, of course—'

'Let us not be too hasty in our actions, Adam,' his grandmother put in firmly.

'Hasty?' he echoed incredulously. 'It appears to me, as the Duke of Sheffield met his end two months ago, that her arrest is long overdue!'

Lady Cicely tutted. 'Adam, I have come to know and like Amanda's governess this past few days, and believe that you are now allowing your...personal involvement to rob you of your natural sense of fairness and logic.'

'Indeed?' He eyed her frostily.

'Most certainly,' she said, unrepentant. 'Think, Adam,' she continued impatiently as he remained impervious to her look of reproach. 'Why would a young lady accused of those crimes now be working in your household as a governess?'

He gave a scornful snort. 'As a safe place to hide from capture, of course.'

'And why would she not have used the money and jewels she is reputed to have stolen to have taken herself as far away from England as possible? To the Continent, at very least? Indeed, that is where the gossip in society these past few months has said she is rumoured to be.'

Adam gave a sudden frown as the logic of his grandmother's comments permeated what she had referred to as his 'personal involvement'. 'It is my belief that we should leave it to the relevant authorities to decide as to her guilt or innocence.'

'Did you wish to say something, my dear?' Lady Cicely prompted as Elena gave a strangled sound of protest at Adam's suggestion.

Elena swallowed before answering. 'Only that the authority to which Lord Hawthorne refers consists of my cousin Neville, the new Duke of Sheffield, and that he—that he—' She swallowed anxiously. 'He is the same gentleman who, for reasons of his own, levelled the accusations of murder and theft against me at the outset!'

'Can that possibly be so, Adam?' Lady Cicely looked wide-eyed at her grandson. 'Surely, for the sake of impartiality, that cannot be allowed?'

He shrugged. 'I know nothing as to the authority in Yorkshire.'

This past few minutes had been more excruciatingly painful for Elena than she could ever have imagined. As well as having to live through some of the events of two months ago she also had to listen to and see, in Adam's cold and remorseless eyes, his condemnation of her as being the guilty party, without so much as a second thought or doubt. It was beyond bearing, when only hours ago Elena had believed herself to be falling in love with him.

A shy and hesitant love, which now withered and died in her breast as if it had never been. 'If you did, then you would know that my cousin Neville has inherited my grandfather's magisterial role in that area, as well as his title and estates,' she spoke flatly, unemotionally—indeed, what point was there in her pleading when Adam so obviously believed her to be guilty without benefit of a trial? 'And that, once safely in his custody, no matter what the evidence, I have every reason to believe he will not hesitate to ensure that I am immediately hanged by the neck until I am completely dead.'

Adam's gaze moved instinctively to that long and delicate throat, wincing slightly as he easily imagined the crudeness of a thick rope about it, squeezing and bruising that soft and ivory flesh until all life had been extinguished from the young and beautiful woman to whom it belonged.

He shuddered at the very thought of it…

Chapter Fourteen

'I believe that a certain amount of hysteria has been allowed to enter into this conversation—'

'Hysteria?' Elena stared at Adam incredulously as she began to pace the bedchamber, her skirts swishing about her ankles at the briskness of the movement. 'Perhaps you, too, would feel less than calm, sir, at thoughts of your own demise in such a horrible fashion?' Her eyes glittered brightly, partly with anger, and partly with those unshed tears Elena refused to allow to fall.

'Hold your tongue, Adam.' His grandmother rounded on him with unaccustomed sharpness, as he would have replied. 'And let me remind you that you certainly liked Miss Matthews well enough—perhaps too well!—before being told of her identity.' Her expression gentled as she turned back to a now blushing Elena. 'I knew and liked your mother and father very much, child.'

Elena felt an emotional lump rise in her throat. 'It is very kind of you to say so.'

'Not at all.' Lady Cicely reached out to clasp both of

her hands in her own, at the same time halting Elena's pacing. 'Your grandmother—Jane—was also a friend of mine in her younger days. And your grandfather—'

'How long is this trip down memory lane going to last, Grandmama?' Adam asked with a sigh.

Lady Cicely's eyes, so like his own, flashed as she cast him a brief and censorious glance. 'Perhaps if you had not become so rigid in your thinking, Adam, you would not only see, but also hear that I am endeavouring to point out that Miss Matthews has a fine pedigree—'

'I believe that every family, even those in possession of a "fine pedigree", has been known to have its black sheep, Grandmama.'

'Your sarcastic sense of humour is not welcome in this conversation, Adam!'

Elena stared at Lady Cicely. The older woman did not truly believe that her grandson was jesting? For, if she did—

'Admittedly it is usually a gentleman who is referred to as such,' Adam continued regardless, 'but I see no reason why it should not occasionally be—'

'Adam!'

'Very well, Grandmama.' He sketched her a mocking bow, that levity swiftly fading as he turned to Elena. 'May I ask what has happened to the real Mrs Leighton?'

'She is in Scotland, living with the parents of her dead husband.'

'And you know this because...?'

'Because I was acquainted with the Bambury family and so was aware of Mrs Leighton's decision not to accompany them to the Continent.'

'I am relieved to hear it.' Adam frowned. 'My grandmother is obviously of the opinion that the respectability of your antecedents renders you incapable of murdering anyone.'

Elena looked at him guardedly, no longer sure herself as to whether he was jesting or serious, and the cool derision in his expression did not give an indication either way. She drew in a deep breath before speaking. 'Even without my antecedents I am incapable of harming so much as a fly—' She broke off as she recalled the blows and scratches she had rained upon Neville as she'd attempted to fight off his attack. 'Unless I am sorely provoked,' she corrected huskily.

Adam raised dark brows. 'And were you given such provocation by your grandfather?'

She hesitated. 'No.'

His eyes narrowed shrewdly. 'By another person?'

Her lids lowered. 'Yes.'

'Would you care to tell us who that person is?'

Could she tell the Hawthornes the awful truth of what had really happened two months ago?

Elena looked first at Lady Cicely, seeing only gentleness and understanding in that lady's countenance, before turning to Adam; his mood was now much harder to gauge, hooded lids lowered in order to shield the emotion in his eyes, his general demeanour unreadable.

But what other choice did Elena have other than to confide in these people? She either told them the truth and threw herself upon the mercy of their compassion, or she found herself removed from Cambridgeshire forthwith and placed in Neville's vindictive clutches, where she knew she would receive no mercy whatsoever.

Elena drew in a deep and controlling breath, determined to relate past events with a calmness and precision Adam would appreciate, if not condone. Where to start, that was the problem.

Adam kept his gaze narrowed as he watched the conflicting emotions flickering across Elena's face, as he waited for her to answer. Or not. He hoped she did as he had no idea how to proceed if she did not.

Contrary to what his grandmother might think, he was not in the least unemotional about this situation. If anything, he felt too much. The surprise of learning Elena's true identity as well as the shock of realising she had been accused of a terrible crime.

Admittedly, Adam's immediate reaction had been to go into protective-father mode; but what parent would not feel concerned at learning their child had, for the past few weeks, been in the care of a woman who was accused of murdering her own relative?

But, despite his grandmother's rebuke, his own good sense had prevailed almost immediately. Elena Leighton, as he had known her to be until a few minutes ago, had shown nothing but kindness and concern in regard to Amanda's happiness; indeed, she had made every effort to bring father and daughter closer together, and he had bought the very pony upon which Amanda was now riding because Elena had told him it was his daughter's fondest desire to have a pony of her own.

And as for the woman he had made love to last night—

Adam drew in a deep, controlling breath as he thought of that woman. A shy and yet responsive young woman, who had given as much pleasure as she had received. A woman who had asked nothing of him in return. Not last night. Nor when they had spoken again this morning. She had even decided to leave his employment rather than be the cause of any further embarrassment to him or his family.

In truth, Adam could not seriously believe that woman to be capable of theft, let alone the murder of her own grandfather.

'Proceed, if you please,' he instructed curtly, only to see Elena flinch as if he had struck her, the paleness of her face taking on such a look of fragility, it took every ounce of his will not to stride across the bedchamber and take her into his arms and offer her comfort.

A comfort that would solve nothing, if it should emerge that Elena really was responsible for her grandfather's death, by whatever means. There was also the accusation of theft to consider. But, as his grandmother had already so astutely noted, that accusation did not at all tally with the young woman who had entered his household three weeks ago as a governess. Or the fact that she had not possessed the money with which to replace those black mourning dresses she wore. Mourning dresses which it now appeared she had worn out of respect for her grandfather's death rather than that of a husband…

The confusion of emotions Adam now felt at knowing there was not, nor had there ever been, a husband in Elena's life, was enough to make him scowl anew.

Elena turned away from Adam's harshly condemning face, knowing she would not be able to talk about what had happened to her if she continued to look at him. Instead she walked over to the window of the bedchamber to gaze out over the beautiful rolling grounds at the back of the house. Such an idyllic picture of the Cambridgeshire countryside, when here inside the house, her life was falling apart for the second time in as many months.

This past two months had been an illusion, of course, a delaying of the inevitable—but she knew she could delay it no longer. 'My grandparents had two children, two sons, the younger being my own father, David,' she began, her voice husky but steady enough. 'His older brother, Howard, was killed in a hunting accident many years ago, after which his wife and son moved to live in the Dower House on the Sheffield Park estate. My own father died fighting against Napoleon, and as my mother and I were visiting with my grandfather when we received the news, we remained living with them.'

'Your cousin being the heir?'

Elena could not help but smile tightly at his astuteness in going directly to the heart of the problem. 'My cousin Neville.' She nodded. 'He is not the most likeable of men.' She repressed a shiver at how unlikeable she personally found him.

Oh, Neville was handsome enough, with his golden blond hair and his deep-blue eyes, his regular features and trim form not displeasing to look upon. It was his nature, cruel and vindictive, apparent at an early age, which had always caused Elena to avoid his company even when they were children together. As adults it had quickly become clear to her that Neville intended to rob her of her virginity at the earliest opportunity. A deed he had finally succeeded in doing after their grandfather's funeral in February...

'And I suppose he became your guardian on the death of your grandfather?' Once again Adam showed himself to be a man of both astuteness and intelligence.

'Yes, Neville is now my guardian.' Elena suppressed another shudder at all that now meant to her. 'My grandfather, in his wisdom, left me well provided for and Neville—he made it known to me, shortly after my grandfather's death, that he wished for the two of us to marry.'

'Indeed?'

Elena looked down at her clasped hands, the knuckles showing white even through her gloves. 'It was not a match I either wished for or encouraged.'

'Of course it was not,' Lady Cicely spoke for the first time since Elena had begun her halting explanation. 'I am slightly acquainted with that young gentleman,' she spoke to her grandson, 'and he is not at all the sort of man I would wish any granddaughter of mine, if I had one, to ever contemplate marrying and spending the rest of her life with.'

'I do not recall ever meeting him?' Adam frowned darkly.

'That is because you have chosen not to be in society for so many years, Adam.' There was censure in his grandmother's tone. 'For if you had been, you would know that Neville Matthews is not only a known reprobate, but is also responsible for the ruination of several young ladies in society! Edith St Just will not so much as have his presence in her ballroom, let alone seated at her dinner table,' she added as if that settled the matter regarding Neville Matthews's nature and reputation.

Which, Adam acknowledged ruefully, it probably did; Edith St Just, the Dowager Duchess of Royston, was not only a close friend of his own grandmother, but also a much-respected matriarch of society, and if the Dowager Duchess had decided Neville Matthews was unacceptable, then so must the majority of society.

And this was the man who was now Elena's guardian? Not only her guardian, but also the man who had wished for her to become his wife? A man known as a reprobate and despoiler of innocents?

Had he—would he have dared to try to despoil her, too? The blood chilled in his veins at the thought.

'Elena?' Adam prompted sharply.

'Lady Cicely has divined his character perfectly,' she confirmed, the slenderness of her back and shoulders now stiff and unapproachable. 'I turned down his offer of marriage, of course. A refusal he did not—did not take kindly to, shall we say. And which, as my legal guardian, he chose to ignore.'

'He is in love with you?'

'Love?' Elena scorned as she finally turned to face him, her face paper-white, and her eyes a dark and unfathomable blue-green. 'I do not believe love to be an emotion Neville is capable of feeling. Self-indulgence. Lust. Greed. Those are the only emotions he understands.'

'Greed?' Adam chose to ignore the first two emotions, for fear of where those thoughts might take him, his gaze intent on the pallor of her face.

She drew in a shaky breath. 'As I said, my grandfather did not wish for me to be left destitute as well as alone after his death and so made financial provision for me in his will. In that, I would come into my own considerable personal fortune on the advent of my coming of age or my marriage, whichever came first.'

'Your grandfather did not expect his demise to occur before your majority.' Adam made it a statement rather than a question.

'No, he did not.'

His eyes narrowed. 'How did he die, Elena?'

Her breath caught in her throat. 'A heart attack, brought on by shock.'

'What sort of shock?'

'Does it matter?' she came back defensively. 'The fact is he died, ten months before my twenty-first birthday. And Neville, as my legal guardian, made it clear to me, after my grandfather's funeral, that he did not intend for any of the Sheffield money to be settled outside of the family and that I was to become his wife as soon as the arrangements for the marriage could be made.'

'A marriage you were opposed to.'

'Oh, yes,' she assured vehemently.

'And so you ran away, taking the money and jewels with you so as to—' Adam broke off, shaking his head. 'You did not take any money or jewels with you, did you?' How could she have done? For, as he had realised earlier, if Elena had stolen those things, then there would have been absolutely no reason for her to seek employment as a governess.

'Neville Matthews made up the story about your having taken the money and jewels,' Lady Cicely stated firmly. 'As he also made up the story of your having been responsible for your grandfather's death.'

Elena turned away, the tears now falling softly down her cheeks as she could no longer bear to so much as look upon the sympathy she saw in that kindly lady's face. 'I—not exactly,' she answered huskily.

'How not exactly?' Adam demanded harshly.

'It is true I did not take anything from the house when I left, apart from a few personal belongings.' Elena gave a shake of her head. 'But if I had not fought off Neville's attentions that evening—if I had not called out for help—if I had not screamed, then my grandfather would not have taxed himself by running to my bedchamber to discover—to see—'

'I believe we have distressed Miss Matthews quite enough for the moment,' Lady Cicely cut in firmly. 'You will go down the stairs for the brandy now, Adam,' she instructed as she crossed the room to Elena's side and placed an arm gently about her shoulders.

Lady Cicely's kindness was too much for Elena to withstand after talking of, remembering, the night of her grandfather's death and the terrible days that had followed, when she had lived in constant fear of what Neville would do next, and she turned in that lady's embrace as she began to sob in earnest. For the death of her grandfather, for all that she had lost, and lastly, because of the disgust she knew would be on Adam's face if she had dared to look at him again.

Which she did not, hearing instead his departure to do as his grandmother bade him and fetch the brandy.

'Now, my dear,' Lady Cicely spoke again with firmness, 'You will tell me exactly what further outrage that excuse for a man inflicted upon you to cause you to run away as you did, without even the means of supporting yourself. A confidence I promise you I shall not share with my grandson, if that is what you wish,' she added at Elena's obvious hesitation.

Elena looked at the older woman searchingly, easily seeing the compassion in that kindly face, but also some of Adam Hawthorne's strength of character in the directness of Lady Cicely's unwavering and encouraging gaze. A compassion and strength, which now gave her the courage to tell Lady Cicely the whole truth of the day of her grandfather's funeral, when she had been left with no choice but to run away from Sheffield Park, penniless and alone.

'I understand from my own conversation with the gentleman that you spoke with Jeremiah prior to my own conversation with him?'

Elena could discern none of Adam's feelings on the matter as she looked across at him from the doorway of his study, where she had been summoned by Jeffries to attend him after earlier refusing to join the family for dinner.

She had known she would have to see and speak with Adam again some time during this evening, of course, and had chosen not to burden the dinner table with her presence, but rather accept Lady Cicely's suggestion that she have a tray sent up to her bedchamber. Not that Elena had been in the least hungry, but she had not wished to disappoint Lady Cicely when she had been so kind to her.

Unfortunately, with only a single candle alight on the front of Adam's desk, his face remained in shadow, so making it impossible for Elena to read his expression to gauge what he might be feeling. 'I thought it best that I try to reassure him, yes,' she confirmed.

He nodded. 'Come in and close the door behind you. There is absolutely no reason why the whole of my household should be privy to our conversation,' he added gently once Elena had done as he requested. 'And having now spoken to Jeremiah yourself, you will also know that Matthews dismissed the majority of your grandfather's household staff seven weeks ago, and replaced them with his own?'

She gave a sigh. 'Yes.'

'What do you make of such behaviour?'

Elena frowned slightly, having expected Adam's next question to be something entirely different. And her own feelings, upon learning of the summary dismissal of the household staff that had been so loyal to her grandfather for so many years, had been ones of distress. Mrs Hodges, for example, had been housekeeper at Sheffield Park for many years, and only two years away from her retirement, when she might have expected to receive a small pension to keep her. Instead, after being dismissed, she had been left with no pension and no choice but to go and live with her eldest son in Skegness. Younger members of staff, like Jeremiah, had simply been tossed out into the world, to seek other employment where they could.

She gave a shrug. 'I would say that it is a typical example of Neville's complete disregard for the welfare of others.'

'And that is all you make of it?'

Elena frowned slightly. 'What else should I make of it?'

'The possibility that Matthews perhaps dismissed the staff at Sheffield Park so that they could not be called to give evidence in your favour at your trial?'

Elena's stomach cramped nauseously at the mention

of a trial. 'I believe it is not uncommon for the new in-cumbent to replace the original servants with his own?'

'Not uncommon, no,' Adam allowed grimly. 'But in this particular instance, it is certainly convenient.'

'Not to those household servants.'

'No,' he acknowledged. 'Jeremiah also seemed to be of the opinion that you were incapable of harming a single silver hair upon your grandfather's head.'

Elena's chin rose defensively. 'Then Jeremiah is an excellent judge of character.'

Adam gave a tight smile at the implied criticism of him. 'My grandmother has also informed me that she still intends for you to travel back to London with her when she leaves here tomorrow morning.'

'I have not encouraged her in that decision—'

'Did I say that you had?'

'No, but—' Elena grimaced. 'I accept that you can-not be best pleased at the idea.'

'And would my displeasure bother you?'

'Of course it would bother—' She broke off abruptly to draw in several calming breaths. 'I am sure that you would much rather I just removed myself from here without involving any of your family further in my— in my personal problems.'

As Lady Cicely had encouraged her to do, Elena had confided the whole of the truth as to the reason for her hasty flight from Sheffield Park two months ago, se-cure in the knowledge that Lady Cicely would not break her promise to her. Nor did she believe for a moment that that dear lady had broken that promise. No, Elena had no doubt that Adam's request for her to attend him immediately in his study once dinner had ended was as a direct result of his conversation with Jeremiah. A conversation he had not indicated yet whether or not he believed.

'You appear to be attributing me with thoughts and wishes which I do not believe I have expressed, either by word or deed.'

Elena wished that she could at least see Adam's face clearly rather than just those hollows and shadows created by the flickering candlelight. 'Perhaps you have not stated them,' she allowed. 'But that does not mean you have not thought them.'

'Indeed,' Adam allowed drily after a brief pause, no longer sure what he 'thought' about this situation. His conversation with the groom had been…enlightening, to say the least, that gentleman having immediately leapt to Elena's defence, after expressing his delight in knowing that no harm had come to her since her disappearance from Yorkshire.

That Lady Cicely knew more of that situation than he, Adam had no doubts. He was also certain that Elena did not intend to share those same confidences with him. So Adam had little choice but to draw his own conclusions regarding the reasons for Elena's flight from the unwanted attentions of her cousin.

And, in view of his grandmother's summing up of that young man's character, a damning statement of fact completely vindicated by the Dowager Duchess of Royston's social aversion to Sheffield, those conclusions were extremely unpleasant ones.

All the more so when Adam considered the physical liberties he himself had taken with Elena so recently.

It was a wonder she had not run screaming into the night, if what he suspected had happened to her should prove to be correct.

Just the possibility of it was enough to warn Adam to exert caution with her now. 'I have no objection to your accompanying my grandmother to London tomorrow,' he stated evenly. 'Although I have reservations as to what she hopes to accomplish by it. No matter what the circumstances leading up to your leaving Sheffield Park…' he scowled as she saw Elena flinch '…the fact remains, innocent or guilty, that you still have the accusation of murder and theft to answer before you may even begin to think of rejoining society.'

She gave him a sad smile. 'I have never been a part of society, my lord,' she explained as he raised a questioning brow. 'My father's death, followed by my mother's, and then my grandfather's, has meant that I have never been out of mourning long enough to ever venture into society.'

'You have not missed much,' Adam drawled dismissively. 'But the fact remains, you must eventually return to Yorkshire in order to answer the charges made against you.'

She repressed a shudder. 'Where my cousin Neville is now magistrate.'

'That is…unfortunate.' Adam nodded grimly at this

reminder. 'But that does not prevent you from being represented by a reputable lawyer, a man who is able to point out the unfairness of such a trial taking place in that vicinity, given the circumstances.'

She released a shaky breath. 'With Neville in charge of my fortune until I reach the age of one and twenty, I do not have the means to employ such a lawyer—'

'But I do.' Adam stood up decisively.

Elena blinked as he suddenly loomed very large and intimidating in the small confines of his private study. 'You—you would be willing to help me in that regard?'

'I feel someone must,' he stated grimly. 'And if I do not do so, then I believe my grandmother will choose to embroil herself in this affair even more than she has already done,' he added.

It was too much to hope, Elena acknowledged heavily, that Adam had made his offer of help because he believed her to be innocent of the accusations; instead he made it clear he was intervening solely to prevent his grandmother from involving herself any further in the tangle of Elena's affairs.

Adam knew, by the fact Elena now avoided meeting his gaze, that she believed his interest in this matter to be for his grandmother's benefit only. An understandable assumption for her to have made, given the circumstances. It was also an erroneous one.

The truth of the matter was, Adam dared not show any sign of personal preference for Elena in this situation, for fear that Matthews, once he knew of the Hawthorne family's intervention in his affairs, should then claim that Adam's interest in Elena was far from impartial.

Which it undoubtedly was.

Despite his initial reaction earlier, to learning Elena's identity, Adam's natural sense of logic had very quickly reasserted itself, allowing him to see her as incapable of killing anyone, let alone the grandfather she had so obviously loved.

Nor, despite their intimacies the previous night, had she asked anything of him, as so many women would have done, other than that he at least listen to what she had to say in her defence, before he condemned her.

That Elena had been treated so cruelly, and by one who should have been her protector, filled Adam with a burning rage completely at odds with the veneer of cool practicality he now presented to her. But he had no choice but to present that side to her, and everyone else, if he were to be of any help to her in this matter.

'It is very kind of you, my lord—'

'Kindness, be damned!' he growled, wishing he dared take her in his arms and comfort her, but knowing that he could not, dare not, for fear he would want so much more from her if he once touched her again. For this to work at all he must remain aloof, from both her and her present situation. 'I am not a kind man—'

'I beg to differ.'

'The truth is, I have never cared for men of Matthews's ilk.'

'You have only heard what manner of man I believe him to be.'

'An opinion that my grandmother and the Dowager Duchess of Royston share.'

'Even so—'

'Do not forget I have also spoken to Jeremiah,' Adam bit out firmly. 'He is to return to Warwick tomorrow morning, but he has promised to be available if his testament as to your character should be needed at your trial—Elena!' He barely had the chance to move forwards in time to catch her, as her face paled and she swayed on her feet, as if in danger of fainting a second time today.

A move Adam knew to be a mistake the moment he held her in his arms again. He smelt and felt the softness of her dark hair beneath his chin, a mixture of lemons and flowers and ebony silk, as he lifted her lightness up into his arms and carried her across to the chair beside the unlit fireplace, before sitting down with her fragility cradled against his chest as she began to cry.

'You really must cease your tears now,' he murmured gruffly several minutes later as he offered her his silk handkerchief.

Elena felt as if her heart were breaking, the tight control she had kept about her emotions this past two months having disintegrated completely under first Lady Cicely's, and now Adam's kindness. Admittedly, Adam claimed he was offering his assistance in an effort to spare his grandmother from any further involvement in her scandalous affairs, but his reasons for that kindness were unimportant at this moment; Elena felt as if she had been alone, and lonely, for so long now, her emotions frozen, that any show of kindness, for whatever reason, was sure to be her undoing.

As it had been, the tears she should have shed two months ago, for the loss of her grandfather, and her innocence, were now falling hotly, and unchecked, wetting Adam's waistcoat and shirt, she realised as she felt that dampness beneath her cheek.

She sat up to take Adam's handkerchief and begin mopping up those tears. 'I am so sorry—'

'There is no need for apology,' he rasped, stilling the movements of her hand against his chest.

'But—' The words froze on Elena's lips as she looked up to find Adam staring down at her intently in the candlelight even as she felt the wild tattoo of his heartbeat beneath the palm of her hand. An intensity of gaze levelled on the fullness of those parted lips even as she felt the stirring, swelling, of Adam's arousal beneath the roundness of her bottom. 'Adam…?' she breathed her uncertainty at his physical response.

His jaw clenched. 'I believe it is time—past time!— you retired for the night.'

'But—'

'Do not argue, Elena—just go!'

The tightness of his jaw and lips might be telling her to go, but the arms he still kept about her, and the increased swell of his arousal beneath her bottom, said the opposite. 'Could I not just sit here, with you, for a little while longer?'

He bared his teeth in a humourless smile. 'I believe we both know that would not be a good idea.' As if in confirmation of that claim, the stiffness of his erection moved hard and demanding against her tender flesh.

Elena looked up at him shyly in the candlelight, at this physical display, despite all that he had learnt and heard of her today, that Adam still desired her. Against his will, perhaps, if his coolness towards her earlier today at luncheon, and the grimness of his expression now, was an indication, but that physical evidence of his desire was undeniable. Of course, physical desire was still not the love she had last night hungered for and craved from this man, but it was so much more than Elena had believed she would ever know from him again.

Besides which, Neville's actions two months ago had ensured that in future she could never ask, or expect, anything more than desire from any man! 'I believe it is.' She settled more comfortably against him.

Adam breathed in deeply through his nose, his normal iron control far more tenuous than he would have wished it to be as Elena snuggled against the warmth of his chest, knowing he should insist that she go, that she leave him, but for the moment unable to find the words, or the willpower, to insist she do so.

'Why were you so aloof during luncheon today?'

Adam flinched. His intention earlier today, of distancing himself from Elena, in an effort to put their relationship back on an acceptable footing, had been rendered completely redundant in light of her revelations this afternoon.

He no longer had any choice in the matter; he had to remain aloof from her, for Elena's own benefit as much as his own.

He dug deep inside himself to add the necessary steel to that resolve as he grasped hold of Elena's arms and raised her to her feet before standing up himself and moving away from her. 'I should have thought that was obvious.'

'Not to me.' She looked utterly bewildered.

Adam's mouth firmed. He had to be cruel to be kind and force her away from him before he kissed her again and they were both lost. 'Because I had decided you are not a woman I wish to become involved with, either as Mrs Elena Leighton or Miss Magdelena Matthews.'

Elena drew into herself as if struck, as Adam's complete rejection of her hit with the force of a blow, bringing a return of those stinging tears to her eyes. Tears she could not allow Adam to see fall for a second time. 'I am sorry if I—I shall do as you suggest and return upstairs to my bedchamber.'

He nodded. 'Amanda and I will accompany the two of you to London tomorrow. I really cannot allow my grandmother to go haring about the English countryside alone in the company of a young woman who has been accused of murder!'

Elena gave a pained gasp even as her face paled once again.

Causing Adam to clench his hands at his sides in an

effort to prevent himself from going to her and taking her in his arms once more; he dared not allow himself to so much as touch Elena again until this situation had been sorted out once and for all. Her safety came first. She was in such terrible danger from that villainous cousin of hers.

He had every intention of ensuring that she would be safe, and as soon as possible.

Chapter Fifteen

'This has just arrived for you.' Lady Cicely smiled warmly as she bustled into the bedchamber Elena had occupied this past four days and nights at the lady's London house in Grosvenor Square, her arms occupied with carrying a large oblong box.

Since she'd been here Elena had not so much as set eyes upon that lady's grandson. Nor had he spoken a single word to her during their two-day journey back to town, Adam having ridden on horseback whilst the three ladies travelled in the carriage, and his parting had been brusque in the extreme once they reached Lady Cicely's home. Elena had been left in a constant state of nerves as to what he intended doing with the information he now had as to her real identity.

'For me…?' Elena now eyed the older woman doubtfully as Lady Cicely placed the large box down upon the bedcovers.

She nodded. 'Open it up and let us take a look inside.'

'But who can it be from?' Elena eyed the box as if were a snake about to strike.

'Who else should it be from but Adam, of course,' Lady Cicely said impatiently. 'I do so hope that for once he paid heed to my instructions…' she added worriedly.

Elena felt her heart sink to the black boots she wore with one of the black gowns she had once again donned before travelling back to London, the pretty new gowns and bonnets Adam had purchased for her seeming entirely inappropriate to her present situation. 'Adam? I mean, Lord Hawthorne has sent me a gift?'

She was even less inclined to open the box now that she knew who it came from.

Lady Cicely made herself comfortable on the side of the bed. 'Are you not curious to see what is inside?' she encouraged.

It would be very rude of her, in view of this lady's kindness to her, to reply as she wished to, with 'not in the least'! For Elena could not think of anything that Adam might wish to send to her which in the least warranted Lady Cicely's present air of expectation.

'I do not understand…' Several minutes later she stared down nonplussed at the beautiful gown of white silk and lace that had been revealed nestled within the tissue paper inside the box, a turquoise ribbon sewn beneath the bodice, several matching ribbons accompanying it obviously intended to adorn her hair.

'He did listen!' Lady Cicely nodded approvingly. 'And the ribbon is a nice touch.' She held up one of the hair ribbons. 'An exact match in colour with your eyes.

Perhaps there is hope for my grandson, after all,' she added speculatively.

Elena looked dazed. 'Why would Lord Hawthorne order an evening gown made and be delivered to me here...?'

'So that you may wear it when Adam escorts us to dinner this evening, of course.' Lady Cicely stood up briskly. 'I shall send my own maid to attend you, for you must look your very best—does the gown not meet with your approval, my dear?' She frowned as Elena simply continued to stare down at the gown.

'It is a beautiful gown.' She nodded distractedly.

'But?'

'But you must know, as must Lord Hawthorne, that I cannot be seen out and about with you in London, this evening or any other. Not only have I not been presented at Court, but for obvious reasons I am like to be arrested if I so much as show my face in society.' She had not even stepped outside of this house since arriving back in London. Indeed, Elena had spent those same four days constantly waiting for the sound of the knock upon the door, which would herald the arrival of the authorities, come to arrest her and lock her away in a prison cell.

'You will not be seen out and about in town, and you are allowed to attend a private dinner party without being presented,' Lady Cicely assured her.

Elena made no attempt to hide her bewilderment at this plan. 'As what? I would not be invited to a private dinner party as Mrs Elena Leighton and I certainly cannot attend as Miss Magdelena Matthews.'

Lady Cicely grasped both Elena's hands in her own, her expression intense. 'Do you trust me not to do anything which would bring you further unhappiness?'

'Of course.'

The older woman nodded her satisfaction with the swiftness of her answer. 'And do you trust Adam to do the same?'

Elena hesitated, unsure of her feelings towards Adam Hawthorne since the evening he had stated his own lack of interest in continuing any sort of relationship, even friendship, with her. 'I trust him not to do anything which would bring *you* unhappiness,' she finally answered guardedly.

Lady Cicely smiled ruefully. 'Your manners do you great credit, my dear,' she said. 'And I will admit that Adam has been irritating in his absence recently, but—'

'I expected nothing less,' Elena assured hastily. 'He has already been more than kind in allowing me to remain here with you for this amount of time.'

'Nevertheless, he could have been a little less…elusive.' Lady Cicely pursed her lips disapprovingly. 'But, he did make the arrangements for the dinner party this evening, so I expect I shall forgive him for—'

'We are dining at Lord Hawthorne's home tonight?' Elena gasped.

'Oh, no, my dear Elena.' Lady Cicely beamed. 'Tonight we are to dine at the home of my dear friend, Edith St Just, the Dowager Duchess of Royston!'

'Is it Lord Hawthorne's intention to publicly humiliate me by having me arrested in front of witnesses?'

Elena backed away, from both Lady Cicely and the box containing that beautiful silk evening gown, tears now glistening in the deep and pained blue-green of her eyes.

Lady Cicely looked shocked. 'How could you think I would ever allow such a thing to happen? Or that Adam would ever do something so callously unfeeling?'

Elena had no idea what Adam was capable of anymore, as she no longer felt as if she knew him at all; certainly the man who had dismissed her so coldly that last evening at Hawthorne Hall had not been the same caring and sensitive man who had made love to her the evening before.

She shook her head. 'Then I do not understand the purpose of my inclusion in this private dinner party this evening.'

Lady Cicely wrinkled her nose. 'And, for the moment, I am not at liberty to tell you, I am afraid.'

Elena looked vexed. 'In that case I believe I would rather not accept the dowager duchess's invitation.'

'That will not do at all, my dear Elena,' Lady Cicely tutted. 'Indeed, there would be no purpose in the dinner taking place at all if you were not present.'

'But—'

'I believe, by insisting you be allowed to stay here with her, that my grandmother has given you her trust, unconditionally,' Adam Hawthorne said from across the room. 'Is it too much for her to ask that you now do the same for her?'

Elena had spun round at the first sound of his voice, a guilty blush colouring her cheeks before she paled, as she wondered how much of their conversation he had overheard.

Her breath stilled in her throat, as she now took in his appearance in black evening clothes and snowy-white linen, the darkness of his hair fashionably dishevelled about his ears and across his brow, the eyes beneath of a chilling grey as he returned her gaze with his usual haughty arrogance.

She moistened her lips with the tip of her tongue before speaking. 'I did not in the least mean to cast doubts upon Lady Cicely's good intentions.'

'Only my own?' Adam guessed drily as he easily took in the scene before him: the evening gown revealed inside the open box placed atop the bed, the pallor of Elena's face against the black gown she presently wore, his grandmother's expression of exasperation as she looked across the bedchamber at him. 'Would you leave us alone for a moment, Grandmama?'

She frowned her disapproval. 'Is that wise, Adam?'

'I am sure it is not,' he allowed ruefully, 'But Miss Matthews's present demeanour makes it necessary.'

'Very well.' His grandmother gave Elena's hand a reassuring squeeze before she crossed the room with a swish of her taffeta skirts. 'Five minutes and I shall be sending my maid to attend Elena,' she warned softly.

His gaze remained steadily fixed on Elena as he gave his grandmother an acknowledging inclination of his head, waiting only until they were alone before speaking again. 'Do you not like the gown?'

'The gown is…lovely, **as** I am sure you are aware,'

she dismissed agitatedly. 'It is the reason it's here that I find so…unacceptable.'

His mouth tightened. 'The dowager duchess does you a great honour by inviting you into her home.'

Elena may have spent most of her life hidden away in the country, but even there she had heard of how coveted invitations were to the Dowager Duchess of Royston's rare private dinner parties—making her own invitation this evening all the more extraordinary. 'Is she aware of *whom* she is inviting?'

'Yes.'

She spread her hands. 'I am not even acquainted with the lady.'

'But I am. As is my grandmother. And you are currently a guest in my grandmother's home…'

'And I understand from your grandmother that you are the one who instigated the dowager duchess's invitation—'

'*That* is something she should not have told you!' He scowled darkly.

'Why are you doing this?' Elena groaned. 'Is it as punishment for the deception I practised upon you when I took up employment in your household?'

His mouth tightened. 'If there was time I would put you over my knee for the insult you have just given me,' he growled. 'As it is, you have precisely one hour to bathe, change into the gown in that box and arrange the ribbons in your hair, all in readiness for dining out this evening.'

'You cannot make me go.' Her chin rose in challenge as she met his gaze defiantly.

'No?'

Elena felt a cold shiver down her spine at the soft menace she detected in his tone. 'Can you not understand that I do not wish to embarrass the dowager duchess, let alone myself, by appearing as a guest in her home?'

It had taken Adam the whole of the past four days to make arrangements for this evening's dinner party and he did not intend to allow Elena's stubbornness to jeopardise all that he had put in place. Nor could he tell her of those arrangements, for if he did, he knew she would certainly refuse to attend.

'How is Amanda?' Elena enquired. 'I have sorely missed her company recently.'

'As she has missed yours,' he said. 'And do not change the subject, Elena.' He crossed the room in long, predatory strides, until he stood only inches away from her, not quite touching, but close enough that he could feel the heat of her body. As Elena could no doubt feel his. 'Do you trust me?'

Her eyes widened. 'Your grandmother has just asked me that very same question.'

He reached out to smooth the frown from her brow, fingers lingering on the warmth of that silky-smooth skin. 'And what answer did you give?'

Her gaze lowered. 'That I believed you could be trusted not to cause Lady Cicely any unhappiness or embarrassment.'

His mouth twisted wryly. 'That is something, I suppose.' His hand fell back to his side as a knock sounded
on the bedchamber door. 'That will be my grandmother's maid come to attend you. You have one hour to
make yourself ready, Elena,' he repeated. 'And I should
warn you that I will not appreciate it if you put me to
the trouble of having to come back up here and button
you into that gown myself!'

'You would not dare!' She gasped indignantly.

'I think you know that I would.'

Elena glared at him, knowing by the implacability
of that unblinking silver gaze that Adam meant exactly
what he said.

She drew in a ragged breath. 'Very well, I shall be
ready to leave in one hour. But—'

'Pity,' he drawled. 'I believe I should, after all, have
enjoyed helping you into your gown. Not as much as I
would enjoy helping you out of it, of course, but that is
perhaps something for another time…' Adam sketched
her a mocking bow as she gasped again, his gaze lingering on those parted lips for several long seconds
before he turned to cross the room and open the door
to admit the maid.

Elena studied her appearance critically in the mir-
ror once Lady Cicely's maid had left to attend her mistress. The ivory of her skin appeared almost translucent
against the white-silk gown, the turquoise ribbons, beneath the low bodice of the gown and threaded through
the darkness of her simply styled curls, enlarging and

emphasising the colour of her eyes framed by stunningly long lashes.

She looked...innocently virginal, Elena realised with a choked sob. A young lady poised on the brink of womanhood. Something she was not now, nor ever could be again.

'You look very beautiful.'

Elena turned slowly to face Adam as he stood in the open doorway, no longer surprised at the manner in which he walked in and out of her bedchamber as though he had the right to do so. 'Thank you, my lord.' She gave an elegant curtsy, silky dark lashes lowered so that he should not see the tears still glittering in her eyes.

To say that Adam had been rendered breathless by the beauty of Elena's appearance would be an understatement. This evening, in the white silk gown, she looked every inch the duke's granddaughter that she undoubtedly was: cool, delicately elegant, innocently ravishing.

'I have something for you. There is no need for you to look so alarmed, Elena,' he soothed as he quickly crossed the room to her side.

She kept her lashes lowered. 'You have been kind enough already in giving me this gown.'

Not nearly kind enough, Adam groaned inwardly, wishing he might shower her with all the kindnesses that had been absent from her life recently, as she was forced to run, and then hide, from the man who had

made her life so unbearable after the death of her grandfather.

His gaze hardened, mouth thinning, as he thought
of the things he would like to do to that man for daring
to harm so much as one dark curl upon Elena's head.
'I wish you to wear this single strand of pearls—they
were my mother's,' he explained as she raised startled
lashes to look at the pearl necklace he had withdrawn
from the pocket of his evening jacket. 'She wore them
on the evening of her début into society.'

Elena shook her head in denial. 'Then I could not
possibly wear them.'

'Of course you can.'

'No!' She moved away from him. 'I have allowed
you to bully me into wearing this gown and attending
the dinner party, but I will not—' Her voice broke emotionally. 'I cannot—I simply cannot wear your mother's pearls!'

Adam knew by the stubborn fragility of her expression, and the determination in her gaze, that she meant
every word she said. Nor did he mean to 'bully' her—it
was the last thing he wished to do; for this one evening
he simply needed her to do as he asked without further
argument or objection. 'Very well,' he acquiesced as he
slipped the pearl necklace back inside his pocket. 'Shall
we go downstairs now and wait for my grandmother to
join us…?' He held out his arm to her.

Elena stared at the strength of that arm, knowing
that once she placed her hand upon it she would have

committed herself to spending the evening at the home of Edith St Just, the Dowager Duchess of Royston. She had no idea who the other guests were to be this evening, but she had no doubt that the arrival of Miss Magdelena Matthews in their midst would be a sensation which would keep the tongues wagging for weeks, if not months, to come.

Her gaze moved higher, to the unyielding hardness of Adam's arrogantly handsome face, the steadiness of that grey gaze asking—no, demanding!—that she do as he requested without further protest.

'I give you my word I will not allow any harm to come to you this evening,' he murmured encouragingly.

A frown creased her brow. 'And how do you intend to prevent that from happening?'

'Can you not trust me enough to see that it does not?'

Once again Adam asked that she trust him. When they had spoken together six days ago he had dismissed the passion they had shared, out of hand. When they'd parted four days ago he had been barely civil to her. And now, after days of silence, he asked that she trust him.

Could she, dare she now put her trust in him?

What other choice did she have?

Absolutely none, came the unequivocal answer as she moved her hand up slowly, hesitantly, and placed it upon Adam's forearm, allowing him to escort her from the safety of her bedchamber.

'Your grandfather was one of the gentlemen whose offer I considered accepting when I was a gel!' the Dowager Duchess of Royston informed her briskly upon introduction, a briskness which appeared to be her usual manner. 'I admit to being quite put out when Jane Witherspoon whisked him out from beneath my nose and married him.'

And an impressive nose it was too, Elena thought admiringly, Edith St Just's a forceful beauty rather than one of pale delicacy, as her own grandmother's had been. 'They were very happy together,' she assured shyly, slightly disconcerted by the forthright manner of the dowager duchess's greeting, after spending most of the carriage ride, to that lady's magnificent house, worrying as to what sort of reception she might expect from her hostess.

'Well, of course they were, George and I would never have suited. Both too fond of our own way.' The older woman smiled before turning to kiss Lady Cicely affectionately upon one powdered cheek, then stepping back to give Adam a considering glance. 'We have succeeded in bringing you back into society again at last, I see, Hawthorne.'

He smiled ruefully. 'It is for this one evening only, your Grace.'

'Then we must make the most of your company "for this one evening only",' the dowager duchess came back drily. 'Come, Cicely, let us take Miss Matthews and introduce her to my other guests.' She moved ahead of them, cutting a swathe through the other ten or so guests gathered in the salon.

Much like a battleship sailing through the midst

of smaller, less prepossessing vessels, Elena thought dazedly as she found herself moving further and further away from Adam's side.

'I believe I understand more what this evening is all about now that I have seen the young lady in question...'

Adam turned slightly to look at Justin St Just, as the duke moved to stand beside him. 'Indeed?'

The other man grinned at him. 'Do not take that arrogant tone with me, Thorne, when any man with eyes in his head can see and appreciate that Miss Magdelena Matthews is a rare beauty.'

'A rare beauty who has been much wronged,' Adam reminded him grimly.

The other man sobered instantly, his expression becoming almost as severe as Adam's own. 'Which is why we are all here, is it not? The duke, the earl, the judge, the lawyer, the doctor? As well as several of my grandmother's closest friends, to act as witness to the proceedings? Indeed, I cut short my own escape to the country in order that I might be of assistance.'

Adam forced some of the tension from his shoulders as he reminded himself that Royston, despite his words of admiration for Elena, was not his enemy, that the other man had indeed brought himself back to town, at the risk of facing more of the dowager duchess's marriage machinations, solely at Adam's request. 'I apologise for my churlishness. It is only—' He gave a shake of his head. 'The reproachful looks Elena cast in my direction, during the carriage ride here, lead me to the conclusion that she believes I have only forced her into coming here this evening because I somehow intend to cause her further humiliation.'

The duke gave him a reassuring slap on the shoulder. 'She will understand exactly why we are all here before this evening is over.'

Adam glanced across to where Elena and Lady Cicely were presently engaged in conversation with Judge Lord Terence Soames and Lady Soames, as well as the Dowager Countess of Chambourne, and her grandson Lord Christian Ambrose, the Earl of Chambourne, and Lady Sylviana Moorland, the lady to whom he had recently become betrothed. Elena's expression appeared to be one of shy pleasure as she found herself welcomed by the prestigious company in which she now found herself, instead of rebuffed, as she must fully have expected to be. 'I can only hope that you are right,' he murmured bleakly.

Adam's plans for this evening had been made carefully and cautiously, with only a handful of people knowing the true reason they were all gathered together here at the dowager duchess's home. Elena had not been one of them. For her own sake, admittedly, but Adam was not sure that she would agree with that decision once she became fully aware of why they were all here. The secrecy was a risk, a calculated risk on Adam's part, and not one he was at all sure would ultimately pay off.

'Too late for second thoughts now, Thorne,' Justin murmured beside him as he turned towards the door. 'I believe I hear our guest of honour arriving.' The duke wasted no more time on further conversation, but strode quickly across the room to stand at Elena's side.

Just in time, as the salon door was opened by the butler and the last of the dinner guests, a tall and confident young gentleman, in possession of a blond-haired blue-eyed handsomeness, stepped into the room at the same time as his presence was sonorously announced by the dowager duchess's butler.

'His Grace, the Duke of Sheffield.'

Chapter Sixteen

It seemed that, in the brief passing of a second, the evening that Elena was finding to be a surprisingly pleasant one had now turned into her worst nightmare. Her face paled to a deathly white as she looked across the room at the man who was her nemesis.

'Steady.'

She was barely aware of the gentleman who had moved to stand beside her, nor did she acknowledge the firm grip he took of her elbow as she swayed on her slippered feet. She had eyes and ears for only one man in the room. Her cousin. Neville Matthews. The eleventh Duke of Sheffield. The man who had stolen so much from her. Not only her inheritance and her identity, but, worst of all, her innocence…

His shrewd blue gaze moved restlessly about a room that had fallen silent at his arrival, nodding haughty acknowledgement as he recognised several of the other guests, that arrogant gaze then passing dismissively over Elena before just as quickly shifting back again.

Elena found it impossible to turn away as she saw the malevolent gleam that instantly appeared in those narrowed blue eyes and felt much like the mouse that found itself mesmerised by the eyes of the cat stalking it. If not for the increased firmness of that grip upon her elbow, she knew her legs would surely have given way beneath her. As it was, she could neither move nor breathe, but only continue to stare at Neville with ever-increasing dread as she waited for him to speak, to denounce her to every other person in the room.

'What are *you* doing here?' Neville's words, no more than a vicious whisper, was nevertheless still heard by every person gathered in the dowager duchess's beautifully appointed but otherwise silent salon. When Elena made no reply—she could not have spoken if her very life had depended upon it, which it perhaps did—his contemptuous gaze shifted to his hostess for the evening. 'I am sure you can have no idea of the deception which has been practised upon you this evening, madam, but I am sorry to inform you that your grandson appears to have brought a wanted fugitive into your home!'

'Steady,' that reassuring voice once again murmured at Elena's side.

A voice, she realised, from Neville's accusation, that must surely belong to none other than Justin St Just, the dowager duchess's grandson.

She blinked her uncertainty, unsure of how that gentleman came to be standing next to her at all. Or why the Duke of Royston should have chosen to take such a proprietary hold upon her elbow, when the two of them had never met, let alone been formally introduced.

'Which fugitive would you be referring to, Sheffield?' Edith St Just was the one to coolly answer the accusation.

Neville shot Elena a scowling glance. 'My cousin, Miss Magdelena Matthews, is the woman now standing beside your grandson!'

The elderly lady gave Elena a cursory glance before turning back to Neville. 'And?'

'And she is both a murderess and a thief, madam!' A flush of displeasure had darkened Neville's cheeks. Obviously he had expected a completely different reaction to his triumphant announcement.

'I do not know much about the affair, but gossip would seem to imply that it is only an accusation rather than accepted fact.' Adam stepped forwards into the middle of the room, placing himself firmly between the cousins. 'And was it not you who levelled that particular accusation against Miss Matthews?'

Elena's heart began to beat rapidly in her chest as she looked across at Adam, the first glimmer of hope beginning to brighten the darkness which she had felt surrounding her since they had left Cambridgeshire.

Trust him, Adam had requested of her earlier this evening, when Elena had questioned his reasons for insisting she attend this dinner party. Could he—dare she hope that he had been referring to this present situation when he made that request? That he had known all along that Neville was to be here this evening? That he had perhaps planned for this very confrontation to happen?

'This is none of your concern, Hawthorne.' Neville looked surprised by the other man's intervention.

Adam raised dark brows, his expression bland. 'I should have thought it to be the concern of any decent member of society?'

Neville gave him a pitying glance. 'From which you are known to have voluntarily absented yourself these past years.'

Adam smiled humourlessly. 'And what bearing can that possibly have upon any of this?'

'I merely mentioned it in passing.' Neville looked more than a little irritated as he once again turned the focus of his attention on Elena and the man standing so solidly at her side. 'I am surprised at you, Royston, for knowingly bringing such a woman into your grand-mother's home—'

'I would prefer—no, I positively insist, that you ad-dress me as your Grace.' Ice literally dripped from the Justin's coldly contemptuous voice.

The other man scowled. 'As your equal in rank—'

'I doubt there is another man alive equal to the depths to which you have fallen, Sheffield,' the duke informed him scathingly.

An angry flush now darkened Neville's cheeks. 'I did not come here to be insulted by one such as you—'

'Have a care, Sheffield,' Justin warned.

'This is ridiculous!' Neville shifted impatiently as he turned to the other guests in the room. 'The woman standing beside Royston has been sought this past two months, for both murder and theft. She is—'

'Innocent of both those charges!' Elena pulled out of the duke's grasp as she stepped forwards, her cheeks flushed as she faced up to the man she knew to be responsible for all that he now accused her of. Accusations, which she had listened to silently, her eyes downcast, as she was filled with tortured mortification at having such personal things discussed in such exalted company. But she could not just stand by and listen any longer, had to at least try to defend herself. 'It was your own behaviour, when you—when you attacked me, that so upset our grandfather he had a heart attack and died! And it was you who threatened to have me locked in the asylum if I did not agree to marry you!'

'I threatened the asylum because I believe you to be mentally ill, madam,' Neville announced scathingly. 'The fact that you ran away is in itself evidence of your guilt.'

'Not so.' Elena gave a fierce shake of her head. 'It was you who made it impossible for me to remain in Yorkshire!' She could not bring herself to say in what manner he had gone about that. 'And you made up those terrible things about me so that I could not make any accusations regarding your own monstrous behaviour towards me following our grandfather's funeral!' She was breathing hard in her agitation.

His jaw tightened. 'As already stated, you are deranged, madam.'

'And yet you wished to make her your wife? That

...es not make any sense at all.' Adam spoke softly,
...lled with pride for Elena, as she stood up to her ac-
...user so bravely. A pride he dared not show. Not yet…

...heffield scowled darkly. 'Perhaps we should take
...ersation somewhere less public?'

Matth...ed to their hostess. 'Your Grace?'

...to hear the re... remained stoically imperious. 'I be-
guests, receiving se... much, that it would be in Miss
before turning back to Nei...' if my guests and I remained
light of your other comments, that ...ds of confirmation,
Miss Matthews?'

'I was unaware of her dangerous mental state when
I made the offer.'

'Correct me if I am wrong, but it sounded as if your
offer of marriage was made to Miss Matthews immediately after your grandfather's death?' the dowager
countess said with deceptive mildness.

'What does it matter when I offered for her, when
that offer, for obvious reasons, has since been withdrawn?' Sheffield's top lip curled with distaste.

Edith St Just raised grey brows. 'I should have
thought it was of great significance, if you made the
offer of marriage whilst believing Miss Matthews to be
deranged and responsible for the death of your grandfather.'

Sheffield scowled darkly. 'I do not have to justify
my actions to you, madam—'

'I believe the dowager duchess is merely seek[ing to] clarify the sequence of events,' Adam put i[n,] not wishing for Sheffield to become so a[rou]-... he turned and walked out. Having c[os] man's would not do at all.

He did not remember meeting [li]ke him in the fore this evening, but just a f[ew] ever have liked, company and he knew th[at] his treatment of Elena. least. That he was not a[...] even without the kn[ock] out, and spoken with, several Indeed, Adam h[ad] these past few days, some of them members of [c]ould testify, and would if necessary, as women [...] to the vicious depravity of Sheffield's behaviour.

Having now met the man, Adam could see that he was beyond arrogant, and his past behaviour surely implied he believed himself to be above the law of the land, too. If anyone present this evening were to be called 'mentally ill' or 'deranged', then it was surely this man?

'I believe we were talking of your offer of marriage to Miss Matthews while fully believing that she was responsible for the demise of the grandfather you shared?' He gave the man another prod.

Neville's hands clenched at his sides even as he glared his anger at Adam. 'If we must finish this conversation, then should we not at least excuse the ladies from any indelicacies that might follow?'

'I believe I may speak for all of the ladies present,'

the dowager duchess answ

we are none of us so delicat.

Sheffield gave a sneering sn.

be it, madam!'

'Indeed,' she said regally.

'Very well,' he snapped his displea

for Elena because it was always intended t.

one day marry—'

'Intended by whom?' Adam prompted.

'By all of the family, of course.'

'I understood that there was only your grandfatr.

yourself and Miss Matthews left alive in that family?

Miss Matthews does not appear to me to be a chit just

out of the schoolroom and I do not recall your grand-

father making arrangements for that match before his

death?'

'Because he was too damned soft to force her when

she declined the match!' Neville muttered disgustedly.

Adam raised his brows. 'You did not agree with his

showing such an indulgence of emotions towards his

only granddaughter?'

The other man snorted. 'Not when it resulted in the

old fool accepting her refusal and then settling half the

Sheffield money on her in his will!'

'Perhaps he made such a decision so that Miss Mat-

thews might be independent after his death? Because

Miss Matthews had voiced her aversion to marrying

you? Her aversion to *you*?' Adam goaded again with as

light a touch as possible in the circumstances. 'I seem

to recall Miss Matthews stating earlier that it was wit-

…ich resulted in the duke's
…t death?'

…o remain averse to me for long
…ath, I assure you, Hawthorne,' the

…

…kept a tight rein on his own temper;
…nged to reach out and squeeze the life out
…use for a man, it would not serve his purpose.
…, at least.

…ville gave Elena a sweeping knowing glance. 'Per-
…ps you should try her for yourself once Royston has
finished with her. I believe you will find that, like all
women, she is only too willing after the initial fight.'
He gave an arrogantly mocking smile as one of the female guests gave an audible gasp.

'You like your women to fight you, do you, Matthews?' Adam's voice had now taken on a dangerous
edge.

'It adds a certain…spice, yes.' Neville gave a confident smile, still certain his position as a duke gave him
an iron-clad protection.

'You do not see it as a sign that they are possibly
unwilling?'

The other man gave Elena another scathing glance.
'Elena fought a little more than most, admittedly, and
earned herself a few bruises for her trouble. But that
was only to be expected. I have found that virgins are
always the most skittish.' He gave a feral smile. 'Married ladies are much more eager to try new things. Your

own wife, for example, very much enjoyed a little rough play in the bedchamber—'

'I believe you are right, Sheffield, in that we have all heard quite enough!' the Duke of Royston rasped, turning slightly to nod at Adam, the two men then moving forwards to link an arm each under Neville's, before then walking him backwards towards the open doorway, his booted heels dragging on the carpet.

'What the—! Unhand me at once!' the other man demanded furiously as he fought to free himself from their steely grasp. 'At once, do you hear!'

'Oh, I assure you, we have all heard you, very loud and very clear,' Adam said icily as the three men stood in the doorway. 'We have heard your contempt for your grandfather. We have heard how it was your attack upon Miss Matthews which caused your grandfather's collapse and death. We have heard you admit to later threatening Elena with the asylum if she would not consent to marry you. We have heard of your brutality when she continued to refuse. We have also heard how you made the accusations against her as a way of covering up your own contemptible behaviour towards her.' He looked at the other man with cold, merciless eyes. 'Feel free to correct me if I have missed anything out?'

Elena felt numbed by this past few minutes, hardly daring to believe she might now be free of Neville and his lies.

'I am the Duke of Sheffield,' he now shouted angrily, 'and I will simply deny any and all accusations you might care to make against me—'

'You may deny it all you like, young man.' A grey-haired gentleman stepped forwards, his expression grim. 'I assure you, it will not do you a bit of good. Not when I, Judge Lord Terence Soames, will be one of the people giving evidence against you.'

'As will the Duke of Royston,' that gentleman assured coldly.

'And Sir Michael Bennett, lawyer.'

'And Dr Jonathan Graves.'

'And Lord Christian Ambrose, Earl of Chambourne.'

Elena was completely dazed as each gentleman stepped forwards to bow respectfully towards her before turning to look at Neville with complete contempt.

Surely the presence this evening of all these eminent gentlemen could not be coincidental?

'We shall remove him from the sight of all the decent people in this room, gentlemen,' the judge instructed as he crossed the room, pausing in front of Elena to take her hand gently in both of his much larger ones. 'You are a very brave young woman,' he complimented gently. 'And I trust you will accept my word that this excuse for a man…' his eyes turned steely as he glanced at Neville '…shall never again be allowed to threaten or bother you.'

She gave a tremulous smile. 'You are very kind.'

His expression softened. 'I believe kindness is the least that all in society should give you in future.'

'Which I shall personally ensure that they do,' Edith St Just spoke imperiously. 'Now remove that distasteful object from my home at your earliest convenience, if you please, Hawthorne.' She looked down the length of her impressive nose at the still-struggling Neville Matthews.

'Your Grace.' Adam bowed briefly to the dowager duchess before glancing at Elena, relieved to see that she appeared to be recovering some of the colour back in her cheeks.

And hoping, sincerely hoping, as he and Royston carried away a protesting and vengeful Matthews, that she would one day forgive him for the ordeal he had put her through this evening...

'I feel as if I dreamt the first part of this evening.' Elena looked up at Adam uncertainly.

He had ridden back in the carriage with Elena and Lady Cicely at the end of the evening, the elderly lady having then announced that she was more than ready for her bed, after all the excitement, and would see them both in the morning, leaving Elena and Adam to retire to the privacy of the library.

Exciting was not quite how Elena would have described the events of the evening just passed. Terrifying. Shocking. Ultimately filled with a surprising warmth and kindness, as Edith St Just's guests made her feel welcome in their midst, both during the dinner the dowager duchess had insisted would be served, and afterwards, when the ladies had all retired to the salon for tea and conversation, leaving the men at the table to enjoy their brandy and cigars.

As if Neville had never so much as been in their

midst this evening, let alone been revealed as the ego-
tistical monster that he was.

'Do you think you will ever be able to forgive me?'
Adam looked down searchingly into her face, which
seemed dominated by her huge blue-green eyes.

If he had needed further proof that Elena had been
raised as the granddaughter of a duke—which he had
not—then it had been all too apparent this evening,
when he and Royston had rejoined the dinner guests to
find Elena guarded on either side by Lady Cicely and
Edith St Just, as they discussed fashions with several
of the other ladies, prior to dinner being served. Adam
believed that only a young woman of refinement and
innocence could possibly have behaved in such a poised
manner only minutes after being publicly flayed by her
nearest living relative.

And only someone who knew Elena well would have
noticed the way in which she kept her gloved hands
tightly clasped together in order to hide their trembling.
Or the way she smiled while at the same time tears
shimmered unshed in her eyes.

Tears which even now glistened in those beautiful
blue-green eyes as she answered him. 'Forgive you?'
she repeated incredulously.

He nodded. 'I wanted to tell you what I had planned
for this evening, but dared not, for fear that you might
alert Matthews, by some word or gesture, as to what
was about to happen. I wished him to believe that you
were as stunned as he by your meeting, and that it was
Royston with whom you were acquainted rather than

myself, so that I was then able to lull him into a false impression of a lack of knowledge of the situation on my part—not difficult to do when, as he stated, I have long been absent from society.'

Neville's remark about Adam's wife had given Elena a glimmer of the possible reason for that lengthy absence. 'I am heartily sorry that in the end Neville chose to make some personal remarks to you.'

'I have found that men of his nature cannot resist boasting of their conquests, willing and unwilling, given the opportunity to do so.' His lip turned back with distaste. 'In truth, it seems it would be difficult to find a gentleman in society with whom my wife had not been intimate!'

Elena gave a pained wince. 'It was nevertheless poor recompense for your efforts on my behalf.'

He sighed. 'I am long past being concerned over such remarks.'

Nevertheless, Elena knew it could not have been easy for Adam to have to listen to them again this evening and from such a vile man as her cousin.

'You do understand the reason for not revealing to you beforehand my intention of exposing Matthews this evening?'

'Oh, yes.' Elena nodded. 'Did Lady Cicely and the dowager duchess know of your plan?'

He nodded confirmation. 'Invitations from the dowager duchess are much coveted by the *ton*, and we had to find some way to draw Sheffield out from his imposed mourning for your grandfather. Soames, Royston and Chambourne were also aware of my intentions.'

'You have been very busy these past few days,' Elena acknowledged ruefully. She had believed Adam to be avoiding her. Instead, he had spent his time putting together a plan which would ultimately prove her innocent of any wrongdoing. 'I do not know how I shall ever be able to repay you for the way in which you have revealed Neville, to the dowager duchess's guests at least, as the cruel and heartless man that he is.'

'My actions this evening were not done with any thought of being deserving of your gratitude,' Adam said hotly.

Elena flinched as she once again felt the sting of Adam's rejection.

Giving her no choice but to accept that his actions this evening had not been meant personally, but were those of the noble gentlemen he was, and that, believing in her innocence, he had simply felt duty bound to correct the wrong inflicted against her.

She lifted her chin. 'Nevertheless, you have it, my lord, and always will have. As does the Duke of Royston. Judge Lord Soames. Sir Michael Bennett. Doctor Jonathan Graves. And the Earl of Chambourne.'

He nodded. 'Lord Soames believes it best if the worst of your cousin's offences against you were not made public.'

'I am sure he does.' She smiled sadly. 'But I doubt that will be possible after the things that have been said this evening.'

'The dowager duchess's guests were all, I assure you, chosen with their discretion in mind. I have their word that they will none of them ever discuss the events of this evening with anyone else.'

'For which I am very grateful.' She nodded. 'Unfortunately, that silence will also mean that I am not absolved of the crime in the eyes of the rest of society.'

Adam's mouth tightened. 'I believe we might find a way of achieving that too. With your agreement.'

Her gaze sharpened. 'My agreement?'

He frowned. 'The situation is a…delicate one. On the one hand we would obviously wish to see Matthews incarcerated for the rest of his life, for causing your grandfather's demise when caught forcing his attentions upon you, and the miseries he has admitted inflicting upon you afterwards. On the other hand there is your own reputation. We can prove to society that you are not a murderess or a thief, but it would be at the cost of—'

'Revealing my lack of—of physical innocence,' Elena supplied huskily, her face now rather wan.

Adam's eyes darkened to a stormy grey. 'Your innocence is not in question —'

'How can you, of all people, possibly say that?' she choked.

'Elena—'

'Just tell me Lord Soames's solution to the problem, if you please,' she asked curtly, no longer able to meet that stormy grey gaze as she turned away. 'It has been a stressful evening and I am very tired.'

Of course she was tired after such an emotional

evening and Adam was a fool for not realising it before now. 'Soames has suggested that Sheffield make a heartfelt apology to you in the newspapers, explaining that his emotions were overset after the death of your paternal grandfather and causing him to wrongly accuse you, that your grandfather had been ill for some time and had succumbed to that illness. That he, Matthews, was also mistaken about any jewels and money having been taken when you chose to leave, both having now been safely found in a hidden safe in your grandfather's bedchamber. After which Matthews will remove himself to the Continent for the rest of his natural life.'

'How would we explain my disappearance this past two months?'

'That you have been living in the country, in private mourning for your grandfather, and did not know of the rumours and accusations circulating against you.'

Elena gave a pained wince. 'Do you think Neville would ever accept such a proposal?'

'At the risk of a public trial, which Matthews will most certainly lose, and which would result in his being incarcerated for some considerable time, or worse? Yes, I believe he might be…persuaded, into accepting Lord Soames's proposal,' Adam confirmed ruthlessly.

She arched dark brows. 'And do you think that society would believe any of it?'

'I think that the unknowing will believe what the Dowager Duchess of Royston tells them to believe,' he admitted drily.

'And the rest?'

'Already know Matthews for the out-and-out bounder that he is and will just be relieved to have him removed from decent society!' Adam scowled as he recalled now knowing of the scoundrel's past association with Fanny, along with some of the tales about him he had heard recently. Tales which had led Adam to believe, no matter how cruelly Elena had been treated by Matthews, that she had at least been spared some of the man's darker depravities. Although only the lord knew she had suffered badly enough at the bastard's hands!

'What do you think I should do?'

'It is not for me to say.'

'But it is.' Elena insisted firmly. 'You asked earlier that I trust you. I did then and I still do. As such, I would welcome your opinion on this, too.'

Adam turned away, knowing exactly what he wished for Elena to do, both now and in the future, but also knowing he could not impose upon her newly found freedom by verbally expressing those wishes to her now. That he could never do so.

The first part of Elena's life had been a protected and loving one, initially with both her parents, then with her mother and grandfather following her father's death. This past few years had robbed her of her mother, and more recently her grandfather, her innocence, and her very existence, when she was forced to flee the only home she was familiar with to take on the name and life of another woman so that she might hide from the man who should have been protecting her, but had instead wounded her deeply.

With the Dowager Duchess of Royston, Lady Cicely Hawthorne and Lady Jocelyn Ambrose as her sponsors, Elena's future in society was assured. She would likely fall in love with a handsome and uncomplicated young gentleman, one unencumbered by a scandalous first wife and a six-year-old daughter from that marriage. As such, Adam's advice to Elena must be given unselfishly, with only her future happiness in mind.

He turned decisively. 'I believe it to be in your very best interest to accept Soames's suggestion.'

Elena looked at him wordlessly for several seconds, before nodding equally as decisively, her gloved hands tightly clasped together. 'Then that is what I shall do. Thank you, Adam. For everything that you have done for me tonight.'

Which was, Adam accepted heavily, his cue to depart…

Chapter Seventeen

'I do not wish to intrude, Adam, but I really need you to explain to me exactly what it is you think you are doing.' Lady Cicely swept into the privacy of Adam's study at his London home during the first week of June, looking remarkably spry for a woman of almost seventy years, in her gown and bonnet of pale blue and her parasol of cream lace.

Adam sat back slowly in the chair behind his desk, having seen very little of his grandmother during the month of May, her time being spent much in the society Adam still chose not to be a part of. 'I am checking estate accounts—'

'I did not mean at this precise moment.' His grandmother eyed him impatiently. 'You were primarily responsible for returning Miss Magdelena Matthews to society some weeks ago—and you have completely ignored her existence ever since!'

He could never 'ignore' Elena's existence. How could he, when he had spent every waking moment of this past month, thinking about her! 'I think you are exaggerating, Grandmama,' he drawled. 'Nor do I think that Miss Matthews needs or requires any more gentlemen to tell her how beautiful she is.' His jaw tightened grimly.

'Ah.' Lady Cicely beamed her satisfaction.

Adam frowned warily. 'What does that mean?'

She continued to smile at him. 'It means that you appear to be as miserable as Elena is.'

He looked startled. 'I beg your pardon...?'

'You heard me,' Lady Cicely repeated remorselessly. 'Which is a little frustrating, as it happens.' She frowned. 'Edith, Jocelyn and I have worked tirelessly these past few weeks to see that Elena was launched into society, since it was decided that three months of mourning for her grandfather would suffice. We wished to have her formally presented as soon as was possible after that dreadful man rescinded all of his accusations and fled to the Continent. I am not sure if I said so at the time, but I am very proud of you, Adam, for the efficient way in which you cleared Elena of all wrongdoing.'

'No, you did not say, Grandmama,' he acknowledged drily. 'And I was only too pleased to remove Sheffield from Elena's life,' he added with satisfaction.

'I am sure you were.' Lady Cicely gave an appreciative chuckle, before sobering. 'Anyway, Elena has become quite the thing and I believe several young gentlemen may already be about to offer for her—did you just *growl*, Adam?' She raised mock-surprised grey brows.

He had, damn it! At the mere thought of Elena accepting the offer of one of those young cubs he had only a month ago decided would be the best thing for her.

Best for Elena, perhaps.

Not for Adam. He had missed her presence in his home these past five weeks. Not just the passion they had shared. He had also missed their lively conversations—occasions when Elena invariably upbraided him over some mistake or other on his part, usually regarding Amanda. And he knew that Amanda had missed Elena, too. Although his grandmother had taken the little girl out on several occasions, allowing Elena and Amanda to spend time together in her home.

Occasions when his young daughter would return home to talk of nothing else but 'Miss Matthews' this and 'Miss Matthews' that—with the resilience of most young children, Amanda had accepted the change of her old governess's name and circumstance, without blinking a silken eyelash—all succeeding in emphasising the hollow in Adam's chest at his own lack of even the sight of 'Miss Matthews'.

In a word, Adam felt…lonely for Elena.

He gave his a grandmother a self-derisive smile. 'I believe it may have been, yes, Grandmama.'

She gave an exasperated shake of her head. 'I do not understand you at all, Adam! Why do you sit here moping, day after day, night after night, when you might have attended any number of social occasions and so spent time with Elena yourself? After which you could have—'

'Could have what, Grandmama?' he cut in harshly.

'I am a widower, with a young daughter and a scandalous marriage behind me; do you not think that Elena
has had enough scandal in her life recently, without the
notorious Lord Hawthorne showing her his marked attentions?' For Adam had no doubt it would be marked;
he could not bear to be in the same room with Elena
and watch other gentlemen, more eligible and younger
gentlemen than he, fawn over and covet her. 'It will not
do, Grandmama.'

'And if it is you whom Elena wants?'

Adam looked at her sharply, hopefully, before he
as quickly dampened down that hope. 'If she ever felt
even the smallest measure of affection for me, then I
am sure it has been forgotten by now.'

Lady Cicely gave him a reproving look. 'Are all
young men as ignorant in their knowledge of women
as you appear to be?'

'Grandmama!' He eyed her incredulously.

'I am not about to apologise, Adam, so you may take
that offended expression off your face!' She eyed him
impatiently. 'Elena does not have a "small measure of
affection" for you—'

'Good,' he grated through gritted teeth.

'—but instead, it's clear she feels emotions of the
enduring and faithful kind,' his grandmother continued. 'No, you shall hear me out, Adam,' she added determinedly as he would have interrupted once more.
'Elena is not one of those flirtatious young débutantes
who appear in society at the start of each new Season, but a poised young lady of almost one and twenty.

Moreover, she is a young lady to whom life has dealt a harsh hand—'

'Which is why I have no intention of taking advantage of the gratitude she expressed to me when we last spoke together!' Elena's gratitude, whilst better than having her feeling nothing for him at all, was not enough for Adam. Not nearly enough!

Lady Cicely sighed deeply. 'It is my belief that gratitude is definitely not all she feels for you. Far from it! Oh, she has put a brave face on things these past few weeks, accepting all that Edith, Jocelyn and I have arranged for her, has been very gracious to all in society. But we are all three agreed, Elena cannot hide from us the fact that she searches for a particular face every time we attend a party or ball and that her disappointment is palpable when that face is never there.'

'And you believe that face to be my own...?' Adam was almost too afraid to believe what his grandmother was telling him, his own heart pounding furiously in his chest as she imparted this last piece of information to him.

'I know it is,' Lady Cicely stated positively.

'This is not another of your machinations to try to see me married again?' He eyed her suspiciously.

A delicate blush coloured her powdered cheeks. 'No, it is not,' she said huskily. 'My only wish has been to see you happy again, Adam.'

'I was not criticising, Grandmama, merely trying to ascertain whether or not this is all wishful thinking on your part.'

She met Adam's gaze unblinkingly. 'I assure you, it is not.'

Was it possible—could Elena really be missing him as much as he was missing her? Could she feel something more than gratitude for him, after all?

There was only one way for him to find out...

'Your hair is as dark and beautiful as a raven's wing.'

'You are too kind, Lord Randall,' Elena responded politely to the compliment as the two of them stood talking together at the musical soirée being given by his mother; it was Elena's usual response to the effusive praise and admiration which had been showered upon her over the last few weeks by so many of the eligible gentlemen of the *ton*.

It had been a very busy time for her, the mornings spent shopping for suitable gowns and other clothing considered necessary by Lady Cicely for her entrance into society, the evenings just as full and busy, Elena's popularity assured as she attended a different social occasion every evening, in the company of Lady Cicely, Lady Edith and Lady Jocelyn.

It should have been every young débutante's dream.

And yet...

There was something missing from Elena's life, an absence which had resulted in her feeling hollow inside, no matter how busy she was, or how effusive and genuine the gentlemen's compliments were.

Because those compliments were never given by the voice she ached to hear again. And the eyes, which gazed so admiringly into hers, were never of a soft dove grey. Nor were the hands, which lightly clasped hers in greeting or during a dance, ever the hands she longed to feel again.

Because they did not belong to Adam.

It was silly of her, Elena knew, to hunger for the sound, the sight, the touch, of a man who obviously had not given her a second thought since the evening of Neville's denouncement—yet she could not stop herself from doing so.

She longed to see Adam again, to speak with him— oh Lord, if she could just *see* him again! Just once—

'Lord Adam Hawthorne.'

'What the devil!'

Elena did not so much as spare another thought for Lord Randall, let alone have any interest in his sudden exclamation, as she instead turned sharply, as had all of the *ton*, to stare across to where Adam stood so tall and handsome in the doorway.

Her heart leapt with happiness at her first sight of him in weeks, that happiness glowing in her eyes as she drank in her fill of the man she knew she loved so deeply he seemed to have taken up residence in her heart, so that she could no longer see and think of anything but him.

Adam…

Adam paid not the slightest heed to the stunned silence which had fallen over the Countess of Livingstone's crowded salon after the butler had announced his presence. The *ton* were obviously extremely surprised to see him here, the first society function he had attended in the past four years, but Adam had eyes and ears for only one person in the room.

Elena.

Looking more wonderful, more beautiful than he had even imagined these past long weeks, in a gown of the softest turquoise, the darkness of her hair secured in a fashionable abundance of curls upon her crown, her eyes glowing that same deep, luminous turquoise as she gazed back at him in unadulterated pleasure.

Adam continued to meet that glowing gaze as, nodding tersely to his twittering hostess, he began to stride purposefully across the room to where Elena now stood alone, a blush in her cheeks and a welcoming smile parting those full and rosy-red lips by the time he reached her side.

They continued to drink their fill of each other with their eyes for several long, telling moments, totally unaware as the hushed conversation—speculative now—resumed around them.

'Elena—'

'Adam!'

They both began talking at the same time, only to both stop at the same time, too. Elena started chuckling, Adam joining in seconds later. 'Please tell me that I am not imagining your pleasure in seeing me again!' he urged gruffly.

She met his gaze unwaveringly. 'You are not.'

His breath left him in a relieved sigh. 'It is so very

good to see you again, too, Elena.' His gaze roamed hungrily over her face. 'And looking every inch the much-praised and admired Miss Magdelena Matthews.'

Her smile faltered slightly. 'Thank you, but I—I—'

'Elena?' He looked at her concernedly as he reached out to grasp both her gloved hands in his own.

'I have missed you so, Adam!' The air seemed to be forced from her lungs. 'I—'

'I love you, Elena.' Adam could no longer bear to see that pained look in her eyes.

'You do?' Elena looked up at him wondrously.

'I should have told you before,' he confirmed huskily. 'But I did not want you to think—I could not bear to think that you might feel kindly towards me because you felt grateful for—for—' He shook his head, not wishing to talk of Neville Matthews's treatment of her now, or his own part in removing the bounder from her life once and for all time. 'And so I stayed away,' he continued determinedly. 'Wished for you to go out into the society to which you belonged, to find a more suitable gentleman to love you, to marry—' He ceased speaking as Elena released one of her hands to place gentle fingertips against his lips.

'I shall never marry, Adam.' Elena gave a sad shake of her head, her heart heavy.

'Why the hell not?' he demanded incredulously.

'We have never spoken of it openly but—you know the reason I can never marry, Adam!' Tears stung her eyes. 'I am no longer innocent!'

'That is not of your doing!'

She gave another despondent shake of her head. 'It does not matter whose fault it is.'

'Elena, I know what happened to you and it does not matter to me. You are everything that is good and beautiful, and—'

'And I shall never marry now,' she repeated firmly. 'Indeed, these past few weeks of missing you I have several times considered accepting the offer you once made for me to become your—'

'Do not say it!' Adam commanded. 'I must have been insane to have ever made you such an offer. I wish for you to be my wife, Elena, not my mistress.'

'You know I cannot.' Elena's heart felt as if it were breaking, as she listened to Adam tell her that he loved her, but knowing she could never be a proper wife to him. No matter how much she might long to be. 'Besides which, you do not intend ever marrying again, remember, and are quite happy for your third cousin Wilfred to inherit the title,' she reminded him in a broken attempt at teasing.

'To the devil with Wilfred!'

'People are staring, Adam,' she admonished softly, lashes lowering as she became aware of curious stares.

'Then let them stare!'

'Perhaps we should remove ourselves somewhere more private…?' Elena murmured.

Adam looked about them, conversation once again ceasing as he boldly met, and challenged, those curious stares, pausing briefly as he met that of his grandmother, before he turned back to a now white-faced

Elena. 'I love you, Elena, dare I hope that you—could you ever love me in return?' he begged.

'I already love you. So very much, my darling Adam.' She looked up at him glowingly. 'More that words alone can ever express.'

Adam looked down at her hungrily for several long seconds, seeing that love for him blazing unconditionally in those beautiful turquoise eyes.

His fingers tightened about hers as he straightened to give her a respectful bow before dropping down on to one knee in front of her. She heard the gasps around them before the room once again fell deathly silent. Adam continued to look up at Elena as she stared down at him in shocked disbelief. 'I love you, Miss Magdelena Matthews, will you do me the honour of becoming my wife?' he spoke loudly enough for all in the room to hear.

The tears fell unchecked down Elena's cheeks as she continued to gaze down into the dear beloved face of the wonderful gentleman whom she loved with all of her heart. The same gentleman who had stated several times how much he hated any public display, that he never intended to marry again, but who was now on bended knee in front of her before many of the *ton*, as he asked her to become his wife.

And he asked in the full knowledge of what had been done to her. Indeed, he stated that her lack of innocence did not matter to him, that he loved her and wished to marry her.

Was it possible that she might accept? That she might

become Adam's wife, his to love, and for her to love him, for the rest of their lives?

She raised her eyes to look quickly across the room to where Ladies Cicely, Jocelyn and Edith stood together, three dear and beloved friends who knew all there was to know of her past, and whom Elena had come to deeply respect and love.

One by one they gave brief, approving nods, Lady Cicely's accompanied by a glowing smile.

'Elena, please…!' Adam encouraged hoarsely.

She turned back to him, her fingers tightening about his. 'I love you, Adam, and, yes, I will marry you—' She got no further as Adam rose swiftly to his feet before sweeping her up into his arms and kissing her with all the hunger and longing she could ever have wanted.

Chapter Eighteen

One day later—the London home of Lady Cicely Hawthorne

'So, Edith, Adam is to marry Elena as soon as the banns have been read, which now leaves only Royston's future marriage to be settled.' Lady Cicely could not stop smiling, thinking about her own grandson's future nuptials.

'And only weeks of the Season left in which to do it,' Lady Jocelyn put in sympathetically.

'Plenty of time,' Lady Edith dismissed airily.

'And are you still of a mind that it will be to the lady whose name is written on the piece of paper you left in the care of Jocelyn's butler?' Lady Cicely looked doubtful.

'I am more certain of it than ever.' The dowager duchess gave an imperious nod of her regal head.

Eleanor—Ellie—Rosewood, stepniece and companion to the dowager duchess, and deeply in love herself with Justin St Just, felt her heart go cold at the determination she saw in that dear lady's face…

* * * * *

REQUEST YOUR FREE BOOKS!

 HARLEQUIN® HISTORICAL:
Where love is timeless

2 FREE NOVELS PLUS 2 **FREE GIFTS!**

YES! Please send me 2 FREE Harlequin® Historical novels and my 2 FREE gifts (gifts are worth about $10). After receiving them, if I don't wish to receive any more books, I can return the shipping statement marked "cancel." If I don't cancel, I will receive 6 brand-new novels every month and be billed just $5.44 per book in the U.S. or $5.74 per book in Canada. That's a savings of at least 16% off the cover price! It's quite a bargain! Shipping and handling is just 50¢ per book in the U.S. and 75¢ per book in Canada.* I understand that accepting the 2 free books and gifts places me under no obligation to buy anything. I can always return a shipment and cancel at any time. Even if I never buy another book, the two free books and gifts are mine to keep forever.

246/349 HDN F4ZY

Name _____ (PLEASE PRINT)

Address _____ Apt. #

City _____ State/Prov. _____ Zip/Postal Code

Signature (if under 18, a parent or guardian must sign)

Mail to the **Harlequin® Reader Service:**
IN U.S.A.: P.O. Box 1867, Buffalo, NY 14240-1867
IN CANADA: P.O. Box 609, Fort Erie, Ontario L2A 5X3

Want to try two free books from another line?
Call 1-800-873-8635 or visit www.ReaderService.com.

* Terms and prices subject to change without notice. Prices do not include applicable taxes. Sales tax applicable in N.Y. Canadian residents will be charged applicable taxes. Offer not valid in Quebec. This offer is limited to one order per household. Not valid for current subscribers to Harlequin Historical books. All orders subject to credit approval. Credit or debit balances in a customer's account(s) may be offset by any other outstanding balance owed by or to the customer. Please allow 4 to 6 weeks for delivery. Offer available while quantities last.

Your Privacy—The Harlequin® Reader Service is committed to protecting your privacy. Our Privacy Policy is available online at www.ReaderService.com or upon request from the Harlequin Reader Service.

We make a portion of our mailing list available to reputable third parties that offer products we believe may interest you. If you prefer that we not exchange your name with third parties, or if you wish to clarify or modify your communication preferences, please visit us at www.ReaderService.com/consumerschoice or write to us at Harlequin Reader Service Preference Service, P.O. Box 9062, Buffalo, NY 14269. Include your complete name and address.

HH13R

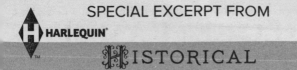
*Sophia James takes you on a delicious journey of scandal,
deception and overwhelming desire in*
MISTRESS AT MIDNIGHT

"And what is our full story, my lord?" Alone, Aurelia felt
braver, their history built up in layers, one upon the other
and all beginning with the kiss at Taylor's Gap.

"Our story?" He turned the words so that each one
of them was carefully pronounced, his eyes grave. "Our
story is unfinished and ill concluded, any hint of what
might have been between us buried beneath duty and lies."
She stood very still.

"Debts of ill repute and payments for silence are things I
am trying to rid myself of, Mrs. St. Harlow, and if the reasons
for my cousin's death are going to be pegged to any future
problems then I would rather not know of them. For years
deception has been my companion, you see, and now I find I
need something different altogether."

"You need honesty?"

The simple question was quietly asked, a pledge that she
knew she would never be able to give him with her mother
and her father and the faithless arrogance of her dead husband.

"I do."

Honesty and innocence and pure, untainted goodness.
Lady Elizabeth Berkeley.

She suddenly and clearly understood why Lord Hawkhurst
had chosen the girl and all hope was lost.

"Would you dance with me again, Mrs. St. Harlow?"

"Yes." She had heard another waltz strike up, the first

chords of Strauss drifting about the room. Aurelia placed her fingers upon his offered arm and they walked onto the floor, the lights dim here and the glow of candles evoking some nighttime grotto far from London town. She hoped that he would not feel the rapid beat of her heart as he brought her into his arms, closer than she expected, farther apart than she wanted.

No one else existed in that room as the music swirled about them and he led her into the steps, the smell of soap and brandy vying for an ascendance, his body hard beneath his superfine jacket.

They were hardly strangers. Not quite lovers. There was a danger in it Aurelia found exhilarating and forbidden. Pushing against him so that he might feel the curve of her breasts, she watched his expression change.

Feminine power was surprisingly easy, the potency of her own body something she had never considered before because Charles had left her so very damaged.

"Keep doing that and I will drag you off home before you know what has happened to you and you will not have a chance to change it."

Look for Sophia James's
MISTRESS AT MIDNIGHT
Coming September 2013
from Harlequin Historical

SADDLE UP AND READ 'EM!

This summer, get your fix of Western reads and pick up a cowboy from some of your favorite authors!

In September look for:

STERN by Brenda Jackson
The Westmorelands
Harlequin Desire

COWBOY REDEMPTION by Elle James
Covert Cowboys Inc.
Harlequin Intrigue

CALLAHAN COWBOY TRIPLETS by Tina Leonard
Callahan Cowboys
Harlequin American Romance

THE BALLAD OF EMMA O'TOOL by Elizabeth Lane
Harlequin Historical

*Look for these great Western reads and more
available wherever books are sold or visit*
www.Harlequin.com/Westerns

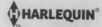
HARLEQUIN®

ℋISTORICAL

Where love is timeless

COMING SEPTEMBER 2013

The Ballad of Emma O'Toole
BY ELIZABETH LANE

HIGH-STAKES MARRIAGE

After he shoots a man, the stakes for gambler Logan Devereaux
have never been higher. On trial for his life, he's offered a
shocking alternative form of restitution…marriage to his
victim's pregnant sweetheart!

Beautiful Emma O'Toole has sworn vengeance against him—
and when a newspaper man puts her tragic story to song the
whole nation waits to see what she'll do. Their marriage is the
riskiest gamble Logan's ever taken, but he'll put everything he's
got on the line for a chance at winning Emma's heart.

Available wherever books and ebooks are sold.